All She Wanted

INTREPID WOMEN
BOOK 6

MEYERS SECURITY

KATHRYN JANE

ALL SHE WANTED

Intrepid Women Series, Book 6

A Meyers Security Story

By: Kathryn Jane

Cover by The Killion Group

Electronic ISBN: 978-0-9949209-1-1

Print ISBN: 978-0-9949209-2-8

http://kathrynjane.com

OTHER BOOKS BY KATHRYN JANE

Do Not Tell Me No
Touch Me
Daring To Love
Voices
Lies
All She Wanted
Secrets (Fall 2016)

To Nancy Drew and Trixie Beldon.

Thank you for teaching me that girls could have adventures,
solve mysteries, and be heroes too!

The Intrepid Women series,
is dedicated to an amazing, courageous, one of a kind friend.
Anne, I miss you still

.

CHAPTER 1

"I. Don't. Do. Christmas."

Angie resisted the impulse to argue. Their relationship had been on his terms for years, and for a very good reason. But this time Dr. Matthias Alejandro Martinez was just being stubborn.

And she still had four months to strategize. To convince him how important it was to spend Christmas at the ranch with her and their son. Until now, she'd never argued, never asked for anything, believed she had no choice but to go along with him because that's what you did when you were in love with a heart-stoppingly gorgeous man who didn't exist in the real world.

"Are we good here?"

Oh, not by a long shot, pal. "You know I have to be gone, like, ten minutes ago."

He reached out with the sureness of an old lover and ran a fingertip along her jawbone, cupped her chin. "Will you kiss me goodbye?"

He always asked, never took. And, dammit, she

couldn't look into those serious blue eyes and deny the man anything. He'd been making her crazy for years, so why would it change now? She lifted to her tiptoes, and slid her fingers into the thick, unruly hair brushing the back of his white collar. "I hate you," she said and dragged his mouth down to hers.

"I know." Hands on her butt, he lifted her off her feet, and just when she was afraid the top of her head was going to blow off, the vibration of his cell made her groan.

"You programmed that, didn't you?"

He set her down with a sexy chuckle and slipped on heavy, black-rimmed glasses to check the display. "I have to take this."

"No worries. I need to be gone anyway."

Before she could turn away, he caught her hand, ran his teeth across the knuckles, then put the phone on speaker. "Martinez, stand by."

Angie closed the door softly behind her and made it halfway to the stairwell before she stopped. She could go back, make him understand how important Christmas was for her, why she was making plans in September. She gave her head a shake. No. And no point standing here looking like an idiot, either. Every inch of this place was on video monitor…except for the offices, washrooms and private suites. ETCETERA acknowledged few boundaries, but certain privacies *were* respected.

By the time she traversed a complex network of tunnels and reached the secure warehouse where her ride was stashed, she'd managed—as always—to put things in perspective. She loved a man who couldn't follow the regular rules of relationships. A man who lived outside societal norms, underground—

literally—and she was one of the few people who even knew he was alive.

She pressed her hand against the black surface of the biometric palm reader and waited until the door of the man trap opened. Once inside, she stared into the retina scanner until it beeped, then waited beside her reflection on the wall of one-way glass.

She wasn't one to primp in front of a mirror, but she did run her fingers through her short hair to straighten what *she* called a man-cut—but Matt called sexy when he had his mouth on her sensitive neck.

Suddenly overwarm, she undid the top button of her flight suit, pushed up the sleeves, and sighed with relief when the lock finally snicked open.

She nodded to the guard on duty. "I'll have the machine out of here in five."

"Need help?"

"Thanks, but I've got it." She strode to the small but powerful black helicopter—nicknamed the Bug—and pushed buttons on the portable landing mat where it was perched. She was grateful to be back functioning in a way that made sense. Every action had a purpose and a consequence. Order mattered. Machines and flight she understood, but people confused the hell out of her.

The door lifted and the craft slid out into the bright light of day, where she went through the well-ordered steps, beginning with a walk-around, then climbing in to deal with switches, buttons, gauges and readings. Like a familiar dance, she sailed through the steps, and once the rotor RPMs were in the green, lifted off and navigated the crowded urban airspace.

Not until reaching a comfortable cruising altitude did she allow herself to tune back in to her personal life. To Matthias and the Christmas Dilemma.

One disadvantage of loving a man with a brilliant mind was the sound reasoning for his decisions. But Angie never backed away from a challenge. Ever. And losing gracefully was something she'd never been very good at.

Fortunately, the flight was long, and by the time her corner of NE Texas came into sight, she had a plan.

Landing at the ranch's airfield felt odd, because she most often flew the Steed, and it resided conveniently beside her house—that way, she was always ready when a call-out came.

She grinned. Being a part of her family's security company, and their go-to helo pilot, was a huge responsibility, and the world's greatest job. Plus, she had a great kid, so life was good…but it would be perfect when she got to introduce Matt to her family this Christmas.

Angie was still smiling while she tucked the copter safely in the hangar and hopped on a four-wheeler to zip home through the late summer heat with dust billowing in her wake.

Her son, Dhillon, would know by now that she was back, but he'd wait for her at the big house. She always needed alone time first, to decompress, and she'd been blessed with a kid who didn't need to be hit over the head before he caught on. Not that she was the kind of woman who pussy-footed around, dropping hints. She'd encountered that type, and they drove her nuts. Nope, when Angie had something to say, she said it. Saved a freaking lot of time and aggravation that way.

The house greeted her with comfortable silence.

The kind she could sink into after several days of intense training, a long flight, and time spent with her charming prince.

Her family called him her mystery man, because they'd never met him. Which brought her back to the subject of Christmas. The last time her brothers had teased her for not bringing him around, and suggested he was a figment of her imagination, she'd done something rash. Told them he'd be here for Christmas this year.

What the heck had she been thinking? Huh. Not thinking was the problem. She'd been caught up in the vision of a full-blown, old-fashioned family Christmas. Her two older brothers would be there with their wives and kids, and Angie had this crazy flash of Matt being there with her and their son.

She plunked down at the kitchen table with her laptop, a handful of Consuelo's oatmeal cookies, a large glass of lukewarm water, and an ice-cold beer. She filled in the Bug's logbook and her own, then completed the more annoying forms that would account for her trip and airtime. "Training" covered a vast amount of area, and with the blessing of Julia—her mother, family matriarch, and company president—she wrote that same word in a dozen different boxes.

Had she been training? Hell, yes. Was that all she'd been up to? Hell no. She guzzled the water and set the empty glass aside, ticked hydration off a checklist in her mind, and munched a cookie while she finished the Meyers paperwork and got started on the report for ETC, filling in the data regarding her extrasensory training progress.

When she was done, she popped the top off the

beer and took a long swallow, savoring the cool while it slid all the way to her belly, then opened her messages.

The one from Dhillon made her grin. HEY, MOM. I KNOW YOU WANT TO REST, BUT YOU CAN DO THAT POOLSIDE. YOU GOTTA SEE WHAT I TAUGHT CHANCE TODAY! COME ON, THERE'S LOTS OF COOKIES AND ICE-COLD…COKE.

She snorted at the winky-face he'd added. She wasn't much of a drinker, but a beer was her go-to after a long flight, and her kid knew it. She sent him a reply. "FEET UP AND RELAXING FOR ANOTHER FIFTEEN, THEN I'LL BE LOOKING FOR RED MEAT. GET THE GRILL FIRED UP."

RELAX HERE. COME ON!

She laughed. What the heck. Brooding wasn't possible with Dhillon around.

***

Back at ETC, Matthias pushed away from his desk, and would have gone to stare out the window if there'd been one. But when you worked underground, there were only panels of glass with holographic images of mountains to give the illusion of being able to see outdoors.

He shoved his hair away from his face and, for just a moment, longed for wind against his skin. Let himself imagine air crisp with autumn driving back the heat, and a mountain trail beneath his wheels, steep drops, sharp curves, and long climbs. Winding his way through the trees, thinking about Angie, trying to figure out what to do about her.

The distraction was especially enticing for a day

like today, when she'd been driving him nuts about going to the family deal at the ranch.

She'd been happy with the way things were, or relatively so, until recently, when two of her brothers and a cousin who worked with her at Meyers had each done the traditional marriage and kids thing. He got that.

And while Angie *used* to be comfortable in the role of single parent, lately it seemed to trouble her that there was no one to catch her if she fell.

But Matthias wouldn't step up to the plate. Couldn't. Had no choice.

And wasn't that half the problem? His perspective was skewed, twisted, warped, tarnished…or whatever other word stood for his world being completely unlike that of normal people. Yeah, Angie'd hit him with the popular phrase "normal is just a setting on your dryer," but everything about his life *was* different. He didn't experience living the way anyone else did.

Besides having comfortable furniture and recessed screens with pleasant outdoor images, his private suite wasn't much different from his office. At least in his lab he felt at home, sometimes not leaving it for days, and when he had to because his eyes would no longer focus, he'd grab his bike and hit the mountain trails—the ones programed into the simulator.

He shook off the dismal thoughts and got back to work. Checked his inbox, sent most of the files to folders for future perusal, then cruised through the one his mentor and boss, Dr. Christopher Kelton, had asked him to review.

Classified information about a potential new

recruit for ETC. Her gift was precognition, but she had issues with control. She was hoping ETC would help her get a handle on the visions currently messing with her daily life. But ETC, in Matthias's estimation, had strung her along. Kept her there for a full week and put her through all the testing, even though it was obvious she wasn't going to fit their program. Matthias hated when this kind of thing happened, because he was the one expected to magically find a way to turn her into a useful tool. Otherwise, her experiences there among them would have to be erased from her mind. A practice he believed was completely unethical.

Among other things, Matthias's talent's lay in the spin. The packaging required to make sure the wrong impressions about ETCETERA never leaked out. Could he sell ice to Alaska? Probably.

He half-laughed. But he couldn't seem to convince a sexy, sweet, pig-headed, half-pint redhead with bright green eyes and a giant economy-sized ego that he would not be going to her family home for Christmas. Ever.

CHAPTER 2

When Angie arrived poolside, her stomach growled happily at the smoky aroma of burgers.

"Hey, Mom, watch this!" Dhillon leaped off the diving board and tossed a Frisbee, which his dry-land-only dog caught smartly just before the kid cannonballed into the water. Chance jogged over to Angie with the toy and a silly grin. "Glad you finally gave up your dignity, pal. This is way more fun, huh?" The tall, leggy greyhound dropped the toy and shook, even though he wasn't wet.

"Mom, toss it here and watch, I almost had him in with me earlier."

"Dog's not that dumb," said Angie's sister, Eve, from her spot at the shallow end, farthest from the splash zone. Angie wandered over to drop onto the chair beside her.

"He bends just enough to keep Dhillon happy. Which I'm sure won't include getting in the water."

"He's bred for speed, not aquatics." And although he was very fast, he'd failed at the racetrack because somewhere along the line he'd missed out on his ration of prey instinct. Nothing they'd done could convince him to chase the fake rabbit. The family had been skeptical when Quinn's wife, Rachel, brought him home. Afraid he'd chase the cats, or other small animals, but he'd proven to be a perfect gentleman, a truly gentle soul.

Eve laughed. "I'll never forget the failed life jacket idea." When they strapped it on him, poor Chance had frozen in place, as though his joints had locked up like one of those crazy fainting goats, and no amount of coaxing could make him move. So, in order to allow the dog to be poolside without worry of someone drowning while attempting a rescue if he fell in, a new tool had been added. Designed by Eve and built by their youngest brothers, it was a long pole with a net big enough to drop over the dog. To date, it had been used only twice, both times to rescue ducklings unable to get out on their own.

"Hey, Mom, can you check the burgers for me? Pleeeease."

She nodded with a wry smile. Tough for a kid to juggle fun and responsibility, and, heck, she had been away. "Yeah, I've got it."

"Thanks," he said, hopping out and leaving a wet trail back to the board, where he launched himself, again tossing the toy to the dog.

"There's a tick under the column for manners," said Eve. "He's okay, that kid of yours."

"Yeah, in spite of the guys," she said with a laugh.

Her brothers spent plenty of quality time with him, making sure he grew up the way they did, wild and free, with a great sense of adventure. They'd been "super" uncles from the day Dhillon was born—probably worried there wasn't enough testosterone in his life. Then, after the incident with his heart, they'd worked even harder to make sure his childhood was normal, and prevent Angie from becoming a helicopter mom. They'd had great fun making jokes, because she *was* one of three helicopter pilots among the siblings.

It had been so hard at first. Letting go. Having him out of sight. Terrified his heart could stop again, even though the surgery to repair the abnormality had been successful and there'd been no residual effects. Besides the thin white streak in his hair.

She shook off the dark thoughts and went to tend the grill. Was pleased to see he'd spaced the meat well, and kept the heat low enough to prevent burning the outside while the inside stayed raw.

"Where's the vegetables, hotshot?"

"In the fridge."

She pulled out the tray of skewered veggie chunks and slid it onto the wide counter of the outdoor kitchen. "Nice work."

"I made two without onions for you guys."

"Appreciated. You forgot the zucchini on a couple of these."

"Funny, Mom. It's a trade-off. There's just as much good stuff in the onion as in the zoo-chunks."

"Okay, point to you then."

He was probably disappointed she hadn't argued so he could spew the numbers he'd no doubt memorized. Kid had a wicked brain. Made her second-guess herself sometimes about homeschooling. But to have him away from the ranch for most of the day wasn't feasible. She'd be a wreck.

She shuddered at the thought of him going to college eventually. Hell, it was only a few years off. She was already supplementing his official classwork with projects for him to research, since he was so far ahead of where he should be for his age. She told herself it was good preparation for college. But in reality she just wanted to keep him home and busy until he was at least eighteen. Then what? Fear slid into her gut like old fryer grease.

Can't go there. Not yet. No point borrowing trouble.

"Angie." Eve's tone was sharp. "Stop it."

Angie shook it off. "Thanks." Sometimes it was a good thing to have a sister who picked up all of her emotions. But not always. She flipped the burgers, then laid down the veggie kabobs, enjoying the sizzle and waft of the super-mouthwatering smoke.

By the time Julia and Consuelo joined them, dinner was almost ready. Dhillon set the table, then ran back to the pool to show them Chance's new trick. Chance obligingly waited and caught the Frisbee just before the deck became soaked by one teenaged cannonball.

"Ain't that something?" said Consuelo. "The danged dog's smiling."

"He loves pleasing that boy," said Julia.

Angie was always amazed when her mother allowed her soft side to show. It didn't happen often, but was a good reminder that there was a lot more to Julia than what she allowed others to see.

"How's Dad doing?"

Julia's face softened even more. "Well. Really well."

"Do you think he'll ever move home again?"

"Not to this house. We're going to build a new

one, a private and secure oasis."

James had made an amazing recovery after bottoming out a couple of years earlier. Mixing alcohol with his medications in an attempt to cope with his PTSD, he'd spiraled out of control and wound up on the street. Family intervention had backfired, and when he took off from rehab, they thought they'd lost him for good. Luckily, he stumbled upon a program that matched vets with special service dogs. With Swagger, a rescued and retrained mutt at his side, James was inching his way back to his family.

"Where are you going to build?"

"The knoll beyond the stables." Not surprising, since James would feel more secure where he could see anyone approaching. "Your father has designed a rancher with three rooms on each side of the main living area. On one side will be the master bedroom, an office, and his den. On the other, guest bedrooms, because he hopes to one day have his grandchildren come for sleepovers."

"Does Swagger get his own room?"

"No. He sleeps beside the bed, and wakes your father up if he's having nightmares. It's amazing to see."

"Chance does that too," said Dhillon.

While Angie battled back the first response— which would have been "What nightmares?"—Eve shot her a look, and said, "That's awesome. How do you think he knows?"

He frowned. "I read that they react to changes in our energy field."

"How do you think that works?" asked Eve.

"Probably kind of like the aura stuff, where

different colors mix when a guy's anxious or something." He shrugged. "No matter, though, I'm just always happy that I get to wake up and don't have to stay in the nightmare any longer."

Angie schooled her voice into a tone of simple curiosity. "What are the nightmares like?" Not *about*, as that would be asking for personal information.

"Usually the same old stuff from when my heart stopped and I saw the ghosts waiting for me. Spooky, but not all bloody and mean like zombie stuff on TV."

Eve's voice was carefully even. "I end up going to the fridge for food to shake off my bad dreams. Maybe I should get a dog. Then I wouldn't have to do the killer workouts to keep from bursting out of my clothes."

"I don't even get out of bed. Chance just climbs in with me and I go right back to sleep."

"You and your grandfather have a lot in common," said Julia. "Have you given any thought to what you want to do with yourself once you've finished growing into your feet?"

Dhillon looked down and wiggled his toes. "I want to be a doctor."

Well, wasn't that interesting?

"Ah, following in your aunt, Eve's footsteps, then. You didn't catch your mom's flying bug?"

"Not really. I thought about doing the family thing, you know, Special Forces and stuff, but I'm not big on following orders." He shrugged. "I'd rather be able to fix people. It would be way frosty if I could do it the way Rachel does, but I haven't been able to tap into that kind of extra power. I guess I'll have to go the college and med school route."

Dhillon wanted to be a doctor. Still stunned, Angie tried to ignore the heavy thumping of her heart while she served up supper, and hoped everyone would be too distracted to notice she was having trouble breathing.

"Angie?" Eve popped the top off a can of soda and passed it to her.

She stared at it as though not sure what to do.

"Drink."

Right. She took a long swallow. He wanted to go to medical school. How crazy was that? His father was a doctor, and a research scientist. But Dhillon didn't know that. He wasn't even aware that he'd met his father. Become friends with the man who was responsible for—

"Genetics are a crazy thing," said Eve. She was the only one who knew.

Angie finally managed to speak. "When did you decide on the doctor thing?"

"It sorta started back when my heart stopped. There were so many of them in and out of my room that week, and they were super cool. Freaky smart, and talked to me like I had a brain. Wasn't just hey, there's that kid with the faulty ticker." He took a man-sized bite of his burger and talked around it.

"I want to do that. Fix people because they matter. You know, like the kid in the room with me, the one with the weird disease. Even when they knew they couldn't fix him, they kept trying to do stuff to make it easier for him. Always tried to make him laugh. And the best is the DNA stuff. I did a bunch of research when Meyers had that case with the horses getting switched.

"And I really like Doctor Matt." He glanced at

his grandmother. "He's the one doing the research thing at ETC."

Oh boy. Angie's heart clutched. This isn't the time to burst into tears. Do something. Anything. She dropped her burger in her lap, swiped at the splotch of ketchup and mustard with her napkin, then bolted for the bathroom.

CHAPTER 3

Matthias stowed his bike in the SUV parked beside the well-hidden landing strip south of Whistler, British Columbia. He gave the pilot a wave before climbing into the vehicle and following directions he'd committed to memory. Within minutes, he was northbound on Highway 99. Huge pine, fir, and cedar trees bordered the long stretch of pavement, and majestic mountains towered above.

When he spotted a couple of deer grazing along the shoulder, seemingly oblivious to the cars whizzing by, he wished he could pull over to watch them. Wanted to observe their behavior, whether they maintained a certain distance from the traffic, or...

Knock it off, Martinez, you're on holiday.

When the odometer showed exactly seventy-four kilometers, he turned right, followed a winding road until he saw a plain metal mailbox with the number thirty-one painted on the side. Drove the long, curved driveway to a safe house belonging to his friends Logan and Grace.

Determined not to waste a minute of his freedom, he quickly checked through every room, changed his clothes, stowed his overnight bag, and grabbed a sandwich and drinks from the well-stocked fridge. Tossing them into a small backpack that already held his emergency gear—clothes, shoes, ID, and sat phone—he headed out the door and reset security.

Steel gray skies might have put some people off, but that, thought Matt as he put a water bottle in the holder and swung his leg over, would just make more room for him, and the less he encountered other riders, the better. Shoving off, he sucked in a long, slow breath of clean, fresh air—completely different from the recycled stuff he lived with twenty-four seven.

What began as a smile moved right through grin and into laughter as he picked up speed and shot down the driveway.

Freedom! He threw back his head and howled.

***

By the time he came upon the first bike path, he was warmed up, and muscle memory had taken over the gear changes. He pushed for more speed on the flat ground, and delighted in the roaring of wind in his ears, the subtle bite of autumn chilling his face and hands, and the crunch of gravel beneath his wheels. Life pumped through his veins, tension drained away, and sheer joy took over before he even got to the challenging mountainous terrain.

He tightened the strap on his helmet and took a swallow of water before starting the long and grueling climb. He couldn't risk taking a lift since there was still a crime group after him.

The alpine switchback he'd chosen was known by few, used by fewer, and would take him around the back and up to the top. He knew every twist and turn from studying satellite maps and taking daily virtual rides on the simulator.

But that was no more like the actual experience than watching a hockey game was remotely like being on the ice.

He'd expected the physiological effects of the altitude and the extreme exercise—straining quads, windpipe fully expanded, lungs begging for more oxygen, and sweat burning his eyes. But he hadn't counted on the sheer exhilaration, the lightening of his being, and feeling so fucking alive.

At the top he paused and rested, overwhelmed by the sheer vastness of the peaks and valleys surrounding him, the brilliant blue of a lake far below, and the utter silence enveloping him. Mesmerized, he didn't move.

If a high-powered rifle with a mega-scope was trained on him because he was reckless enough to be out in the open? He didn't care. He'd die a happy man.

The smile started slow and grew until laughter erupted yet again. Shoot me now, he thought, and I won't have to worry about Angie trying to get me to the ranch. And what the hell *was* he going to do about that?

Reality seeped in. He always did what needed to be done, of course. Stayed out of the light. Made sure the sinister force he had no control over couldn't find him. But wasn't he tired of living that way? Tired of ducking and dodging an invisible power?

Was it a mistake to allow himself to dream? This ride—hell, the whole trip—was about him cracking open a door that had stayed shut, locked tight, for far, far too long. Lulled him into accepting his fate, kept him deeply entrenched in work, and his research, and the belief that what he was doing was important.

Well, it was. But there was more. Substantially more, and wasn't it about time he started claiming what was his? Maybe.

Time to stop thinking. He clipped his water bottle back in place, and pushed off.

While making his way toward the black diamond trail, he came across his first pile of bear scat, right there on the path. He stopped and scanned for footprints in the dust, spotted several large ones but no small—hopefully that meant Yogi was travelling without the missus and the kids. Good grief, he was channeling Angie.

He did a careful perusal of the area and, seeing no signs of wildlife, carried on and started pedaling hard. He'd slow down later, on the ride back, when his lungs were a fiery pit in his chest and his muscles were screaming for pity. That's when he'd take in more of the scenery, absorb the tranquility.

For now, he put all his attention on his route. A long, curved slope morphing into a sharp turn tested one set of skills before catapulting him over the edge and asking for something entirely different. This was where the mountain was known for winning most of the battles, but he was prepared to ride it to the bottom while his joints absorbed the concussion of bumps and dips.

On a long downhill straightaway he nearly shot

his arms towards the sky with a shout of joy, but his hands stayed welded to the grips. It didn't get any better than this.

But he was wrong. The bend at the bottom was long and slow, where you're supposed to be able to catch your breath, but his lodged in his throat when he caught sight of another rider standing just off the trail. How the—?

"Hey, cowboy, want some company?"

"How the hell—?"

Angie's grin was a face-splitter. "Didn't take much to figure out where you were headed. You've been riding this for weeks in the sim-lab."

"I should be furious."

"But you're not."

How could he be? He loved spending time with her at ETC, but seeing her here, looking fresh and just a bit wild, was whetting another appetite. "You look good outdoors."

"Gotta say the same back atcha. Nearly swallowed my tongue watching you."

"Come here." He held out his hand, and when she put hers in it, he drew her against him for a warm, welcoming kiss. "I should be pissed," he muttered.

"Should…never did like that word."

He couldn't resist sliding his hands over her very fine ass. "We can't stay here this way. Someone will run us down."

"Then let's get a move on."

Watching her throat as she drank from her water bottle, heat spread. He cleared his throat. "I, ah, didn't know you rode."

"Dhillon got me into it a few years ago. Just on the ranch, though, nothing as spectacular as this. I got here a few days ago and took some coaching on practice runs to hone my skills—as the pamphlet promised—on lesser terrain." With a cheeky smile she donned her helmet, hopped on her bike, and took off like a runaway horse.

Matthias was quick to follow, but nearly missed a gear when he took in her rear view. "That is one fine—" he gave his head a shake. "Probably going to break my neck now for sure."

But he didn't, and an hour later he drew alongside where she'd stopped on a wider trail. "There's a good spot up ahead if you want a break," he said.

"I'd rather just stop here instead of where I'm *supposed* to stop."

He nodded. "I hear ya. I've lived within parameters set by others for so damn long, I sometimes wonder if I'll ever be able to think for myself."

"Then why not break free?"

"You know why."

She pursed her lips. "Actually, I know the what. But I'm not sure I understand the why."

"They're one and the same. I'm hiding from people who want me dead."

"Could you change that?"

"Only by moving from their peripheral vision into the cross hairs. He shrugged. "I've been off their radar for so long now, I doubt they're even actively searching for me anymore."

"Then why stay in hiding?"

"Because."

"Great answer. Makes you sound like a parent."

His throat thickened. "I am."

"But—"

"Angie, what I do is important. I can't just walk away from it. People depend on me. I shouldn't even *be* out here indulging myself and risking being seen. I'll never be free. I've resigned myself to living out my days underground because I have a purpose. Every bit of my research is for my son. He's the reason I do it. The reason I live in a glorified bunker, and put in fourteen-hour days searching for minuscule clues in test results."

"But Dhillon's fully recovered and a perfectly normal kid, Matt."

As always, her use of the shortened version of the name hit him in the solar plexus. Why was it such a big deal? Not like it was even his real name. But it made him hers somehow.

Frustrated, Angie studied the face so familiar, yet today so new, and unease slid between them. "I wonder if I even know you anymore," she said. "Maybe I never did."

She'd always believed that one day wanting a life with her and Dhillon would be enough to make him stop running, stop hiding from the organized crime group who'd made him choose a life underground.

But maybe she'd been wrong. Maybe there would never be anything but stolen moments like these. No quiet evenings at home, no family dinners, or any of the other everyday things she'd imagined. Dreamed of. Prayed for. Maybe days like today were the most they'd ever have. And even that was because *she'd* engineered the trip to surprise him. It had nothing to do with him choosing to spend time with her.

"Tell me what's wrong. Why my life in hiding is

suddenly bothering you? What's different today?"

She could have laughed to cover up, but didn't. "Aside from the incredible scenery, the sheer celebration of being in your company where we can talk and breathe and just *be* without windowless walls and cameras and processed air?"

She had become what he wanted and needed. Had changed who she was for someone she only thought she knew. In her heart she'd believed, dammit. She swallowed the rising fear. "I don't understand what makes you tick. I don't know how to predict your next move. And I'm not sure if I want to continue being what you need me to be." She huffed out a breath. "Here I thought I was setting myself up for a fabulous few days of freedom with you, and now I'm fighting a primal instinct to point my wheels downhill and not look back. I must be losing my mind."

She scrubbed her hands over her face. "What I thought I wanted isn't here." With one final glance at his expressionless face, she said, "I have to go."

Tears blinded her to the trail, forced her to slow her frantic pace. Bumps and turns had her blinking frantically, clearing her vision for self-preservation. She needed to focus on the miles of dirt and rock between her and where she was staying, needed to suck it up until she got there.

When she finally reached the bottom, she stopped. Looked up to where she'd left him. But of course he wasn't there. Maybe he never had been. Wasn't she in love with a mirage? A man who didn't exist? She gave her head a shake and started along the wide path to her condo.

She'd been strong for so long, been the one with

the backbone, the family member everyone depended on to help them when things were rough. She'd survived the shock of becoming a mom before she was old enough to drive, the terror of Dhillon's near death, a gunshot wound, and dozens of life and death Meyers missions. But having her dream shattered after foolishly holding onto it for so many years was like the camel's proverbial straw, and she buckled under the weight.

Hands shaking as she unraveled, she tugged off the helmet, hung it on the handlebar and leaned the bike against the patio table. Tears blinded her while she struggled with the door lock, and a sob escaped when she finally got it to open. She stumbled inside and twisted the deadbolt.

Sank to the floor and shattered.

Like Dresden on concrete.

Tears poured, and soul-deep cries wracked her body as she lay curled in a ball, mourning the loss of a dream.

***

Matthias had watched until she was out of sight, instinctively knowing better than to follow, but his gut also told him he needed to fix whatever she thought was broken. Even though they could never have a life together in the traditional sense, they were a couple in their own weird way, and he wasn't about to let her forget that. He loved her—and not just because of Dhillon.

He loved her tenacity, her ingrained sense of right and wrong, the way she stood up for the underdog without going against those on top. Her sense of self was a remarkable thing, and her belief in *him* occasionally took him out at the knees.

But something had broken, and he needed to fix it.

The shine had worn off his ride, and he didn't take time to enjoy his surroundings on the way back. It was cold on the north side, reminding him summer was long over and snow would soon cover the mountain from top to bottom—he glanced up at the clear blue sky—but not today. The ominous clouds of earlier had cleared on his ride up, adding to the euphoria, as though the universe had gifted him one perfect day.

A day gone dark like a bad dream. He needed to think. And he had to find her—that would be the easy part.

By the time he retraced his path back to the house, he'd worked out some of the details. First stop, call Logan on the landline to find out where Angie was staying—the man knew everything, or could at least track down the information. Then Matthias would go to her and get her to explain *exactly* what the problem was.

But what he saw when he was halfway up the driveway made his heart sink. Logan was there waiting for him. Pacing in front of the house.

Vacation was obviously over. He'd have to go back.

Hey.

Instead of responding telepathically, Logan simply watched Matthias until he came to a stop, then said, "There's a problem."

"Figured."

"Angie's missing."

Relief spread. "She's here. In Whistler, I mean."

Logan shook his head. "Was."

"Is. We were on the mountain together only," he glanced at his watch, "about an hour ago, maybe an hour twenty."

"Her GPS was hot on screen all day on the mountain and back to her condo. Ten minutes later she was on the Sea to Sky highway, southbound."

Shit. She'd been mad, but he hadn't expected her to take off. He propped the bike alongside the porch and hung his helmet on the handle.

"When she passed right through the populated areas and onto open highway—a flag went up in the Meyers control room, and they haven't been able to raise her."

Adrenaline surged through Matt's system and words failed him. Angie worked for—was an integral part of—her family's security company. She wouldn't ignore communications. Going dark was simply never done unless answering would put a life in danger.

Logan was standing by the driver's door of the SUV. "Keys?"

Matt fished them from his pack, tossed them to his friend, and swung around to get in the passenger side.

As they barreled down the driveway, Logan said, "We've got a team on the road coming north from Vancouver. You and I will check out the condo, then head south to get behind her in case she doubles back."

"She was pissed at me for some reason. Which is probably why she bolted." His gut clenched.

"Possible." When a steady beeping tone came from Logan's phone he said, "That's an update." He flicked the speaker button without taking his eyes off the road. "Go ahead."

"Signal's gone black. Northbound team setting up at Porteau Cove as planned. Over."

"Copy." He stuffed the phone back in his pocket. "They're staging a motorcycle crash so they can block the highway down to single lane, and check all vehicles."

"What aren't you telling me?"

Logan sighed. "Meyers Security has strict protocols about changing locations, and she failed to adhere to any of them."

"She was here on personal time, and she's pissed at me."

"Rules are twenty-four seven, three sixty-five. No exceptions. Angie might be a bit of a rebel, but this kind of move is out of character. She knows the cavalry will be called out if she's incommunicado. And nobody wants them showing up."

"We were together today, in public. Granted we were on the side of a mountain in the middle of nowhere, but anything long-range could have picked us up." Had she been kidnapped to draw him out?

At the condo, they found no hint of struggle. Her biking clothes were in a heap on the tiled floor along with a couple of damp towels, and the rest of her belongings were neatly packed in a black duffle on the bed.

Logan attached a small device to the landline and was on a call with Meyers control when a door slammed.

He disconnected, and had a gun in his hand almost before Matthias could blink.

A silence both eerie and expected blanketed

them until Logan suddenly grinned and shouted. "Hey, Angie, it's Logan. We're upstairs."

He slipped the weapon back under his jacket and stepped out into the clear while footsteps pounded up the stairs.

She came into sight, a flurry of motion and anger. "What the—"

"Easy, spitfire. We come in peace." Logan smothered her with a hug and she didn't resist. "Your tracker showed you hitting the road out of town and you didn't answer any calls from Control, so we came to check on you. Give me a sec." He called Meyers, told them to stand down the teams.

Angie rolled her eyes. "That's just not fair. Everybody else screws up all the time and gets away with it, but the one time I do, they send out the freaking troops."

"Because you never screw up," said Logan, and immediately threw Matthias under the bus. "Romeo, here, figured you'd been spotted with him, and it was his fault because he'd ticked you off."

"Thanks, pal," said Matt.

"Don't mention it." His expression went from amused to serious when he turned back to Angie. "What happened, kiddo? Where's your com unit? Your tracker?"

Wasn't this embarrassing, thought Angie as she went to the bathroom and dug her phone from the pile of clothing on the floor. Made her look like she was a pig, when all she'd been was freaking mad at herself once her pity party petered out. She was furious to think she'd become the kind of woman she neither understood nor empathized with. The kind who fell in love with a man and then proceeded to try to change him into what she really wanted.

"When I was in the shower, it dawned on me I'd left my helmet outside, with my tracker in it. But when I went back out I discovered bike and all had been stolen off the patio, and I saw red." She shrugged. "I took off at a run, thinking maybe I could catch the thief, and by the time I slowed down I was halfway into town, so I kept going and reported the theft at the police station."

Thank heavens she'd dressed before leaving the bathroom, or there was a good chance she'd have run outdoors naked—that's how damn mad she'd been.

"Sharp game," said Matthias. "Follow people off the mountain, knowing the first thing they're likely to do is hit the shower. Great window of opportunity for a quick grab and go. Ride off to wherever your vehicle is stashed, and poof. Gone."

She put her hands on her hips and asked Logan, "Do I need to check in?"

"Nope, you're officially no longer missing."

"But my cover's toast, so I have to leave, right?"

"Sorry, kid. Meyers policies and procedures can't be messed with."

"Have I blown it for this safe house too?"

"No sweat. We'll unload it and pick up a couple more."

"You say that as though you're buying and selling socks."

"Grace and I can never have too many safe houses." He frowned for a second, then held up a finger, the universal signal for stand by.

Recognizing that he was having a telepathic conversation, Angie grabbed her shampoo and soap from the shower, stuffed them into her travel bag along with the few other cosmetics she'd left on the counter, and was cramming her biking gear into a plastic bag when Logan finally spoke.

"There's a place northeast of here you can have for a week. Fully secure, less than an hour by air, and has no road access."

Angie looked at Matt. Would it make a difference? Or would getting to really know each other just make it harder to live without him—as if that was possible? What the heck did she have to lose? "I'm game if you are," she said.

Matt didn't hesitate. "How do we get there?"

Logan smiled. "Since Trent's already on his way with the Steed to pick you two up, maybe he'll let you have it, and I'll take him back to Meyers."

Angie grinned. She loved the Steed, a high-tech helicopter with capabilities some would call futuristic. It flew faster than any other helo, was nearly silent, and had a reflective surface treatment that made it almost invisible. As a Meyers pilot, she was the primary operator for her favorite bird, and it even had a hangar outside her front door so she could fire it up the instant it was needed. Hers to command.

And there it was, her need for control. The one thing she didn't have in her relationship with Matt— the man she wished could be the father her son deserved.

"Angie?"

"Two minutes to gather my stuff. Here." She passed Matt the case she'd already filled. Years on ops had given her mad skills when it came to traveling light and being prepared to relocate with less than a moment's notice. She took the stairs two at a time, hooking left into the kitchen, grabbed the insulated bag from the fridge. Had it zipped and slung over her shoulder before the guys met her at the door.

Instead of driving south to the airstrip, Logan took them north to a secluded farm, where her brother landed the Steed in a tree-lined field. Once he shut it down, Logan drove closer and parked at the tail.

Angie scooted toward the bird to engage Trent as soon as he climbed out, and when Logan joined them to explain the plan, Matt slipped out of the SUV and around to the other side.

Minutes later, Angie stowed Trent's helmet and dug out her own, gave him a fist bump, then climbed into the seat he'd vacated.

When Matt opened the passenger door, she pointed at the spare helmet on the seat. "That's mandatory, because this buggy internalizes her engine noise." He pulled it on. "And," she said with a smile. "The direct mic means you can't ignore me."

"My lucky day."

Onboard cameras showed the SUV was already halfway back to the highway by the time she finished her checks and was ready to get them airborne. Matt held the paper with the information Logan had given them. But she didn't need it, since she'd already programed the flight into the onboard computer. Maps, directions, and locations were her thing, and no minuscule detail was ever missed.

"Strap in and hang on, cowboy. You're in for a treat."

CHAPTER 4

Angie stood in front of the wide window, and stared out at the valley where they'd landed. Several thousand privately owned acres surrounded the beautiful log house, and it was theirs for an entire week. Who would she be at the end of those seven days? What would her future look like?

Hearing a sound from the kitchen, she turned to find Matt watching her, and she sighed. "I never would have imagined feeling awkward with you. Not in a million years."

His smile was slow as he closed the space between them. "I felt that way every time you came to me. As though, for those first few minutes together, I didn't know where to put my hands, my feet, where to look. And then you smile and I forget everything."

Nearly undone by his words, she almost swerved from what she'd been about to say. But she had to get it out, stepped back to keep him from touching her. "I have a confession," she said, then barreled on before she lost her nerve. "I've been under the misguided impression that we had, in spite of continuing to deceive my family and countless others, always been honest with each other. But somehow I've managed to trick myself, and you by default."

Concern was something she was used to seeing on his gorgeous face, but confusion was an addition she could blame herself for. And fix.

"You said, right from the beginning, that you couldn't have a real relationship with me. That any time we had together would be moments stolen from the reality of our lives. A few hours at most." She smiled. "And I loved every single glorious minute. Savored and relived them second by second until we could be together again. I was good with what we had. After all, I had Dhillon, the best of both of us, so being with you twice a year was like caramel sauce and whipped cream on top of an amazing chocolate fudge brownie. Perfection kicked up a dozen notches."

He sat on the arm of the long leather sofa. "I'm hearing past tense."

She couldn't stay still. Wandered to the shelves lining the interior walls and ran a fingertip over a tiny figurine of a warrior on horseback, a teepee, and a buffalo…while she gathered the strength to finish what she needed to say.

"When we met that first time at ETC, I was barely recovered from Dhillon's—" She hesitated, always loath to say the words. "That day when his heart stopped changed everything about me. It just took a while for me to notice. Anyway, even weeks later, when I walked into your office at ETC and realized it was you across the desk, I think I was still running on adrenaline, and you were a gift from the universe. Dhillon's father. The person I'd long ago given up hope of ever seeing again."

Angie moved to the other side of the room, lifted a beautiful agate half the size of her fist, let the weight warm her palm while she studied the different shades of gold highlighted by penetrating light. It looked incredibly strong, but if struck in just the right place would probably explode into hundreds of pieces. That's how she felt.

She set the stone back on its circle of leather. "I'd been building you up in Dhillon's mind for so many years, it was as though you'd been alive in mine forever." That unforgettable day, he'd simply stepped around the desk and opened his arms, then held her while she cried for the first time in years. "There you were. And you still wanted me. It was like a dream come true."

Of *course* she'd agreed to the secrecy he needed. Understood why they couldn't have a normal relationship, or even let Dhillon know who Matt was.

"I'd never depended before. Never leaned on anyone. I'd handled whatever came my way, and, until the day Dhillon collapsed, had been the person to prop up everyone else. I didn't even notice I was becoming dependent on you. Pathetic, when I look back on it." And she didn't do pathetic very well. "I've never had any sympathy for needy females." She tried for a smile but couldn't quite manage one. "I guess the joke's on me."

"You've never been needy," he said. And if she went to him now, she knew he'd kiss her and everything would be better. For the moment. She shook off the temptation.

"That's where you'd be wrong. It's been a long, slow build, but it's there. I just didn't realize it until yesterday."

Matt refilled his water glass, then went to stand in front of the wall of glass. Although facing her, he was backlit, so she couldn't see his features, just his outline. Couldn't judge his mood, but, what the heck, she needed to get everything out, no matter what his reaction.

"I've allowed myself to build our relationship into something it wasn't—in my mind, that is. Because I've been seeing you more frequently, talking to you about Dhillon and our daily lives, I've managed to twist my view of the future to include you in it."

"But I will be." His voice was soft, low, and her heart picked up speed before she managed to squash the hopeless hope.

"I mean as in you being a part of our daily lives."

"Christmas."

But so much more. "That was where it finally manifested. I had this stupid mental image of all of us together for the first time. I imagined surprising Cass by producing her long lost brother, watching your gentle hands while you lifted your nieces to say hello, and Dhillon's face when it sank in that his favorite doc at ETCETERA was actually his father." Her gut churned and she swiped at a tear escaping down her cheek. "I created my own fairy tale, Matt, and didn't even know I was doing it. I've become one of those women who falls in love with someone and then spends her life changing them to fit who she wants them to be. I have no patience for women like that. They're idiots. And so am I. I'm sorry."

He drained his glass and set it on the low sill, then turned back toward her and opened his mouth as though to speak. Instead he shook his head, grabbed the glass, and headed for the kitchen.

She'd bared her soul and he had nothing to say. She should just climb back in the Steed and get the hell gone. She sucked in a deep breath, shoved her fingers through her hair and tried to focus on anything but him.

"The past won't just go away, Angie. It can't be changed, or ignored. I can't unsee an execution."

"Don't you ever wish your life could be different?"

He shook his head. "There would be no point."

"I don't think I could live that way. Without dreams and wishes."

"I have to. But I also get to make a difference. My research has changed lives, given people hope. What more could I ask for?"

What an extraordinary human being he was. He'd gone from being an average ten-year-old boy growing up with his parents and a couple of younger sisters in small town USA, to a solitary man living a hermit's life. Isolated, and content to stay that way.

She went to him, lifted to tiptoes and brushed her mouth across his. "I'm sorry I changed what was between us."

He cupped her face. "I wish I could be what you need." He kissed her gently, then let her go. "Want to walk with me while I take some time to process?"

"You go. I think I'll just hang here for a while. See if I can get a grip on myself. I don't want to completely wreck our time together."

He kissed her again, quick and hard this time. "I still love you."

And then he was gone.

***

Matthias hiked the length of the valley, discovering a whole network of trails leading into the wooded hills, but he wasn't in the mood to explore while Angie's words dogged him.

Obviously he hadn't been paying attention. Should have seen this coming. He couldn't give her a normal relationship. After so many years in witness protection, he didn't know how to live any other way. First there'd been the official version with Meyers Security, then, when he'd taken off on his own, the feds messed up his new ID and nearly got him killed when the Minnows found him. Walked right up and knocked on the door. Lucky for him, his landlady was a busybody and quizzed the two men while they stood on the porch. Matt had gone out a back window with nothing but his go-bag.

From then on he'd stayed ahead of them, created another identity, and never allowed himself to feel comfortable. School, oddly enough—education—was something he'd craved, though, and a chance meeting with Logan gave him the key to the kingdom.

Logan had the ability to pick up thoughts, and he heard Matthias's wishes—there'd still been wishes back then—and struck up a telepathic conversation as easily as nodding and saying good morning to a passerby. Freaked Matt right out, since he'd only ever conversed silently with his siblings, and that had been years before, when they were kids playing silly games.

The only time he wasn't watching his back now was when he was at ETCETERA...and this morning on his bike. He glanced at his watch. Crammed a whole helluva lot into a day, hadn't he? From ETC, to Whistler, a mountain ride, a monumental scare, another flight, and then Angie's revelation.

Night was falling quickly, and out here the only light would be from the stars. He broke into a jog. He'd left Angie alone too long already.

He couldn't help but laugh when he saw her, hands on hips, muttering, and frowning at the stove where steam rose from a couple of pots.

She turned on him. "What's so funny?"

"The ferocious look on your face while you were scolding inanimate objects."

"It's your fault."

"Hey, I just came through the door, and it smells damn good in here."

She scowled. "I've never cooked for you before. We have a teenaged child, and I've never cooked you a meal." She held her hands out, palm up. "And I'm a crappy cook because I only know how to make kid stuff."

"Like I said, it smells good."

"It's pasta sauce from a *jar*," she snapped. "And we're having it with packaged shells of the variety that comes with a three-year shelf life. Is that the kind of meal a woman is supposed to make for a man she—" She shook her head. "For a man she's trying not to scare half to death by turning into a possessive freakoid stalker?"

"It still sounds decent to me." Mostly. "And teamwork's always a good plan, so will you let me help?"

She threw her hands in the air. "Whatever."

He started with the fridge, pawed around and found no meat, but struck gold in the freezer.

"Sausages."

"Frozen, and I'm too hungry to wait for them to thaw."

"We'll cheat." He held them under the cold water tap until he could break them apart, then grabbed a sharp knife and cut them into one-inch chunks.

He dumped the whole works into a skillet with enough water to cover them up about halfway. "Is there a lid for this thing?"

She slid one on and he cranked the burner to high. "Ten minutes," he said and went back to the fridge for a couple of beers. Passed her one. "Want a glass?"

She shook her head, popped the top and took a long swallow. "You know I'm not this person, right? I'm really a shit-together woman with guts and brains, and I pilot helicopters and anything else that flies, and I'm a good mom, and a solid sister, and teammate."

Why was he enjoying watching her unravel? What did that say about him? He lifted the lid and pushed the sausages around while he puzzled his sudden need to have her naked and under him, right here, right now. All red-faced and flustered.

"I love you."

She stopped mid-whatever she'd been saying that he hadn't been listening to. "You can't do that. You can't just say those words and make everything better."

"Not my intention. But looking at you in this unusual state, the words just came out, because I do. Love you. No matter if you're queen of the skies or a slightly frustrated version of yourself with tomato sauce on your face." He wiped the single drop from the edge of her jaw with his fingertip.

"Oh, man. I'm toast." She rubbed the center of her chest, and he fought the urge put his hand over hers, step in, meet her mouth. "Uh, toast," she said. "Garlic. We can make some if you like. How hungry are you?"

He was starving for the taste of her. Most times they met, they'd be naked together within minutes, sometimes spending the entire time in bed—once they got that far. At the moment, what he wanted was to lift her onto the counter, peel off her clothes.

"Do you want garlic toast?"

He blinked. Got a grip, although not in the way he'd prefer. "No, thanks." Just a taste. He cupped her chin. Kissed her softly while he fought the need to sink in, take, give. And she sighed, nearly undoing his resolve. Instead he wrapped her tight in his arms, tucking her in under his chin and simply holding on. Enjoying the feel of her, the fruity scent of her hair, and her heart beating against his.

Until the pasta water boiled over with a hiss.

She spun away, grabbed the lid off, and stirred, while he dumped the sausages into the red sauce.

They worked together then, him straining water from the big pot, and setting the table while she dished up.

"We should have wine with pasta," she said.

"You don't like wine."

"True, but..."

He smiled at her. "This isn't a date, Angie. It's you and me getting a rare opportunity to spend real time together. Time to learn more about each other than our sexual preferences."

She grinned. "I bet if we did the math, we'd

discover about ninety percent of the time we've spent together we've been bare-assed naked."

Ninety-five. He'd had his mouth on every part of her, but didn't know what side of the bed she preferred to sleep on. "If you want to finish your supper, I suggest a change of subject."

Heat darkened her eyes to the color of the forest, and he knew she was feeling the same thing he was. He could touch her in just the right place— "You've got about ten seconds."

She hopped up and scooted to the kitchen. "You want another beer?"

"No thanks."

"Soda? Water?"

"Nope, I'm good."

"Dhillon would drink soda with every meal if I let him. Such a contradiction for a kid who spouts the scientific facts about stuff like that, but he loves both soda and potato chips anyway."

"It's called being a teenager. He can't help it. Next he'll be sneaking out at night."

"Oh, no," she said. "That won't be happening in my house. Even though we're totally safe on the ranch, right down to seismic cables around the entire place, I have excellent security on the house."

It was his turn to smile. "The boy is an electronic wizard with superior hacking skills. Don't think for a minute he can't reprogram, bypass, or disable anything you can throw in front of him."

She simply stared at him, then said, "He wouldn't dare."

"I don't know him anywhere near as well as you do, but I think he would dare." He held up a hand. "That is, providing he was sure he wouldn't worry you. You and your peace of mind are important to him. I suspect that's because of the heart incident. When he came to, he saw you scared, and that frightened him. He'd never intentionally do anything to put that fear back on your face."

"He told you that?"

"Not in those exact words, but the subject was touched on during one of our debriefs. We were talking about a personal sense of security and what could jeopardize that, how to avoid it."

"What's it like for you, having him in one of your programs when he doesn't have a clue you're his dad?" She held up her hand. "I'm looking for more than your stock, 'okay.' No quick answer this time."

He set down his fork, used the napkin, and leaned back in his chair. "I thought it would be weird at first, but it wasn't. He was just a kid. We had no connection. I found myself studying him when he wasn't looking, but for the most part, it was more as a scientist. Searching for similarities, but not familiarities.

"To me, he was *your* son. Not mine. I was no more than what some call a sperm donor. I get it," he said, holding up a hand to ward off the inevitable barrage, "that probably pisses you off, but you're the one who wanted more." He ignored her raised eyebrows.

"He said he wanted to be in my program so he could help others with the same heart abnormality. But he was jazzed by the whole ETCETERA thing. Kept asking questions about the facility, the people." He smiled. "Every time someone new joined us, he'd try to quiz me about what their 'specialty' was, and he'd be pissed that he couldn't do any of the cool stuff like telepathy, or telekinesis. I began to worry that he'd have a brain bleed if he tried any harder to move an object with his thoughts, and I never let on that I could hear him telepathically. Just didn't want to open that door. Didn't think it was my place."

He started clearing away their empty plates, loading the dishwasher while he talked. "That was when he started to get under my skin. I found myself looking forward to our sessions. Taking longer with him, which then made me afraid I'd be skewing the test results. I backed off."

He rifled in the freezer and found ice cream. Scooped it into two bowls and set them on the table.

"Sit," said Angie, and he did.

"He called me on it. Came right to my office, the way you would have, and asked why I was avoiding him. I explained about the test subjects all having to have the same exposure to the same stimuli, and he laughed at me. Said he wasn't some lab rat, then he did something that grabbed me by the throat."

He sat in the chair across from me and said words I'd said myself at almost exactly his age, to my father. He said, 'You can't keep me in the dark, or I'll go crazy trying to figure out what's going on. I'm a tough kid, so tell me."

He shoveled ice cream, appreciating the cooling effect on his suddenly raw throat. "Kicked me in the gut, and he saw it. I told him that because I'd had to say the same thing once, I got it. He was good with that as an explanation, but it left me raw. I had a son, and I more than liked him. It grew from there, until even though he still has no idea that I'm his father, he knows I care about him."

She tipped her head. "What about the skew of

your test results?"

"I had to admit to myself that the research would always be flawed, but as long as the pure data was studied by others, it would stand up to any scrutiny. My colleagues will do a good job while I remain, as always, in the shadows."

"Do you ever wish for more? Want the recognition you're due?"

"No."

"What about freedom, Matt, don't you sometimes wish you could move around as you please?"

"That's like asking someone born without sight if they miss being able to see flowers. I was never free. Ever. It's not something I'm familiar with." When she looked doubtful, he continued. "Up until I was ten, my mother ruled, and I did as I was told. I got my sisters up in the morning, got them dressed and fed. I set them up in the playroom before I went to school. I came home at lunch and fed them again. After school I took them outside to play."

"Where was your mother?"

"She slept in until sometime between breakfast and lunch, then left and didn't come home until it was time to prepare supper. That's when I'd get a free half hour or so."

"You looked after Cass and Syd."

He frowned. "Yes. Their names were different then, but we all had to change. For a while that's how my memory was set up. Stuff before we left, and stuff after. Even in my head I couldn't allow images of what I'd seen that day. It was all about leaving instead. I promised Cass I'd come back for her. Syd was too young to understand. But for a very long time, I carried the weight of that promise. Anyhow, that was my regimented life before. And after…well, I couldn't so much as belch out loud, let alone speak to anyone. We were in Meyers witness protection, told where we were going, when we were going, and who we'd be when we got there."

"What about when you bolted from Vegas and Meyers—well, everyone—lost track of you, didn't that give you a taste of freedom?"

"Yes, and it was terrifying."

"Your safety was in your own hands then."

"Exactly. I bet I didn't sleep for more than an hour at a time, and that went on for nearly a year."

"You still don't."

He smiled. "I do when you're not with me."

She came around the table and took his hand. "I need to be with you now. So I'm not liking your chances of getting much sleep for a while, cowboy."

CHAPTER 5

Angie knew he got a solid three hours of sleep after they'd made love again at midnight, because she lay awake next to him. Listening to him breathe and watching the thin bars of red light on the clock radio while the numbers changed.

When he rolled over to spoon her at 4:17, she slid a hand down his long, muscular thigh, and was rewarded with a deep hum. The one thing they'd always have was a deep understanding of each other physically. Their emotional hornet's nest evaporated with the rasp of his jaw on the sensitive flesh where her neck and shoulder came together.

He teased her, awakening that part of her always starving for his touch, and when his mouth warmed her ear, a pleasured sigh escaped and she turned her head to welcome him.

His arms came around her, and soft sounds worked their way up her throat.

"You're purring," he whispered.

"Mmmmm."

His chuckle vibrated against her back. And then his fingertips had her arching, seeking the exquisite pleasure of release, and being rewarded over and over until she was as close to boneless as a human could possibly get and, "OhmyGod," slipped from her lips like a breath.

There was no chuckle now. His entire body was hard with what he held in check. More evidence of what a giving man he was.

She mustered energy, rolled over and pushed him to his back. Slid up his chest until she could see his eyes in the watery light of approaching dawn. "Your turn, cowboy."

She started at his mouth, nibbled lightly, then scorched his lips with a fiery kiss. Pouring emotion and her very being into him. Them.

Paying homage to the man she'd loved since she was barely more than a girl, she began at the rough edge of his jaw and worked down, taking control and pleasuring him, reveling in their intimate knowledge of each other, and when she rose over him she smiled, took him in, and all was well with her world.

***

Waking up to full daylight, she was momentarily saddened by the smooth, cool sheets where Matt had been, but she quickly reminded herself that for the first time since they'd been reunited, they would have more nights together. Days, too, and here she was wasting one.

With a roll and a twist her feet hit the floor and she headed for the shower, but stopped and tipped her head to listen. He was still here, wasn't he?

Of course he was. He'd never leave without saying goodbye.

Feeling fresh from her shower, and thankful the house was well stocked with clothes they could use, she slipped on warm leggings and a cotton sweater long enough to cover her butt. Then she followed the scent of coffee to the kitchen, but bypassed the pot when she spotted Matt through the window.

"Hey, beautiful," he said when she stuck her head out the door. "Come join me."

Who could resist an invitation like that? And why? For starters, no one ever called her beautiful. She'd been labeled 'cute' all her life because, hey, it came with her size. And second, just look at him in those faded jeans, a heavy Irish knit sweater, laced boots, and a smile she could fall into.

The pungent scent of the surrounding pine trees enveloped her while she crossed the deck, took his mug from the arm of the rustic wooden chair, curled into his lap. She took a long sip before tipping her head back and brushing her lips across his. "Good morning."

"And looking better all the time."

"Man, do you practice those lines?"

"No, and that wasn't much of a kiss if it was payment for stealing my coffee."

She kissed him again, this time not stopping until every cell in her body had joined together to sing the Hallelujah Chorus, and a single breathy word was the best she could manage. "Better?"

He leaned his forehead against hers. "And then some."

She passed the mug to him. "I prefer cream and sugar. I'll go get another." But his arm clamped around her.

"Just sit here for a minute. Listen to the silence with me, and think about what you want to do today."

She relaxed against him, rested her head on his shoulder. "It really is nice, isn't it?"

"There's a squirrel watching us. See him?" He pointed to a tree. "On the right, about a foot out from the trunk, halfway up. He was chattering at me for a while, then just sat back to stare. As infrequently as this place is inhabited, I suppose he's decided the house and deck are his territory and we're trespassing."

"Or he's waiting for handouts. I bumped into a bucket of nuts in a closet near the door when I was looking for a broom yesterday. Property management, gangland style—pay up or else—" Oh, God what had she been thinking? She glanced up. His expression was bland. Too bland.

Laying a hand on his cheek she said, "I'm sorry. I didn't mean—"

"I've always wondered why you've never asked me about it."

She gritted her teeth.

"Talk to me." He took her chin between his thumb and forefinger and forced her to meet his direct gaze. "Spill it, lady. I want to know how you feel."

"Fine, then here it is," she blurted. "Why would I waste our precious minutes together talking about the *crooked bastards* who stole your life? Robbed my son of a father. Why would I want to give them any more time than what they've already taken? I wish the whole disgusting works of them would blow themselves to smithereens so you could be free and—"

"Come on, Angie, tell me how you really feel."

The sound that came out of her was half laugh, half snort. "I hate them."

"Why give them that kind of importance? Allowing them into your mind gives them even more power, more of your precious time."

"They've nearly killed Cass more than once. Your other sister has been on the run for the past five years, and your dad is forced to live off the grid in order to stay safe."

He put his palm to hers and linked their fingers. "Syd, in her own words, is living the dream with the man she loves, travelling the world, and having a great life. Cass and Gage—according to what you've told me—are very safe and happy on the ranch with their two little girls, and had a fabulous time visiting with Syd and Wes last year. And my dad…well, he's just crazy content living off the grid and spending half his life in a kayak being—in his words—at one with the Pacific Ocean."

But what about him? Was there any joy in his day-to-day life? Or was he actually happy to be tucked away at ETC instead of being with her and Dhillon? Her heart stuttered.

"Whatever you were just thinking, let it go." He pressed his lips to her forehead.

She leaned away, had to see his face when she spit out the question. "Would you be happier if the Minnows—stupid name for a crime group, if you ask me—didn't exist? Or are you content with your life?"

He smiled. "Yes, I suppose I'd be happier; yes, it's a stupid name; and yes, I'm content with things the way they are."

"Have you ever thought about testifying?"

And there, thought Matthias, was the burning question. "No."

"You've dedicated your life to digging for answers, to finding ways to fix children and give parents the joy of day to day living without fear. Why wouldn't you seek that for yourself?"

"Because there is nothing to testify to."

"You saw a murder, and gave a witness statement."

"I wasn't able to identify any of the people involved, and the case went cold. Nothing I could say would make any difference."

"Then why are you hiding? Why did the Minnows try to kidnap and kill your sister?"

He sighed. He didn't want to waste their time on this subject, but envisioned her storming into a precinct house demanding that they do something. And that just couldn't happen. Ever.

"Much of what you've probably learned from Cass may be misinformation. She was only five."

"She spent years as an adult searching for you and your dad, and dug up every detail she could."

"I doubt she ever learned the truth, because it just wasn't out there to be found." And never would be.

"When I heard people approaching the barn, I hid, because I wasn't supposed to be there. It was private property, and I was a kid snooping around. Looking for the kittens I found the day before. I was in the loft, and peering down between the boards gave me a reasonably clear view of the men who came in." And he nearly shit his pants when he saw the guns.

"There was arguing, and they shoved a man to the floor." He'd never forget the image of the tattoo on the back of the man's neck. A star, highlighted by sunshine slanting through the doorway. "Two men pointed their guns at the back of his head and shot him." So loud. So instant. The body in a heap. And silence as loud as the gunshots had been. He'd jumped at the sound of another gun going off, echoing in his head while he stared at the dead man.

"I stayed for a long time, too terrified to move until it was nearly dark out. Then I ran as fast as my feet would carry me. But I guess I was spotted. A police car pulled into the driveway behind me as I got home. My dad was there, because he'd just come home from work. I threw myself into his arms and started bawling." He'd never cried again. Ever. He rubbed a hand up and down Angie's back.

"Dad kept shoving my face against him while I was blurting out what I'd seen, and I struggled against him, not knowing he was trying to protect me because the cop was there listening. Said we'd have to go to the station and make a statement."

"Why was the cop there?"

"Said he'd seen me crying and running and was worried about me."

"You said you started bawling when you saw your dad." She was quick; he expected no less.

"Exactly." And his dad hadn't missed that either.

"Then what happened?"

"Dad said he'd bring me along. Just wanted a minute to get me cleaned up. We went in the house, and he told Mom to put everything I had on, right down to underwear and shoes, in a bag, get me washed up, and into clean clothes." He smiled then. "My mom wasn't the type to do what she was told, ever. But she never said a word, simply did as he asked. When I came back to the kitchen door, he was on the phone, mostly listening, not saying much." But Matt would never forget the grim look on his face.

"When we went back outside, the cop was still there, and we followed him to the station."

"Did they show you photos to see if you recognized anyone?"

"Yes."

"And?"

He recognized the Minnows, but his dad had warned him to say nothing, and he'd continued that silence. "I couldn't give a positive ID on anyone, but it was on record that I'd been there at the time of the murder."

"Yet they put you in witness protection."

"Not exactly. My dad had been Special Forces. Years later he told me his instincts started screaming the moment he spotted the police car following me. Not taking any chances, he called his connection— your dad—when we were in the house for those few minutes. Meyers set a plan in motion immediately.

"The house was closed up as though we'd gone to bed, and, without using any lights, we were bundled into the car. Dad drove without headlights to where another car met us to take my mom and sisters. Dad and I went the opposite direction. Another guy was waiting for us at a bridge far from town and helped stage the accident, rigged the car to plow through the railing and into the river."

He'd never forget watching it sail out of sight. That was the moment he realized his life would never be the same. But it had been more exciting than scary. Who else got to ride rail cars, bulls, and some of the finest horses on the planet? They'd moved from place to place, picking up work on farms, ranches, and even at a fancy training center where the owner had taken one look at Matt's slight build and decided she'd make a jockey out of him. When they had to hit the road a few months later, there were no regrets, because he'd started to grow again at sixteen, which meant he'd never stay small enough to be a race rider.

"You ended up with Meyers Security because your dad knew mine."

"Exactly."

"And when you spotted your sister in Vegas, you called Dad to set up a meet."

"Losing them was the worst part of running for our lives. I was thrilled to think we could have just a bit of time together, and I was willing to disappear again afterward. But when your dad said it would put them in danger…"

"You were pretty shook up."

He nodded. "Freaked me out. I didn't really care by then if the Minnows found me or killed me. I was living in the moment. But the thought of my baby sisters being in danger rattled me down to my boots. Made me a bit crazy."

"Which is how you ended up with me?"

He chuckled. "You were determined to cheer me up. And irresistible even then. Man, if your dad had caught us, he'd have killed me with his bare hands."

"Likely." She grinned. "Good thing he loves Dhillon so much, or you'd still be on his hit list."

"You were jailbait, and I had no excuse."

"Regrets?"

"Not a single one." He pressed a kiss to the top of her head. "But I'd rather not have to face off against your dad."

She snorted. "James is much tamer these days. Did you deliberately get us off topic?"

"No, but there wasn't much more to tell. Bottom line, what I saw was more complicated than murder, and therefore some powerful people need to keep me quiet. After the incidents with Cass, it was brought to their attention that I'd be a loose cannon if they took away my reasons for staying quiet."

"You did that? Contacted them?"

"My dad did." He lifted the empty coffee cup. "I need more caffeine."

She slipped off his lap. "Me too," she said leading the way into the kitchen. "And food."

"I make a mean omelet."

Pushing open the door, she glanced back at him. "Nice idea if we had eggs, cowboy."

"Then how about I doctor up a can of beans?"

"Anything but hot sauce. And I'll do the toast."

It was comfortable, working together in the kitchen as they had the night before. But today was different somehow, and he was afraid to think about why.

***

Angie was well aware of, and okay with, the gaps in what he'd told her. Grateful for how much he'd shared, and now she understood the police involvement. She shuddered to think of what Matt's dad had gone through while everything unfolded. How terrifying for him as a parent, to split his family up and depend on strangers to keep them safe.

She'd never thought much about Dhillon's grandfather, hadn't known he was Special Forces—which accounted for the presence, guardedness, and quick wit she encountered when she met him briefly a few years earlier. She wondered if there was any chance he might come to the ranch for Christmas. Spend some time with Dhillon and Matt.

Matt. Funny, she never thought of him as Dean anymore. Or any of the other names he had over the years. When he asked her last year to come up with yet another alias, Mathias Alejandro Martinez popped out of her mouth without thought. She loved the way it rolled off her tongue, and hell, who didn't love *Zorro?* She hadn't shared that part with him.

"What are you grinning about?"

"Ah, just thinking about the many names you've had over the years. Kind of like getting a new guy each time." Because somehow he seemed to take on a new persona with each alias.

He frowned at her, as though not certain how to respond. "Is it hard for you?"

She grabbed him by the collar, and, inhaling his familiar masculine scent, dragged him down for a noisy kiss. "Nope. You always smell and taste the same."

"Why helicopters?"

"No segue there," she said.

"Whenever we get a chance to talk it's mostly about Dhillon—which I love, don't get me wrong—but sometimes I wonder about things…like why your passion for helicopters?"

She shrugged and forced a knife through frozen bread. "My sister says it's compensation for being half the size of my personality. She's right in some ways. I'm not limited in a helo. Not tied to the earth, and nothing I can't reach. And there's the incredible freedom that comes with lifting off, skimming the ground, and then zipping higher and higher. I *become* the machine."

He was smiling. "I used to feel that way on horseback. The four legs were mine to operate as I chose. To race up a hill, or spin, or sail over a fence. Freedom, and trust. Celebration of life and movement. Racing faster and faster until tears streamed from my eyes and wind roared in my ears." He stopped. Turned back to stir the food he'd been preparing.

"Do you ever get a chance to ride?"

"Only the mountain bike, and while there's a similar freedom, it's just an object, and can't share the exhilaration the way a horse does."

"If you came to the ranch sometime, we could ride. Dhillon's good on horseback, but he didn't inherit your passion. Or any of mine, for that matter." And then she remembered. "He told us the other day that he's decided to become a doctor so he can fix people. It was like hearing an echo of your voice in my head. You told me a hundred years ago, in that beat-up old camper, that you wanted to be a doctor with an old-fashioned country practice. Do you ever wish you could have gone that way instead?"

"Research suits me better than hands-on. I already get attached enough to my subjects, so I don't think having long-term patient connections would be good for me."

"Even without the Minnows looking over your shoulder?"

He nodded. "It's the emotional connection. I don't think I could leave my work at the office if I had a whole practice worth of people depending on me."

Interesting. "But you have thousands depending on your research." And when he talked about his advancements in predicting and managing rare heart conditions in children, she knew just how invested he was in every life he touched. "How long 'til you're ready over there?"

"Me or the beans?"

"Funny guy. You're always ready."

"Beans in five."

She pushed the bread down in the toaster. They'd have a meal, then maybe a bit of a hike before she tackled any more tough subjects…because the next one would be a doozy.

CHAPTER 6

Matt was impressed with the way Angie pushed up the narrow trail, digging for purchase with every step. Nothing seemed to slow her down when she set her mind on a goal, and that worried him. Sure it would serve her well while hiking the Chilcotins, but in their relationship?

Granted, she hadn't brought up the subject of Christmas with her family since they arrived, but he knew, as surely as she was putting one foot in front of the other, that she had a plan. One she had every intention of implementing.

But thinking about it would only get in the way of now—a place he reverently believed in, because the past and future were beyond his control. He powered up the path behind her and clamped a hand on either side of her waist.

When she spun around with a questioning look, he kissed her, felt her sigh, and lost himself in the moment. Dragged her closer, wrapped her up in his arms, and held on. Devouring the taste, the feel, even her lemony scent, until he finally came up for air.

A breath whooshed out of her and she rested her forehead against his chin. "Where'd that come from?"

"Watching your ass climbing up there in front of me, I needed to remind myself this isn't a dream." He wanted her here and now.

She tipped her head back to study him. "You've got that look in your eye."

"What look?"

"The one that says you want me naked."

"I always want you naked." But this week together was about more than sex. "We should almost be there." They'd found a map of trails and lookout points—for security purposes, of course—but they were using it for adventure and exercise. "Let's keep going. Lead on."

"Now I know you'll be staring at my ass."

"Tell me you didn't already, and I'll call bullshit."

She smiled. "Point to you. Come on, cowboy, let's get to the top of this so I can have my reward." She held up the chocolate bar she found in the freezer. "I'll even share." She continued to lead the way. The scuff and thump of booted feet against rock and the occasional crackle of a dried leaf or twig were the only sounds to accompany them.

And the view when they reached the lookout point was breathtaking. Humbling. Reducing their presence to minuscule dots on a vast landscape. Miles and miles and miles of mountaintops and valleys covered by hundreds of thousands of trees, blended together in a kaleidoscope of deep greens.

They stood shoulder to shoulder, absorbing Mother Nature's magnificence, for a very long time before sitting on a wide flat rock overlooking the valley where their trek had begun. She passed him half the chocolate bar, and he handed her the water bottle without saying a word—a moment of pure pleasure and camaraderie frozen in time.

The air was rich with the earthy scent of fall. Leaves littered the ground, grasses swayed golden, and all but the pines stood naked in the wind. Rough under his hand, the rock held a faint warmth given it by sunshine.

Silence surrounded them, so pure he could hear every breath they took, and he'd hold this moment forever, stored, crystal clear, to take out when he needed to remember the beauty of what he'd had for these few days. Tucked away in his mind, where no one could take it away from him.

When Angie's fingertips feathered across the back of his hand, he turned it over, linked with her in the simplest of ways, and his heart was full.

Then it got better, because she scooted over to sit between his legs and lean against his chest. With his arms looped around her middle and his face beside hers, they took in the beauty around them, within them. *I could die now and it would be okay.* But he had no intention of dying anytime soon.

And in that moment he decided it was time his son knew who he was, and maybe one day he could show him this place, the vastness of the landscape, and tell him this was where he'd been when he decided that protecting a son from his father made absolutely no sense. The boy was smart. Bloody brilliant, actually. And he'd been raised by a family of security specialists. He could be trusted with the truth.

Next time Dhillon came to ETCETERA—with Angie's blessing, of course—they'd talk.

"Where are you?" Her voice was low, almost a whisper.

"I'm here with you."

"You were gone somewhere else for a while. It's a habit I've noticed. Is it work that distracts you? Your research? Or something else?"

He didn't often speak without thinking, but this time, the words had been so close to the surface they slipped out uncensored. "It's about time I came clean with Dhillon."

Even though she hadn't been moving, everything about her stilled.

"Just an idea I thought I'd run by you," he said, stalling until his brain cells shook off the euphoria of the setting. "How would you feel about that?"

Angie's heart pounded against her ribs, and something that was neither a laugh nor a sob fought to escape her throat. She needed to chill. Not scare him. From before Dhillon had been born, she'd dreamed of him knowing his father, dreamed of the man she loved being in their son's life. She'd almost accepted that connecting through the program at ETC was as close as they'd ever get to having a relationship, but maybe there could be more. Did she dare to hope? Dare to trust that Matt wouldn't back away before it actually happened?

She turned to face him. Knelt to bring herself level with his steady gaze. "You're serious?" The man was *always* serious, but this was different. This was her son's life, his understanding of who he was.

"Very."

"Why? Why now?"

"This place. One day I'd love to share this view with my son."

While the words made her warm inside, there was a subtle emptiness that came with them. Was she wrong to wish he'd included her? Was this the time? Would it ruin the moment? Hell, her thoughts had already done that. *Don't be a coward, Angie.* She backed away from him. Got to her feet and stuffed her hands in her pockets.

"Whatever it is, say it."

"You have an annoying habit. One that I've wondered about and, well…" It wasn't like her to dither. She straightened her spine. "When you refer to Dhillon, you always say, 'my son,' never 'our son.' And he's not yours, or mine—he's ours."

Matt blinked. His eyes moved to the left, and then the right, as though he was actually examining his motives. She waited.

"Do you want a reason? Or just an apology, since it really is worthy of one."

"Both."

He took a deep breath and went on. "When I think of you and Dhillon, he's your son. You gave birth to him, raised him, did all the work. I had nothing to do with any of it. But when I think of him as my son, it's because of that newness of getting to know him, even though he doesn't have a clue that he's related to me."

He shoved at his hair the way he did when he was going to tie it back, but then his hands dropped to his sides. This was costing him.

"Here's the hard part. And please consider the source. I'm a man who has lived a very solitary existence."

Okay, she mentally braced herself. "Go ahead, I'm a big girl."

His eyebrows went up but he made no remark about her being small enough to stuff in his pocket—one of his favorite cracks.

"*Our son* refers to far more than biology. It speaks of a partnership, a bond between two people raising a child, making decisions together, tag-teaming each other. I see it in my office. A mother and a father fighting for their child's life. Making decisions, together. And we've never been that. We don't *have* a relationship. We've never been an *us* against the world, a *we* standing together. We are a you and a me. We're separate entities."

The words were a punch to the gut because of their absolute truth. The relationship she'd thought she had with him was largely a product of her imagination. They weren't much more than booty buddies—to anyone on the outside looking in. Or even perhaps from where he viewed them. And in spite of that not being a new thought, hearing him call them separate instead of together ripped a hole in her. Tore a piece from her existence. But tears didn't spring. There wasn't even anger. Just a hollow feeling in her stomach and a strange ache in her chest.

"Say something."

She shook her head and he reached for her but she shot up her hands to ward him off. "No. I don't want you to touch me right now." For fear she would crumble, because something she'd leaned on, held onto, and cherished had suddenly been stripped away, and she teetered on the edge of an unfamiliar abyss.

The idyllic few days they were to spend together like honeymooners had become bleak. Without meaning. She started down the trail. Needed to get to familiar footing. To somewhere she could close a door, lock herself in, and lick her wounds.

He wanted Dhillon, *his* son, but not his son's mother.

Had she just imagined this horror happening? Could it be that—

"Angie."

She spun and watched him come toward her, staring into his dark blue eyes, looking for something to connect with.

His voice was low with emotion. "We need to talk this through."

Backing away from him, she shook her head. "No. I need time to think first." She spun and pressed on toward the house without looking back, knew he hadn't followed her. Just as well. I really need to get my shit together.

But even as she reached the safety of walls and doors, she was coming up blank on how to pull that off.

Staring at her image in the bathroom mirror, she could see no visible difference, but inside, *who she was on the inside*, that's what had changed. A belief she'd held in her heart had evaporated as fast as a chunk of ice on hot pavement. Gone without hope of recovering even a fraction of what had been.

Was she that stupid? Had she really built her life around a mirage? Around something with so little connection to reality that it was gone as easily as a puff of steam? Apparently.

This must be a bit like what Tara experienced when meeting her bio father and finding out the man she imagined hadn't existed anywhere but in her mind. But that had been a *child's* imagination.

"You're a grown woman," she said out loud.

"You don't have nearly the excuse." But she'd only been a girl when the fairy tale began. Born and raised on the ranch, she'd led an extremely sheltered life, until Vegas.

Exhilarated by the bright lights and the sheer energy of the place, she was swept off her feet by a boy barely older than she was—but already a man. A shy, yet self-confident and gorgeous, cowboy. Oh, how they'd laughed and danced that first night. And she'd never forget the moment the talented bull-rider with a tanned face and sure hands had placed a gentle kiss on her mouth and said, "You're so pretty."

She could still see the heat in his eyes, feel the dazzle of his smile as she fell head over heels. Sneaking out of her room later, she'd mustered courage she didn't know she had and gone to the vast parking area to tap on the door of his camper.

He tried to send her away, but she'd been sure of what she wanted, slipped inside and closed the door. Leaned on it, clueless about what to do next, but he touched her face then, and she'd known everything would be okay.

They were together for three nights, three magical nights she stole by lying to her brothers. Then her dad got word of her cousin's helicopter accident and hustled them home. She never had a chance to tell her cowboy she was leaving, to plan to meet again, and thought she'd die of a broken heart. She searched the Meyers databases for information about him, and found nothing but an email sent from an internet café in Vegas, thanking the company for their years of protection, and stating that he'd decided to get on with his life without their assistance now that he was eighteen.

When her mortified family found out she was pregnant, she refused to tell them who the baby's father was. Let them believe it was some randy cowboy she met and had a one-night stand with. But she knew what she'd experienced was much, much, more than that. She'd met the love of her life, and one day they'd have a life together with their child.

He'd stayed there in her mind, his image an integral part of her life. And then one day when she walked into the office of the ETC doctor who was doing research on pediatric cardiac arrest, she'd been stunned to see her son's father on the other side of the desk. Words had stuck in her throat.

They managed to meet privately a few times that year. Then there'd been more opportunities. She shook herself out of the memories.

That was then, and this was now, and she needed to find a way to reconcile the two.

***

Matt used his sleeve to wipe sweat from his face. He'd hiked, pushing for speed and distance, until he could go no farther. And there he was, several rugged miles from the house, when it occurred to him that she might simply leave him here. Fire up the Steed and vanish into the sky.

But would she? That was the fifty-thousand-dollar question, and he was an hour of hard going away from the answer. He was adept at silent communication, but although she'd been training at ETC, he wasn't sure her skills had developed well enough to hear him clearly.

He chose instead to keep his mind's pathways

carefully locked, as they had been since he left headquarters days ago, and trudged on. One foot in front of the other, following the trail back to her. Back to the only woman he'd ever cared about. The mother of his fatherless son.

Was telling Dhillon about their relationship wise? Or self-serving? How would it change the boy's life? And how could they tell him and then expect him to keep it a secret from everyone else?

Matt knew what pressure and secrets did to a young mind. Wasn't it enough he'd survived a near-death experience? It had to help that Matt's research uncovered the cause so they could understand what happened, but was that enough for the kid's peace of mind? Or had he really shrugged it off as history? No big deal?

Dhillon had become an asset, helping with other kids who'd gone through the same thing. Taken on a brotherly role, talking to any and all about the facts and fallacies. Yes, they'd undergone emergency cardiac surgery, but no, it couldn't happen again. It was a genetic fluke, he'd say, no different than one out of a hundred kittens born with a stubby tail, or bicolored eyes. The genes just happened to line up in a precise order and cause a microscopic abnormality in the heart wall.

Matt would be eternally grateful to Quinn's wife, Rachel, and her healing hands. She'd been able to revive Dhillon, keep him alive on the flight to hospital. And a relatively simple surgery repaired his heart.

Coincidentally, Matt had been doing research on heart failure in children, and Dhillon had showed up in the program as an already-diagnosed subject for follow-up.

After Dhillon's data was collected, Matt discovered that the boy's abnormality was the result of the perfect storm. Matt was a carrier, and Angie's genetic makeup was the exact match required for the condition to manifest. If they ever had another son—as it only occurred in boys—he'd be tested upon birth and the defect corrected as soon as possible. Another son.

That should never happen. Not another child to live without a father. And Angie didn't need that kind of pressure. That's why they were careful. Always careful.

Upon reaching the valley floor, he studied the house and saw no signs of life, but what would he be able to see in daylight? He couldn't see the Steed's camouflaged portable hangar from here. Damn chopper with its silent operation capabilities could have left without him hearing a thing while he was in the woods. Even if he'd been out in the open, the special shell would keep it invisible, and hell, she could be firing it up at the end of the valley, right in front of him, and he wouldn't know it.

Nothing he could do about that. He was leg-weary, and desperately needed hydration so he'd be able to think straight, listen, then plead his case.

Huh. Plead ignorance and lack of people skills to cover his insensitivity. Not that what he said wasn't true. But obviously his delivery had been lacking. Seriously lacking, if the way color drained from her face had been any indication. And the memory of that moment made him feel somewhat ill again.

Need water, he thought. Clear the mind.

He shoved open the back door and peeled off

his jacket. Then the soaking wet T-shirt sticking to his skin. Water, then a shower.

He guzzled a full glass, then took another with him, detouring to poke his head in every room, looking for Angie, but she wasn't there.

CHAPTER 7

Angie didn't answer his yell. Let him come and find her, she thought, then nearly laughed out loud when he raced into the Steed's shelter and stopped as though he'd hit an invisible wall.

"You're here."

Oh, what a picture. Naked from the waist up, hair plastered to his head, a wild expression on his face, and nothing on his feet but socks.

"I called. You didn't answer. Don't leave. Please don't leave."

"I'm not leaving. Just doing a bit of maintenance. The Steed centers me when my world tilts on its axis." She frowned. "It did that today. Tilted. And I didn't like it very much."

He took a step toward her and she took one back. "Angie, I—"

"Could use a shower, and some clothes. Go before you freeze to death. I'll be up when I'm finished here." Because the look of him had pushed her just a bit off center again, and she needed to fix that. Needed to be ready to tackle his mind when she went back inside. She needed to understand the *why* behind what he'd said. Only then would she be able to put it away.

He stared at her for a minute, as though trying to decide what to do. Then shrugged. "You scared me."

"Seems we've taken a chip out of each other. Give me a half hour, then we'll see what we can fix."

"I'd rather we talked now, showered later."

"You think you can talk me into water sports?"

"Hope springs?"

She went to him then, couldn't help herself. Hooked a hand around the back of his neck and drew him down, feathered her lips across his. "You're freezing. Come on." She stashed the buffing cloth in the hold, shoved him outside the shelter, fastened the flap, then grabbed his hand and dragged him to the house.

Once inside, he was doing such a lousy job of suppressing the shivers she shoved him in the shower and cranked on the hot water.

"Hey, still dressed here."

"So undress."

She escaped to the kitchen, where she lifted the lid of the slow cooker and stirred the soup she put in after breakfast. She'd pour a couple of bowls full into him, and that should complete the warming process. Fool man, running around outdoors without a shirt or shoes. But it helped that he'd panicked, thinking she'd left him. Yeah. That helped a bunch.

She put a match to the paper and kindling pyramid she built in the fireplace. They could be cozy in here while they talked—while she figured out if there was any hope for their future. She couldn't imagine herself with anyone else, but maybe it was time she stopped living her life according to when she'd get to see him next. Stopped making special arrangements to go to ETCETERA, working on projects there just to be able to see him. Maybe it was time to cut the strings.

Sure, and didn't that thought make her feel like puking. Chill, she told herself, cross the bridges one at a time, and in the order you come to them. Deep breath in. Exhale. And again. She hated when women lost their own identity in a relationship, and she didn't want to be one of them, but it wasn't looking good for her.

Everyone at home thought she was the strong one, the gutsy one, the baby sister who'd tackle anything that came her way, and wasn't defined by a man. Oh, if only they knew what a fake she was.

Sure, she did what she had to do to get by, but over the past few years, everything had begun to revolve around Matt and when she'd be able to see him again. It was as though she'd been living in an alternate universe. Everything was better when she was around him. Brighter, sweeter, more exciting, yet smoother. And the weeks between visits dulled, dragged, and progressed at a much slower pace than they should.

She'd been fine up until she saw an opportunity to be with him more frequently.

She loved the sound of his voice, his laugh, and, oh, especially when she made him laugh in bed. She loved making the mood just a bit crazy by teasing him, being funny. That's when he let his guard down. Had fun. And once in a while she got a glimpse of that wild young cowboy she'd rocked a beat-up old camper with years ago.

Then he strolled into the kitchen wearing nothing but jeans, and she caught a glimpse of a few beads of water clinging to the light dusting of hair on his perfectly masculine chest. She shook her head and pointed at the doorway he'd just come through. "Unfair tactics. Go get a shirt. And socks." There was a vulnerability in naked feet that moved something inside her, something she didn't dare let loose right now, because it would screw up the tone she needed for this serious discussion.

He advanced on her. "You saying you can't resist me?"

"I'm weak."

He took her hand and laid it over his heart where she could feel the rapid beat. "That's what you do to me, even with your clothes on."

Warmth spread, and she pulled away. Stepped back and found herself up against the counter. This wasn't a good idea. "Look, Matt, I need my brain cells to be in charge right now, not my hormones."

He shrugged and leaned just out of the room to grab the shirt he'd apparently left there. "It was worth a try."

"I've never known you to cheat or play dirty before."

"I was hoping for a bit of an edge, that's all. I dug myself a hole earlier, and I'm having trouble figuring how to climb out."

She nodded, then filled a bowl with steaming soup. "If you're about to grovel, you can eat at the same time," she said, setting it on a bright red place mat on the breakfast bar.

He had no experience with groveling. Figured it

meant taking the blame for what was wrong, and swearing to mend what was broken. Not what he had in mind. Couldn't see it working for them, because he needed to explain exactly what he meant. But while he shook out pepper, he considered the option, because it seemed to be what she was expecting.

He tasted the soup, then quickly took a gulp of water to sooth his burning tongue and throat.

"Painful, that stalling tactic," she said, and he glanced over to assess her degree of smugness.

"Yeah." He set down the spoon. "Here's the problem." He put the water glass and the soup bowl side by side. "These are both vessels. They hold liquid, and probably just about the same amount. But they're not really alike at all. This one is made from clay dug out of the ground, then hands shaped it with great care. Whereas this drinking glass is really plastic, and comes from pouring liquid into a mold."

"Where's this going, Martinez?"

Using his last name probably wasn't a good sign. "I was looking for an analogy to explain how differently we grew up. You became an adult at the hands of your family. They helped to create a being able to communicate succinctly with others, and to use a type of reasoning based on vast exposure to other people and their ideas."

"And you didn't have that."

"No. My dad and I functioned well together. He taught me to see the goal, and drive toward it, always being aware that there would be times—" Her raised eyebrows stopped him.

"Aw, hell. What I'm trying to say is—"

"Groveling would be a heck of a lot easier, cowboy."

"But I need you to *understand*. An *us* is a pair who go through daily life together. The ups and downs, the good and the bad. We don't have that." He held up his hand. "I'm not saying I wouldn't love to have that with you, but up until the last couple of days, all our time together came as special moments." He groaned. "Yes, this is special, too, but bear with me. They were snapshots of perfection. We'd be together for a set number of hours, celebrate each other, make love as many times as physically possible, and then we'd each get on with our individual lives." His thoughts from when he was hiking alone came back to him.

"Think of our times together as being photographs—moments in time. There are eighty-six thousand, four hundred seconds in a day. Even if a photo captured a full second, which it doesn't, it would represent less than one eighty-six-thousandths of a day.

"Up until we crossed paths in Whistler this week, we'd been together for approximately ninety-seven hours in a twelve-month period. That's ninety-seven out of eight thousand, seven hundred and sixty hours. Less than two percent of our lives were spent together. We were apart for ninety-eight percent of the time.

"Added to that, as I've already said, those hours are nearly perfect. We're not dealing with reality at all, then. Hell, we barely put on clothes."

Her sigh was heartfelt. "There's no argument for that."

"And as for referring to Dhillon as *my* son, that comes from catching myself when I'm about to call him *your* son, because you told me he wasn't just yours, he was mine too." His throat was suddenly dry. But instead of reaching for the water, he had to finish this out. "Does it make sense why I never felt I had the right to call him *ours*?"

She nodded. "Sure. Well, aside from the numbers, and the fact that you just rattled them off to distract me. Now I'll explain my perspective." When she braced her elbows on the counter and pressed her fingertips together, he wished he had a cold beer instead of water. But drank anyway.

"In the beginning, I had a wonderful, simple scenario built in my head. You'd show up at the ranch one day and claim us as yours, then we'd live happily ever after."

He grimaced. Yes, he thought about her a lot, even back then, wanted her again, but he'd been completely occupied with scrambling to stay one step ahead of the Minnows. Then he met Logan and grabbed the opportunity to get an education while under the protection of ETC.

"Yeah. Pretty hokey," she said. "And then, after years of no contact, and the dust growing thick on my fairy tale, the moment I bumped into you again, it started to grow legs. Over the last year, when we got together a lot more often—which I thought was way more than a grand total of ninety-six hours—I began to dream of us having life together, because you were always there in my head. I thought about you when I was on ops, when I was home with Dhillon, with other family members. Always wondering…what would it be like if Matt were here with me right this minute? I turned into the proverbial love-sick teenager."

What the hell was he supposed to say to that?

Did he love her? Sure. Would he love to have a life with her and Dhillon on the outside, in the real world? That was a yes, but with a qualifier—only if it was safe. And it wasn't. Which was why he never entertained those kinds of thoughts.

"Do you ever wonder what if?"

Boggy ground. "I don't have much of an imagination. But if it means anything, I hate when you have to leave me. My apartment seems lifeless without you in it. I usually pull a couple of all-nighters in the lab because I can't stand to go home to the emptiness." That's as close as he ever felt to being imprisoned, and the only times he ever got angry about the kind of life he was forced to live. But then the research would swallow him, and the anger would dissipate.

Her expression made it abundantly clear his answer wasn't what she was hoping for, but it was better than she expected. Then she opened another can of worms. "I've never been with anyone but you."

He nearly groaned out loud. Set the spoon down and pushed away the bowl of tepid soup. "I'm sorry I have to ask, but is that something I'm supposed to respond to?"

Her face twisted into a smile. "Well, a 'neither have I' would have been nice, but then I'd have felt sorry for you. According to my brothers, celibacy is tougher for men."

He bit the bullet. "I can honestly say there has been no one but you since we reconnected."

She nodded. "That's good. Now I won't have to kill you and leave your body in the hills for the wolves and bears to clean up."

"Nice. Thanks for that. But I'd be an awful big carcass for a shrimp like you to drag into the hills."

"There's a four-wheeler in the shed."

He laughed. "Does this mean we're getting back on track finally?"

"We've got at least a couple of wheels out of the mud."

He leaned back in his chair. "If I was at home, I'd dump this soup back in the pot to reheat it with the rest."

"I live with a male child and grew up with brothers, so you can't gross me out. Besides, your spoon only dipped in there a couple of times, plus…well, let's just say as intimate partners, we've swapped spit countless times. Toss it in."

He did, then laid a hand on either side of her face and said, "I want to kiss you."

She met him halfway, with a sweet sound in her throat that had his heart slamming into hers. She moved him. This remarkable, feisty woman moved him like no other, and he wanted her. But he'd promised himself he wouldn't go there, wouldn't go to sex as the default when things got awkward or complicated. They needed this time almost as much as he needed to have his hands on her. Hers on him. He kissed her nose and returned to the soup pot. Cranked up the heat and stirred until it was ready again.

***

Gradually, the wariness between them wore off, and they grew comfortable again. Maybe not quite the same as before, but close.

He'd always thought of her as a brilliant spark of light flitting in and out of his life, and now he also recognized her depth, and the child inside the woman who'd been forced to grow up too fast because she had to be a mother.

For him, growing up quickly began that day in the barn, but got real when he left his dad and struck out on his own at sixteen. Then at eighteen, after breaking away from Meyers protection he had to keep moving in order to stay ahead of the Minnows. Until he heard another man's voice in his head.

To say he'd been suspicious was a monumental understatement. But in time he grew accustomed to the man's presence, had considered some of his advice, and they eventually met. If it hadn't been for that meeting years ago, he'd still be alone, a weathered wrangler pushing cattle on some ranch or other, still looking over his shoulder. Waiting for the men with the guns to find him.

But here he was with Angie, and she wanted more. Wanted him in her life, along with the son they'd created together. Did he dare allow himself to be seduced by something he'd never dreamed was a possibility?

She slid onto his lap. Snuggled in.

And he wondered about the men with the guns.

CHAPTER 8

Matthias had no idea what to say when, on their third evening together, Angie began sorting through a stack of board games.

"You can learn a lot about a person by how they play," she said.

Perhaps she'd spent too many years in the company of a child. With not nearly enough adult interaction. Having the opposite experience, Matt knew nothing about games unless they were something to do with a deck of cards.

"Your pick," she said, spreading out a collection of boxes.

"I have no preference. I don't know any of these."

"You're not getting out of making a decision. Pick one."

He studied both her and the collection for a clue. "Twister," he said. It seemed to be about bright colors and laughing faces.

She slanted him a sideways look. "You're

claiming you've never played this."

"Never even heard of it."

"Then all I can say is either your instincts are very impressive, or you were reading my mind."

Not hard to guess when she'd been staring at the box. "So, how does it work?"

She grinned. "Start by taking off your shoes. Might as well lose the socks too."

"Seriously?"

With instructions explained, they began, and he milked his grand advantage, easily reaching from corner to corner while she stretched underneath him. At one point he held her completely in his grasp, and kudos to her for turning tables on him, pressing upward as she laughed.

When he finally conceded and declared her the winner, she claimed him as her prize and had him kneel on the rug in front of the fire.

She leaned against him and breathed words into his ear. "I've always had this fantasy. Just you and me, in a remote cabin in the woods, snowed in."

"It's not snowing," he whispered.

"That's okay, I have a vivid imagination." She slipped her hands under the bottom edge of his shirt and slid it up over his head. Then tipped him backwards and followed him down. "First I want your mouth." Hers descended, and she took his bottom lip between her teeth. Teased.

When he went for the buttons on her shirt she pushed his hand away. "Not yet, cowboy. First I'm going to drive you to the very edge of crazy."

And she did. With her mouth, her hands, slowly working her way down to the waistband of his jeans. Teasing along the edge.

"You know what playing that game taught me about you?"

From seduction to conversation in one point two seconds. He shook his head and rose up on an elbow to stare at her.

Her laugh was deadly sexy, and the few brain cells he'd had a grip on went south.

"You're fair, and generous, and want to be in control." She undid the snap. Slid down the zipper. "And I'm going to experiment to see how easily you'll give that up."

Give what up?

She stood and grabbed the bottoms of his jeans, tugged. He lifted to help, but she stopped when they were halfway down, wrapped around his knees. "I think that's far enough," she said with a small smile. "It's about control. You have none for the next hour. I suggest you lie back and enjoy."

An hour? He'd be lucky to last ten minutes, he thought, when she tossed aside her own shirt. Spit dried in his throat when she dropped her pants and stood there in front of him wearing the kind of underwear men only see in magazines. Black, shiny, and not much of it. An hour? Not a chance in hell. He caught himself about to reach for her. Settled back. Closed his eyes—almost. "You're killing me."

What began as a smile widened into a grin. "You're gonna live, cowboy, and you're going to thank your lucky stars I have such a wonderful imagination, and fantastic sense of adventure. But you're gonna want to keep your eyes open for this."

He did. And was grateful. He'd never forget what she looked like when—

"Hour and ten," her voice was low, gravely, and

her breath cooled the sweat-dampened skin at the base of his throat. If his muscles hadn't been as limp and useless as overcooked spaghetti, he'd have wrapped his arms around her. Finally catching his breath, he wondered if his eyes had rolled back in his head. He blinked once, twice, and his vision cleared.

If he ever found his voice, he was sure he'd have something to say. Maybe.

"Mmmm."

Exactly, he thought. To the nth degree. And when his body regained solid form again he'd carry her to bed.

He woke up cold, with Angie pressed against his side as though seeking warmth. He scooped her up and carried her to the hot tub they'd fired up earlier, but had yet to use. They'd played games instead, and he would always have a soft spot for that silly plastic sheet with big colored dots on it.

He tapped the stereo button on the way past, and stepped into the heated water with her. She sighed and pressed her soft mouth against his chest.

Music spilled over them. This was the seduction he'd had planned until she changed things. "Too bad you're so sleepy," he said.

"I'm just comfy. What did you have in mind, cowboy?"

He lifted her to straddle his lap. "How about we start here and see where it goes," he said, kissing her slowly.

Days and nights passed, filling him with the unique flavor of the woman Angie was whether mad, sad, sexy, smart, or conniving. They made love, hiked, fished, talked, fought, and made love some more. Until their stolen time ran out.

On their last morning, he sat out on the deck, as had become his habit. First he watched the sunrise wash light and color through the valley. Then, staying statue still, he coaxed the squirrel. They'd done this dance every day, with the nut closer and closer to his hand. Today, with his arm outstretched along the railing, Matt held the prize between the tips of his fingers. "Last chance, pal. It's now or never."

The fluffy tail twitched, the tiny head swung side to side, and bright black eyes stared as if trying to size up his adversary. Then in a blink of rapid movement, he darted, grabbed, and raced away as though a pack of hounds was snapping at his fuzzy behind.

Matt was still chuckling when Angie came out to join him. Her flight suit, although sexy as hell, accentuated the fact they were leaving. Going back to reality. "Were you watching?" he asked.

"Pretty cute," she said. "Snatched and ran like a bandit. Did he add it to his stash?"

"Nope." He pointed up into the pine. "I'd say from the bits of shell flying that he's going to eat this one."

"Dhillon has your knack with animals. We'd have a houseful if I gave in every time he brought a new critter home."

"He just has the dog?"

"Officially, but we're feeding half the barn cats because they follow him to the house. And then there's the ducks. My brothers promised mom they'd dig a pond in my backyard to keep them out of the pool at the big house, where the ducklings can hop in, but can't climb out."

Perfect, he thought. Dhillon got to have what his father had been denied. Matt's mother refused to have animals in the house. Even when he came home with a kitten, she hadn't bent so much as an inch. Made him return it because cats were disgusting creatures, leaving hair everywhere, and constantly licking themselves.

Being a kid who adored animals, he'd tried again with a puppy, and then a full grown dog he found wandering around near his school. He kept it outside, made it a house out of an old packing crate, but his father had given in to the nagging and taken the dog to the pound. Then there'd been a baby bunny. He kept it hidden in his closet for two days before taking it by bus to the other side of town to give it to an animal sanctuary, where a nice lady promised they'd care for it until it was old enough to survive on its own.

Whenever he could get away from sister duty, he'd hung around a barn where there were always cats, kittens, horses—

"Matt?"

He smiled automatically. "Hmm?"

"You okay?"

"Sure."

"You kind of zoned out."

"Sorry."

"Did you have any pets?" Had she picked up on his thoughts?

"No. My mother had a perfect house. Clean. Everything in its place. No room for pets there. And then when Dad and I were on the run, it was impossible. Now I live underground."

"You make it sound as though you're trapped inside a concrete bunker."

"I am."

"It's an underground city, almost."

"Without a sky." He leaned his head back and gazed up into the vast blue, as he had time and time again since they arrived. Sat out on this deck for almost every sunrise and sunset. Sucked in unfiltered air as though stockpiling it for when he went back—like the squirrel stored the nuts.

"I hate that you have to go back there."

He held out a hand. "Come and sit. We can make some more memories." He'd never done that before—consciously thought about later and wanted to take a piece of now to keep him warm when later came. "You're a bad influence on a man who lives in the present." He pressed his lips to the top of her head while she rested against him.

"Could you stay longer? Just a few hours more?"

"Ah, baby, I would if I could. But they're waiting on me with more results. More possibilities to make lives easier, longer, and without the daily stress of unnecessary medications."

He glanced at his watch. It was time for Angie to fly him back to ETCETERA.

***

Angie had her own internal conflict. Hating to part with Matt, but anxious to see their son. She always missed Dhillon when they were apart, but she'd needed this time away for herself, and maybe for the future of their family. She still had no answers, or at least any she chose to accept, but there had to be a way to get Matt his freedom. Or at least get him to understand that he could come to the ranch and be a part of the family that way. The place was more secure than Fort Knox, for heaven's sake.

While they'd walked and talked for hours over the last few days, she'd come to understand how he felt about living the way he did. Put simply, it was a necessary evil, and not one he had any intention of walking away from.

She slipped off his lap and tugged him to his feet. "Let's get a move on then, cowboy."

They did a final walk-through to be certain no evidence of their presence had been left behind—a responsibility neither took lightly. The bulk of the Minnows might be inept idiots, but there were enough dark souls in the group—plus their law enforcement connections—to keep a person vigilant.

As they folded back the Steed's temporary hangar and rolled it up to slide into the storage canister, Angie took a moment to utilize the techniques she'd perfected during some of the special training sessions at ETC. She visualized the expanding of her senses, the accessing of receptors within her mind, and kicking open every door. Channels wide open, she had to steady herself against the blast of information before she could begin sorting.

First she drew out the gentle, steady wave of energy from the earth itself, then a stronger one coming from the vegetation. Moving upwards in power she identified the veil of insects, then the individual presence of mammals—and here she took care to be certain no human energy was intermingled—but there was nothing aside from Matt, and she recognized the nuances of his pattern. She frowned.

"You're broadcasting."

He nodded and stepped back while she slipped the canister lid into place and fastened the safety clips. "You're not."

"And you shouldn't be."

"I was allowing myself a few more minutes of freedom."

She touched his face. "Thank you for the most incredible week of my life. I love you, Matthias Alejandro Martinez, with every fiber of my being." She put a finger to his mouth when he opened it as though to speak words that were hard to say. "What I said is my gift to you, and doesn't require reciprocation."

He took her hand and teased the fingertip with his teeth. "You're one hell of a woman. And I wish I could give you what you want."

A peculiar trickle of strong energy nearly slipped past her. Something she didn't recognize. "Company. Get in."

She fired up the helo as fast as she could, but there were steps that had to be taken unless it was a life or death emergency, and by the time they lifted off, she was sweating.

"Over there," his voice came to her through the speakers built into her helmet. She looked where he was pointing and laughed out loud. A bull moose with a huge rack was meandering down the valley behind a cow. "Must be breeding season," he said, and she laughed.

"ETC doesn't include moose energy and pheromones in their teaching module. I'll have to tell Kelton his program could use an upgrade."

Their conversation stayed on neutral topics right up until the last five minutes of their flight, as though leaving the privacy of the ranch had meant leaving the personal behind as well.

That she longed for one last bit of reassurance irritated her, but she shook it off. "I hate dropping you off this way." She'd rather go to his apartment with him and have a proper goodbye, as planned, but she'd received a coded message from HQ. She was needed at home immediately.

"Duty calls. I'll miss you."

"But you'll be buried in work."

"It won't be enough anymore," he said, and warmth poured through her.

"Thank you." She didn't ask when they could be together again, didn't plead for him to stay with her, although all that and more screamed inside her head. She'd been careful to close down and not broadcast her thoughts throughout the flight. They'd yet to share a telepathic connection, and she decided it was something he would have to initiate. She'd already laid her heart at his feet, and because she understood him better than she had a week ago, she was certain he needed to make the next move.

She concentrated on landing the Steed at a secluded ETCETERA location, where Matt would transfer to one of their helos for the ride to an ETC entrance. Security protocols were stringent, and no one ever returned through the portal they'd departed from unless specifically assigned to do so.

It was incredible to her that they could maintain their extreme levels of security with the vast number of egresses. But they claimed they'd never had a breach.

"Keep your head down," she said, and Matt grabbed the hand she held out. He understood that because she couldn't shut down, their noise barrier helmets would have to stay on, and there's be no goodbye kisses. His gaze met hers, then he grabbed the door handle and was gone. Hunched over to stay safe, he sprinted into an old barn.

Angie swallowed back the sadness that came with knowing something extraordinary had ended. She got down to business. With a shift of her hand and pressure from her feet, she had the helo lifting off, sliding forward and climbing into the sky. Ten minutes out, she contacted Meyers HQ—and everything changed.

CHAPTER 9

Angie stormed into the board room. "What the fuck?"

Gage stood and she punched him in the arm. "You don't get to do that to me, big brother. Not now, not ever. I was on my own time." The text message had been brief.

HQ STAT. D FINE. NO COM.

"We need you here."

"I'm here, and I don't see anyone bleeding to death, or any buildings burned to the ground."

Julia came into the room. "Did you have a good vacation, Angie?"

She spun to face her mother. "I did. But it would have ended better if I hadn't had to fly here at warp speed because of his cryptic message," she said, pointing her thumb at Gage.

"I gave that order."

"What? Why?"

"Because there's been a development in an old case. One that could have a significant impact on this family, and I need you and the Steed to be available at a moment's notice."

"What case? Who?"

Gage's voice had an edge of steel with the slightest hint of unease. "The Minnows."

Angie felt the blood drain from her face. "What?" Something landed in her gut like a ball of molten lava. "Tell me what's happened."

"A letter arrived yesterday addressed to Cassandra, Lola, and Katy." Gage's wife and two-year-old daughters. "Not really a letter. Just a sheet of paper with a crude drawing of a smiling fish, and two child-sized stick figures with their heads lying at their feet."

"The girls."

"Their names were on it. We don't know how the Minnows could have that information."

"Your trip last year to see Cass's sister. Have you checked on Syd?"

"She's fine, and they've already relocated."

"How's Cass doing?"

"At first she was terrified, wanted us to pack up the girls and move to Iceland."

"Really?"

"Lasted about ten minutes, until she got her mama-bear mad on. God help anyone who gets between her and our kids. She'll slice and dice them and feed them to the alligators."

"Alligators?"

"I didn't ask."

"I've seen her fierce. She can be damn scary. Makes you two a formidable pair. She won't run, will she?" Cass *had* struck out on her own once, but that was before she and Gage were married, and at the time she didn't trust him.

"Nope. She knows this is the safest place she can possibly be. We've also checked on her dad, and he's fine. The only person we don't have a connection to is her brother Dean, who is the center of the problem. I just wish we could find him and convince him to talk. Then the whole Minnow problem would go away."

Angie's throat closed up. She hazarded a glance at Julia, and that was apparently the opening she needed. "Which is why I asked Gage to call you in." Eve had obviously told her.

Firmly shoved into a corner, she watched Gage's face while the pieces fell into place, and he muttered. "You said Dhillon's father was a one-night stand with a cowboy in Vegas, but it was Dean, wasn't it?"

She shrugged. "He was a cowboy, but there was an extra night or two."

"And the secrecy about the man you're dating." He shook his head. "How dense could we all be? Dean's been under our noses for years. That's why you've stayed single. It wasn't for Dhillon."

"Careful how you tread, Gage. Everything in my life is about Dhillon." And his father. Weariness seeping into her bones, she dragged out a chair. What now?

"You'll tell Dean what's happened. Get him to settle this." Gage began to pace. "We'll set it up with the authorities. He'll be kept safe from them while he testifies. We'll use multiple safe houses, and work out a plan for moving him daily. With the Steed, we can make it easy." He snapped his fingers. "Grace has lots of properties we can mix with ours, and Logan can—" He stopped, spun and pinned Angie with a look.

"Logan's been in on this the whole time, hasn't he?"

Her gaze stayed steady, giving away nothing, but he went on. "He facilitated the vacation you just had together. You need to call Dean now." He pointed at the landline on the table. "Tell him what's going on."

"Gage," said Julia and her tone managed to convey both censure, and sympathy.

He stuffed his fingers through his hair. "This isn't going to happen, is it? He'd have done it by now, you'd have seen to it if he was ever going to testify and get the Minnows off our backs. I need a minute." He marched from the room and silence eddied thick in his wake.

Julia laid a hand on Angie's shoulder. "Are you okay?"

She nodded. "I need to tell Matt—that's his name now—I need to tell him what's happening, but I can't contact him."

"I'll speak with Grace. She and Logan will take care of it." Telepathically, that was the word she hadn't said out loud. Julia to Grace, Grace to Logan, and Logan to Matthias.

"Matt won't." She shook her head. "He can't testify. It's way more complicated than that." Should she say what she knew? She needed to talk to him first. "Tell Grace I have to talk to him about something he said while we were away."

Julia was watching her carefully, and not for the first time Angie wondered about her mother's powers. Could she pick up thoughts? Or just communicate without speaking? "The training at ECT has helped me understand about the pathways of the mind, but I haven't advanced far enough to get to what you're capable of. So far, I've only learned to access energy and interpret its source."

"Good defensive skills. I'm glad their approach is to arm you before opening you up to more."

"Like training on a single engine fixed-wing before moving up to multiples and then the helos. Makes sense. But—"

"But you want to be able to communicate with the man you love. I'm sure you've been told what you're seeking has more components than a single set of skills. You have to have the wiring already in place, and not all my children do."

"You can tell?"

Her smile went right up to her eyes. "Babies have no secrets from their mother. At least not for the first year. Some of you could hear me. Others couldn't. And there are degrees, as well as other minutiae. Children with imaginary friends may, actually, be communicating with someone telepathically."

"I never had any of those."

"But you have an interesting connection with your son. One you think is just understanding. But, in fact, you read each other very clearly. It's a joy for me to watch."

Gage came back in and ended their conversation by saying, "I want to talk to him, man to man. I need to make him understand that his sister and her children are at risk if he doesn't deal with the Minnows. I want to tell you to take the Steed and go get him, but I want you and the Steed to be here in case I have to suddenly move Cass and the girls.

"I need caffeine." He grabbed a cola from the fridge under the counter in the back corner of the boardroom. Chugged.

"Gage," said Angie. "He, uh, Dean, would do anything to keep Cass and your kids and our son safe. That's why he's stayed hidden all these years. That's why I've never spent more than eight hours at a time with him, up until last week. He's got a new identity, and a vocation. He does important work. People— many people—depend on him for what he does. He makes a difference. He's a caring man, but there's nothing he can do to change the situation with the Minnows."

"Your son. I hadn't thought. Dhillon, Lola, and Katy are double related, which means he's just as much at risk as they are."

"Exactly, with the slight difference that no one knows Dhillon's connection."

"I knew," said Cass, slipping into the room. "I've left the three of them in the kitchen with Consuelo, she's feeding them lunch—and too many cookies, I'm sure." She smiled at Angie.

"Dhillon felt familiar from the very beginning. Which makes sense, because the last time I saw my brother Dean, he was the same age as your son when we first met. And I've always felt that Dhillon and I were tight, like there was an invisible bond between us." She put an arm around her husband. "What really sealed the deal was when you said once that Angie's mystery man was as elusive as my brother Dean." She grinned at Angie. "You nearly choked on your supper."

Angie remembered that incident, along with a few other times when she'd almost given herself away.

Julia cleared her throat. "Lockdown is in order."

Angie's spine tingled. This was real.

With the flick of a switch, Gage sent a signal to notify family, security, and employees that a strict and well-established set of protocols would be adhered to, effective immediately. Every human, animal or machine going on or off the property would be scanned by security.

Calibration of the seismographic cables protecting the perimeter of the vast property was automatically altered so even a rabbit would set off an alarm.

All infrared and heat detection cameras connected to motion detectors were activated, and a family member, or one of the most trusted staff, would be in the security room or the Emergency Operations Center twenty-four seven.

The four of them moved as a group to the EOC, a large boardroom at the most eastern point of the sprawling house that vaguely resembled the spokes of a broken wagon wheel.

Lance, their head of security arrived at the same time, through the outside door.

He exuded power, probably because years in Special Forces stayed with a man. He nodded. "Julia."

"Lance."

"What have we got?"

Gage kept it simple. "A threat to our children that makes it apparent information has leaked from here about them. We'll stay on lockdown until we've identified and removed the problem, and/or eliminated the threat. Either you or a family member will be in here or the security room at all times, monitoring the data. Rotation every two hours." Which would make sure nothing was missed. Staring at security footage could be eye-crossing.

Lance frowned. "The children?"

"Will all wear sensors, and for the most part remain together."

"In the main house," said Angie. Security paranoia was a by-product of her father's PTSD, and he'd drilled them on every aspect of safety.

Julia nodded. "This place is bombproof. You'll all move in for a mini vacation." She smiled. "Consuelo will be in her glory with the children underfoot, and everyone will pitch in to help her when you're not on shift in here. Lance, you'll bunk in the house as well. Everyone, take care of your details, be back here for supper, and be prepared to make camp. Angie, with me."

In her mother's spacious office Angie paced, waiting for Julia to make a telepathic connection with Grace, her niece, and explain the situation to her. Ask her to have Logan connect with Matt.

What would Matt do? How would he respond to the threat? Would he allow her to share what they'd talked about just a few days ago? Would he regret telling her anything?

God, but she needed to see him, feel the heat of him under her hands. She longed to hop in the Steed and go after him, but Dhillon's safety and that of the others had to come first. She could take her son to ETC with her. He'd be safe there, but it would leave one less able body to protect Cass, Lola, and Katy.

At Julia's firm touch on her shoulder, Angie spun from where she'd been staring out the window.

"Grace has explained everything to Logan, and he'll connect with Matthias."

"Considering that telepathy is such a perfect

form of communication, it's a shame to have to introduce a middle man…heck, three. What are the chances something could be misunderstood or left out?"

"Slim. We're very good at this. And Grace thinks with a bit of coaching you and Matt could make your own connection, and we won't be needed."

"How do I get started?"

"As I expected." She smiled, and pointed at one of the white wingback chairs. "Sit." She didn't speak again until Angie was parked on the edge of the seat. "As you've already learned about extra sensory perception, you need to go inside yourself to open channels, become receptive to the possibilities. Grace will target both of us after Logan has spoken with Matt."

Angie slid further into the chair and leaned back, closed her eyes. Took a couple of long, slow breaths. "Okay, ready."

"Clear your mind of everything but my voice while you walk cerebral corridors, looking for doors to open. Listening for voices. There will be dark tunnels, but pay them no mind. Follow the light, and search for colors, since every pathway has its own— not unlike an aura. Look for a golden light, and one slightly darker, nearly brown. They should be very close together."

"I think I see them."

"Follow them, and you may find they blend, but if they separate—" *Follow the darker of the two, and you'll find the doorway partially open. You need to give it a nudge, see it opening, and tell me what's there, but don't speak.*

I see you, here in this room, but nothing else.

Then you have made your first connection. You need to be

very careful now, and work your way back to the more golden light. Follow it and see if you can find the door.

It's there. I see it. But it seems to be firmly closed.

If you can stay where you are, just rest within the pathways, we'll see if Grace will be able to open it for you.

Angie had no concept of time. She looked around, trying to put words to what she saw, but it was like trying to describe a scent. It just was. Well, except for the color. But she saw no others aside from the brown and gold. *What color would Matt be?*

Midnight blue. Hello, Angie.

Grace! Have you spoken with Matt?

Logan has updated him.

What did he say? What about his story?

He said to do whatever's needed to keep the children safe, and suggested taking them to ETCETERA until you can be sure the ranch is the best place for them. He'll make the arrangements a soon as you tell him it's a go.

What about him coming here?

He fears that would put everyone in more jeopardy. He'll be working from where he is to try and resolve the issue instead.

Explain resolve?

Sorry, kiddo, that was all he said.

Thank you, Grace, and thanks to Logan, too.

Julia's voice joined them. *Will we see you anytime soon, Grace?*

No plans, but one never knows. Angie had a mental picture of Grace's smile and the door closing softly.

Wow. I've just had a full, three-way telepathic conversation. I should feel stunned, but it felt normal. Strangely unremarkable.

Come, said her mother. *We have work.*

By suppertime the house was teeming with people. Lola and Katy's giggles mixed with low-pitched adult conversation, and Dhillon was obviously torn between the two camps, craning his neck to hear what was going on, yet unable to resist playtime with his young cousins and the three dogs.

Cass's two resident felines had also been moved to the big house and were currently perched on a bookshelf, watching over the goings on, and keeping an eye on the plates yet to be cleared from the table.

Consuelo's chicken pot pie was legendary, and scraps were slim, but the girls were often too antsy to finish their supper, so the cats would get to help clear the plates of any leftovers.

Under normal conditions, Angie would have enjoyed watching the interaction of her huge family, but tonight there was too much edge and expectation floating among them like sheets of electricity. It was making her head hurt. She should shut down the pathways, but was caught up hoping that once Grace let Matthias know Angie had managed to open a telepathic link, he'd make contact.

She glanced around. This is just how Christmas would be. The whole works together. But then there was her dream of having Matt there with them. First for Christmas morning, with just the three of them at her place, and then the afternoon of food, gifts, and sloth with the entire family.

She glanced at her son. This wouldn't be the year she got to tell him that the doctor, the scientist he idolized, was his father. She had to close her eyes to stop the tears, then looked around suddenly when a tingling began at the back of her neck. And she'd have sworn she felt breath in her ear. She scooted back her chair, slipped off to the bathroom.

Leaning back against the locked door she took a

long, slow breath, another. Slid down until her butt hit the floor, then carefully took the steps she'd only just learned. Followed the pathways, looking for an elusive light edged with midnight blue. Smiled when she found it.

Hey, cowboy.
Tell them.
Gone.

Like a light blinking on for a nanosecond, leaving you wondering if you'd seen it at all. Not what she'd expected. No warmth, no feeling of connectedness. Just two words. Had it been him at all? Maybe her own conscience was playing tricks with her?

No. He'd relayed his message. And in spite of the emptiness seeping inside her like an incoming tide, she'd have to press on. Time mattered.

CHAPTER 10

Her family, thought Angie, not an easy group to play to, but she did love the war room—as Dhillon had dubbed the EOC—and the powerful feeling that came from leading a briefing, or at least having the floor temporarily.

Her oldest brothers Gage and Quinn were most often the ones in control, but they were also used to playing supporting roles. Their wives, Cass and Rachel, were both brilliant women who sat back, listened, and offered constructive ideas, or ran the communications and display equipment.

Trent, one of Angie's younger brothers, was the family's second pilot and a general cast member. Other Meyers were on security missions around the globe and would have to be updated remotely.

For the benefit of Quinn, Rachel, and Trent, Angie started at the beginning, bringing them up to speed on her relationship with Matt.

Angie's brother Quinn was a psychologist who was usually content to sit back and absorb things before sharing his opinion, but this time he jumped right in. "You've been having an ongoing affair with Cassandra's missing brother for all these years and never bothered to let her know he was okay?"

"Well, ouch," she said. "I had no choice."

"Bullshit. You chose to continue seeing him. Secretly."

Quinn and Angie had been tight growing up. He was her go-to brother if she needed anything, and when his wife, Rachel, had disappeared back a few years ago, Angie helped him get through the rough times. But she understood he was only striking out now because his feelings were hurt. Such an important part of her life, and she'd kept it from him. She was sorry it had been necessary, but would do it again in a heartbeat. She loved her brother, but she loved her son and Matthias in a completely different way.

"As you would say, Quinn, I did what I had to do. My apologies to everyone who was hurt by my actions. Moving on, and more relevant to the current situation, is what Matthias has given me permission to share." Now she had their full attention.

"First off, he gave up the name Dean when he was ten, and his current alias is Dr. Matthias Alejandro Martinez. Although the name is fake, the doctorate was earned. And he's worked as a researcher for ETC since he was nineteen. His areas of study include pediatric cardiac arrest. That's how he came back into our lives. Up until Dhillon's surgery, I'd had no contact with him, had no idea where he was. Not since Vegas."

Seeing Quinn's nod helped to dissolve the lump in her gut. At least he believed she hadn't been keeping a secret since Dhillon was born. Although what difference that should make, she didn't know.

"He's stayed in hiding and never offered to testify against the Minnows because it's just not that simple. He was in the hayloft peering through a crack between boards and, although he saw the killing clearly, he didn't see any faces. As a ten-year-old boy, his witness testimony would have carried no weight, and now, over twenty years later, would mean even less. However, the Minnows do know he was aware there were at least two law enforcement officers present. And police involvement is presumably why the case was filed away as cold almost immediately."

"Does he have any idea if the two are still LEOs? Has he… Of course he has," said Gage. "Strike the question."

Angie nodded. "I suspect that he's going layers deeper as we speak, but he has to be very, very careful not to send up flags by trying to access protected information."

"Moving back to the situation at hand," said Julia. "We need to review our visitor records, beginning with today and going back for six months. That gives you each a month, and I want every visitor investigated fully, no matter how well we know them. The only exceptions are family, which includes Grace and Logan."

"Have you ever taken the girls to Haven?" asked Trent. Although Haven was connected to the home ranch, its security situation was different. The facility Rachel and Quinn had founded for the rescue and rehabilitation of humans and animals in need had dozens of people on their visitor and residential rosters. Not quite a revolving door, but close.

"Aside from our trip to Oz last year, they haven't been off the ranch property since they were born."

"Does James know about the letter yet?" Rachel asked Julia. The family patriarch lived in a remote cottage over at Haven now. It was as close as he'd come to moving home since bottoming out and landing on the streets of Seattle a few years ago, and he had a handle on his demons now. Mostly.

"Yes."

"How is he with the idea of a security breach?" He'd come a long way since paranoia and hyper-vigilance ruled his life, and Angie hoped this didn't cause a setback.

"He's handling it." Julia said. "He'll be fine. Swagger's looking after him." He'd made significant progress since getting his service dog. Now he even trained canine companions and partnered them with other PTSD comrades while they participated in Haven's rescue and recovery programs. "I'll keep him up to date on all progress."

She studied the faces of their family. "Your father is no longer fragile, so you can channel some of that worry into identifying who betrayed us. Gage and Cass, you take August-September. Quinn and Rachel, June-July. Angie, May. Trent, April.

"I'll work with Lance for a couple of hours in the security room, while the rest of you work out a schedule to take over later, two-hour shifts. As for the children, Dhillon and Consuelo are watching a movie in the sitting room outside the girl's room. Puck and Stick are in with the little ones, plus they're on monitor. Are you two good with that?"

Gage nodded, and Cass said, "The two mutts will keep them safe, although I'm betting they're both in bed with the kids." Puck and Stick were Black Russian Terriers, and although they resembled big, fluffy teddy bears, they were highly trained personal protection dogs.

"Good. I'm off, then. Anybody gets the slightest whiff of anything, I need to know. Anytime, day or night."

***

Matthias set his glasses aside and rubbed his eyes. He'd been at it since he got back. His gear was still piled in the corner of his office. First he got caught up on work left hanging because he'd needed a break, one that morphed into an amazing collection of memories—snapshots he could take out whenever he wanted.

Then he tackled the task he'd abandoned time and again over the years. He had to get it done this time. Identify the unknowns.

Judging by the fake light behind the equally fake window, it was finally morning. The first one since he'd been with Angie, yet waking up beside her seemed like weeks ago. And it might as well be, because they were—like they said in the movies— worlds apart.

He was wide awake, fifty feet below the tenth green of an exclusive golf course in West Virginia, and she'd be sound asleep at the family ranch in Texas, with his son in the next room. Dhillon's dog would be on the bed with him. He'd bragged once about teaching the greyhound to stay on the floor until after Angie checked on him, then Chance would jump up and snuggle in.

113

Angie would, of course, know exactly what the kid was up to, but she'd let it go because she was a smart mom. She had to be. The whole burden was on her.

But now it was his turn to step up. To find the men who'd changed the lives of his entire family. To do what had to be done so he could have a chance at a life on the outside.

He started by hitting up the head of ETCETERA's security division for access to files on the Minnows dating all the way back to when the group was formed—when a handful of high school bullies figured out how to make a bundle of money by providing the kind of services people in high places wanted.

Protection. And when their services were turned down? No problem. Give the prospective client a nice scare, and they'd come running but—oh, dear, the introductory special price was no longer available. The perfect scenario. Create a product, then create a need for the product.

As a terrified ten-year-old, he'd recognized the mug shots they showed him at the police station that day, the three Minnows—including the one they'd shot, but there had been no names with the photos, which made tracking them down close to impossible. He dug through old files on the group to find the shooters. And there they were, on the screen in front of him. Two death certificates. Both documented as suicide.

Of the three men slightly harder to identify, the ones who had stayed in the doorway, two had been small town cops, and neither spent more than two years on the force after the murder. One of them had gone the politics route, climbing steadily through the ranks, spending time in positions of power where he could manipulate businesses and property owners. The other had stayed in law enforcement, and was at the moment an FBI Special Agent in Charge.

Matt wanted to tag him as responsible for the security breach at Meyers, but reined himself in, because there was still a third total unknown who could just as easily be the culprit. He'd stayed by the door, perhaps as lookout, and never spoke to anyone. Had he been inside when the murder happened? Matt wasn't sure, because his own eyes had been riveted to the men with the guns. But he'd seen the guy after, when he was called over to help carry the dead guy out.

Matt couldn't wait any longer. *Logan?* He glanced at his watch. Six-thirty, surely he'd be up by now?

This better be good, man, or my wife is going to skin you.

Not like a ringing phone had woken her up. Oh. Morning sex. Matt grimaced. *Sorry, but I've got IDs on two of the non-Minnows in the barn. One of them's real power.*

Anyone I know?

Rollins, FBI.

Fuck.

Yeah.

The two shooters apparently killed themselves, and I have nothing on the last man yet. Could be anyone.

If he's alive and not a Minnow, he'd have to be attached to Rollins.

I've been working that angle and coming up empty.

Let's see what the other minds come up with then.

Family's on lockdown.

Good.

Later.

Yeah. Apologies to Grace.
I'll make it up to her.

Matt half-laughed while he secured the portal, and wondered if Angie was up yet. Only five-thirty there. He thought about tickling her psyche. "Don't be stupid," he muttered to himself, wondering when exactly he'd lost his mind.

He dug back into the search, this time bringing up personnel files for the agents Rollins commanded. But it was another dead end.

Maybe the mystery man *was* dead. Or he'd broken free. The former was more probable than the latter, and both impossible to research. Wait a minute. What if—

He logged onto two other computers, searching for obituaries, and for missing persons files in the northeast corner of the country, from the day of the murder onward. White males birth year ranging from twenty to forty years prior to the incident.

The first shock was seeing his father's photo and the accident report filed after their car went into the river. The reporting officer was the one who followed Matt home the day of the murder, and then to the station where they'd been handed over to a detective—a man alive and well, living in a retirement resort in Florida.

The second shock was the picture Matt had been looking for. The missing person file had been opened two days after the murder, and had never been closed. Matt studied the photo of Timothy Leslie Fredrickson. Yes, he remembered that face, but there was something else scratching at him. He combed through the slim file, hoping something would ring a bell. When he came up empty, he searched for any

John Does who could be him, but found no viable options.

Matt went back to the photo. A casual shot of a young man standing beside a car. He lifted every detail he could and made a file with information about the car, the man, and the background. No jewelry, which wasn't uncommon. Button-down shirt in pale blue with a navy tie. Again, standard.

Matt leaned back in his chair. Puzzled. What was it about that face? It was nicely balanced, not much beard growth. Eyes were a plain brown, as was his shoulder-length hair. Average.

With no other lines to tug, Matt decided to play with an age enhancing program and set it to work, requesting samples at five year intervals.

It was the third one that sent Matt's heart to his throat. Fuck. He knew that face.

Time to get the hell out of Dodge. And he needed a ride, fast.

Logan!

***

Angie woke momentarily disoriented, but quickly grounded herself with the memory of moving into the main house the day before. She flung the covers aside and scooted to crack open the door to Dhillon's room, just enough to peek in at him. She had to grin. He was sprawled on his back with both arms stretched out to his sides, and the dog was also belly up with his head resting on the boy's arm.

She closed the door softly and glanced at the bedside clock on her way to the shower. Uh. Why was she up before six in the morning? She could just crawl back under the covers, but instead she'd go and help Consuelo get things together in the kitchen. The house was chock full of people to feed.

"You fall out of bed?" Consuelo asked when Angie arrived in the kitchen before the sky was fully light.

"Something like that. Figured I was already up, so I might as well help you in here."

"I'm doing a breakfast pizza, and a ham and cheese omelet casserole. Plus there's the rest of yesterday's chili, and sandwiches for those who've been up all night and want something more substantial."

"I can handle the casserole." Because it was one of Dhillon's least favorite things, she rarely made it anymore. "You got a recipe for the size you want?"

She pointed to a shelf. "Fill that big blue dish with ham and bread cubes, pour in a dozen eggs whipped with three-quarters of a cup of whole milk, then cover the top with grated cheese and—" She hesitated. "Better leave off the jalapeno bread crumbs, just in case the little ones want some."

"No self-respecting kid will touch a casserole when they know there's sugar-coated cereal in the cupboard."

Consuelo laughed. "I used to make you kids eat one scoop of the good stuff before you got the other." Which was why Angie had a similar rule for Dhillon.

"You've mellowed with grandkids." She didn't miss the woman's instant smile. "Yeah, they're yours, too." Consuelo had come to the remote ranch when Julia was pregnant with Angie, and never left. She became a second mother to all of them, and now their kids had an extra grandmother.

They worked together in a silence broken only by the occasional hum from Consuelo, and were sitting at the table with steaming cups of coffee when Gage joined them. He was just coming off shift in the war room.

"Everything quiet?" Angie asked.

"Nothing out there but coyotes and rabbits." He rubbed at the back of his neck.

"Good. Let's hope it stays that way."

Gage had alternated with Trent from ten pm to six am. Quinn and Angie were up for tonight. He sniffed the air. "Do I smell chili?"

Consuelo started to rise, but Gage stopped her. "No, sit. I'll get it." He filled a bowl and poured a large glass of milk. "Thought I saw a ghost right at sunrise," he said with a frown.

Angie's senses sharpened. "Explain."

"Just a flicker on one of the cameras. Ran it back and forth a dozen times, but there was nothing there."

Trepidation ran Angie's spine like a flame up flimsy curtains. "Why is that punching buttons for me?"

He studied her. "Did for me, too. Shadows can be dust devils." He set aside the food. "Let's go for a drive." He downed the milk, grabbed a handful of cookies from the jar, and two bottles of water from the fridge.

Consuelo waved them away when Angie reached for Gage's bowl. "I'll take care of it. Check in with security, and then get a move on."

Angie stopped and stared at her. "You, too?"

"Probably just channeling from the two of you,

but I'll let the others know when they get up."

Gage nodded. "We'll probably be back before then."

The security jeep they took was loaded with equipment, everything from heat sensors to automatic weapons and GPS tracking devices. James had established the protocols they followed, and it was never a bad thing to be over-equipped, unless of course you were on foot, because that shit was heavy.

They didn't make conversation, since they were also well versed in observation, and both studied terrain, the movement of the wind, the feel of the air.

When he stopped the vehicle, they sat in silence for a couple of minutes, heads turning slightly, then stopping, like wild animals trying to catch the sound or scent of a predator they knew was there.

"Too still," said Angie.

"Yep."

All she could smell was hot earth.

Angie.

She jumped. *Mother.*

We have you on camera. What are you picking up?

Nothing. Less than, actually, and that's weird.

Gage was frowning at her.

"What?"

"You've got that look. Who are you talking to?"

"Julia. She's watching."

He nodded. "Figures. When did you two start?"

"Yesterday. It's freaking weird having her suddenly talking in my head, as though she's looking over my shoulder."

"Spooky."

"You're telling me? Do you have any? Other powers, I mean."

Instead of answering, he held up his hand. Tipped his head.

She touched his arm when she heard it too. The faintest buzz, reminiscent of a very tired bee trapped against a window. But there was no variation in pitch.

When Gage started to step out she grabbed him. "Smells like a setup," she whispered, and he nodded.

They opened the back of the jeep, fired up the comps, and ran diagnostics on the area. Came up with a familiar shape constructed of metal screws, wires, and plastic, but thankfully, no explosives. It was fifty-two feet east, and four feet off the ground.

Gage donned night vision goggles and passed her the heat sensing ones. Then they armed themselves and slowly started through the brush.

Angie could almost feel Julia breathing down their necks. Besides the telepathic connection, she'd be following their every move on-screen, thanks to the GPS tracking devices the two of them wore.

Staying about ten feet to Gage's left, Angie proceeded forward while visually scanning, the same way he was. Sweeping side to side, then doing a slow three-sixty to keep watch over their backs. She heard the sound again.

Gage swung a glance at her, then turned his head to the left. He'd heard it too. Adrenaline pumped. She flexed her fingers against the barrel of the rifle. They altered direction slightly, and crept forward, a single step at a time, scanning the ground and everything above it. They were both well trained, and used what they knew, careful not to follow an anticipated path.

They circled around and approached the sound from the opposite direction, and soon came upon the small drone stuck in a bush. Caged by the dozens of skinny branches.

After carefully checking for wires or traps of any kind, Gage put Angie up on his shoulders to take a couple of photos from above. Then he plucked the drone free and shut it off.

Well?

It was a drone stuck in a bush, Mother.

I don't like it.

Neither do we. We'll put it in a blackout bag and take it to the isolation shed for analysis. The rest of the area appears to be clear.

Security's launching our drones, and moving forward with the nanotechnology. Not even a fly will get inside our perimeter again.

CHAPTER 11

Matthias took apart his computers, damaged them beyond usability, then closed them back up. He knew they were connected to bigger systems, where his browser history could certainly be retrieved, but at least his efforts would make things more difficult for anyone checking up on him.

Then he headed toward his apartment, but went past it to the exit where he'd arranged to meet Logan. Although he'd always been free to move about ETC as he pleased, he still felt like a criminal sneaking out of a building. He schooled his expression for the benefit of the security cameras, nodded and smiled at the few people he passed.

"Hey, you're going the wrong way," said one.

"Pulled an all-nighter in the lab. Need some air, then sleep, much sleep." What he really needed was to get the hell out of here before someone figured out what was wrong. What he'd learned. He refused to allow himself to run up the stairs two at a time, rubbed a hand over his face, then dug at his neck as though to relieve tension—a normal-looking reaction to hours spent going over data.

Almost there.

One more flight of stairs.

Was he clear?

Would Logan be waiting?

Would they be intercepted?

It was insane to be running away from the place where he'd been safe for more than a dozen years. From the people who'd mentored him, given him a purpose, a life, and safety.

Had the safety been a mirage? Instead, was he being kept here so he wouldn't talk? Wouldn't expose people in high places?

He went through the steps. Door one, security pass and biometrics into the man trap. Door two, iris scan. The light blinked green, the lock clicked open, and he stepped out into a cavernous warehouse.

"You need transpo, Doc?" asked the guard at the desk.

Logan wasn't here yet. "Friend's picking me up. Any sign of incoming?" He glanced over the man's shoulder at the computer screen, and, sure enough, there was a fast-moving green dot on the air traffic monitor. He pointed. "That'll be him. I'll use the side door so you don't have to open a bay."

The guard smiled. "You back within twenty-four?"

"You bet." Otherwise, there was paperwork to fill out.

Matt slipped outside, and his heart rate picked up at the sound of a helicopter bearing down. He stuffed his hands in his pockets and watched the bird land. At a signal from the pilot beside Logan, he ducked his head, crouched, and ran under the moving rotors.

"Fucking hell," he said as he grabbed the headset off the backseat and strapped in.

"Hard on a guy's heart?" Logan asked.

"You don't know the half of it. Walking, nearly managing to stroll when what I wanted more than breath was to run, flat out, for the nearest exit. I'd forgotten that feeling."

"Just chill and relax, for the flight at least." Logan turned his attention to the view out the windscreen.

"Yeah, sounds good." He leaned back in his seat. *You don't trust your pilot?*

I don't trust anyone today. Not after the bomb you dropped.

Yeah, kind of sent my day off the rails, too. Didn't dare draw a full breath.

You'll get a chance to relax at Paradise.

You don't think they'll come after me there?

I'm not sure they'll want to. First off, we need to review what you've found and be a hundred and ten percent certain you're right, because there's a chance it's not as bad as it looks.

I learned long ago not to expect the best. Hope had been eradicated from his vocabulary, even the internal one.

I understand, but we need to take the steps to be sure before we open this can of fish. And there's been another development. Security was breached at the ranch last night.

Fear clamped a vise grip on Matt's throat, and words froze there.

Relax. Everyone is fine, but the Minnows breached Meyers security early this morning, and freaked the family pretty good, so they've brought out the big guns, literally and figuratively.

Are they equipped to handle what could come out of ETC?

Yeah. They've engaged their secret weapons of defense. Nano and drone combined with radar, audio, video, infra-red, and seismic accessories to spot anything coming their way.

Good.

Grace is staying open to Julia, so there's a solid communication link.

ETCETERA claims they can intercept telepathy.

Yeah, we'd heard that. And although I think it's a stretch, and nothing more than a tactic to keep their telepaths in line, they'd still have to decipher the messages.

Matt grinned and some of the weight he'd been carrying lifted. *Dhillon has created some amazing codes.* His brow furrowed. *He told me about some of them when he was in my office. They could have been listening.*

Possibly, but no worries there. This is a brand new one he says he didn't tell anyone about yet.

Kid's sharp.

He's been living and breathing security since the day he was born. No small wonder he's ultra-careful about what he shares.

What a damn shame he had to grow up that way. Never trusting anyone. At least Matt had the vague memory of his early years, when his biggest worry was getting busted for trespassing or snitching apples from a neighbor's tree.

Your situation had minimal impact, my friend. He's a Meyers, and security is their personal choice, but also their livelihood. He isn't on the Minnows' radar as far as any of us can tell. And they're not the sharpest set of knives. If they knew about him, we'd know.

But Rollins. He's a smart bastard.

True. So, yeah, pays to be careful.

He could have been working undercover that day and unable to stop the execution.

I'm hoping that was the case, but I won't go blue with it. I've never had any dealings with the man myself, but I did a bit of snooping after you called, and found lots of shadows worth exploring.

Logan went silent while they approached Paradise, and Matt assumed his friend was communicating with his wife. Grace would need to send someone to pick them up, because they'd be landing in a field as far away from the inn as you could get while remaining inside the concrete walls. There was plenty of room for a helipad closer to the main buildings, but with most of the residents being in recovery—young women rescued from human trafficking—Grace kept their living area as stress-free as possible.

***

Grace watched the average-looking blue and white helo touch down, but when the doors slid open and the men hopped out while the rotors were still spinning, she squeezed her eyes shut.

Stayed that way until they jumped into the SUV with her, then pinned Logan with a look. "What the hell was that for?"

He grabbed her hand, kissed the knuckles. "Were you frightened for us?"

"No. Pissed I might have to get blood all over the interior of this thing. It's new."

"Hear that, Matt? The sound of true love."

I don't know why I let you push my buttons. She had a phobia about loading or unloading hot.

Because you love me?

"You come across any more info since this morning?" Grace asked Matt.

"You mean besides the fact two men in very high places were witnesses to the same execution I watched when I was ten? No, thank God. I think that's more than enough."

Grace's stomach hadn't unclenched since Matt shared his findings with them that morning. A powerful man in the FBI on the wrong side of the law was one thing. But Kelton. That hit home because not only was he head of the psych department at ETCETERA, and Matt's mentor, he was also married to Grace's half-sister.

Grace had never trusted him because of the role he played when her father was murdered.

"Any updates from Julia?"

"Not since the drone incident."

"Say what?"

"I haven't had a chance to tell Matt yet."

Grace launched into the story while she drove the winding dirt track, and had barely finished when they arrived at the inn. "There's no one currently in residence—everyone has been relocated until we have a handle on things—so I've set us up in the boardroom and the library."

"I couldn't copy any of my research without leaving evidence behind, but if you give me a computer and about an hour, I can duplicate my notes."

"Sounds good. Then we'll blend it with the data I found and see if we can build something that makes sense of this whole mess," said Grace.

What aren't you telling us? Logan knew her well.

Understood her tone, every nuance.

Just a few odd details. Let him get his stuff down, then I'll show you what I have.

He winked at her. *I've already seen what you have, and it's delectable. No way I'm sharing.*

Pervert.

Once Matt was ensconced in the library, Logan took her hand and led her to the elevator. On the way up to their private penthouse suite he gently cupped her face and kissed her softly. *Missed you.*

You were only gone a few hours.

Still missed you.

***

Matthias made meticulous, detailed notes, and built a timeline with everything he could find, starting the day he witnessed the murder. He noted every Minnow case the FBI had any connection to in the past few years, as well as the info he'd dug up about Rollins. High points in his career, decorations, and promotions.

Then he started on Kelton. Data on the man was scarce, but due to a natural propensity for remembering details, and extensive research training, Matt was able to fill pages with notable memories and the dates to go with them. Memories, dammit, of a man who'd given him everything. A career. A chance to make a difference in the world, and, more important, to the lives of families torn apart by the illness of a child—and the fear that crippled them afterwards.

Kelton had not only facilitated an extraordinary amount of education, but he'd fed Matt's soul by giving him a purpose.

Had it all been a way to keep him quiet? To keep him comfortably underground and prevent exposure of a man who not only attended an execution, but…

Matt shook it off. Research projects required focus, at a level he could not attain if he wasn't able to filter out the personal connection, because his vision would be impaired. Important details couldn't be overlooked. Air, he thought, I need some air.

He pushed open the French doors and stepped out into manicured gardens perfectly suited to the fancy old inn, reminiscent of those he'd seen on his internet travels of Europe. Hedges trimmed to angles of mathematical precision, rose blossoms in every conceivable shade of pink, names of which only women seemed to know. Even the stones underfoot were arranged in meticulous patterns. Everything about it, even the heavy scent of roses, was extremely unlike the Grace he knew, but his friendship with her had been limited to short intervals of time spent with her and Logan. And social skills, drawing people out in order to learn about them, wasn't something he'd had any real experience with.

Books had been his greatest source of information about people and societal interactions, and clearly they hadn't exposed him to the realities of individual diversity and contradictions.

He strolled, taking in the beauty of the roses and the comfortable predictability of the layout. There were other flowers, the names of which he didn't know, and stone benches, inviting in theory, but being stone, not a place to rest for more than a few moments.

Unless, apparently, you were a large, white cat.

He studied the animal while it studied him in return. "Am I interrupting your nap?" asked Matt, and he was rewarded with a one front leg outstretched, toes spread, delightful feline yawn.

"I'm Matt," he said, holding out one hand.

The cat sniffed at it, then bumped it with his forehead.

"Ah, so you're a friendly fellow." Matt sat on the hard seat and stroked the purring cat, who eventually flopped over and appeared to be offering its stomach for a rub. "You know, I've been tricked by that move before." He tentatively rubbed under the cat's chin first, then allowed his hand to trail across the beast's underside.

"Be nice, Careless," said Grace, approaching from the direction Matt had come. "He's usually good, but once in a while he goes for blood."

"There was a kitten years ago who set me up that way. He'd seem to be begging for a belly rub, then latch on to me with four sets of claws and his pointy baby teeth. But he was feral, sort of." He'd been taming the whole litter he found in the barn, and they'd been such fun to play with.

"Standard procedure, I think. But this guy's getting on in years, and kindness usually supersedes his wild side. He's even nicer to the dog these days."

"His name's Careless?"

"Long story, but basically he couldn't care less about the silly dog, or much of anything else. He's a solitary fellow, but does enjoy occasional companionship...on his own terms, of course."

"Nice gardens."

"If you're into stuffy."

"You aren't?"

"Not really. Come on." She led him past the hedges. "This is more my thing." Flowers of every shape, size and color lined a mulched pathway cut between huge willow trees. As they walked, they came upon alcoves with wicker chairs and odd sculptures of metal, rock and wood. "This looks much more like you."

"Thanks." She met his gaze directly. "You ready to get to work?"

"Yeah, no point putting off the inevitable."

"It might not turn out to be as bad as you expect."

"It's hard to see my mentor in a bad light."

"You are aware that he and I have a personal connection, in that he's married to my sister."

Matt stopped, studied her for a moment. "I'm sorry. I hadn't thought about how this was affecting you."

Her half-laugh was accompanied by a wry expression. "It may also interest you to know Kelton and I have always had a rocky relationship. He's controlling, and I don't care for the way he treats most humans as underlings." She sighed. "That said, I'm still conflicted about this whole mess, so I'll be glad to get it sorted out."

The three of them spent the afternoon fleshing out the timeline, both on the computer, and by using dozens of colorful sticky notes on the walls of the boardroom, because Matt preferred to see a picture of the whole.

He added a marker for when the Minnows had kidnapped and tried to kill his sister Cassandra. Luckily, she was a smart and resourceful woman, and managed to escape, although not unscathed.

And now they were after her children. All in order to get to him. He shook it off. Focus.

"This is the first Minnow encounter since Cass got away from them? Four years is a long time. Makes me wonder why."

Grace nodded, and Logan answered. "There have been other small incidents which they never took credit for, but it's suspected the Minnows were behind them. We'll have to get those dates from Meyers."

"Last year, when they went to visit Sydney, was the first time Cass left the ranch in…what, two years?" she asked Logan.

"Closer to three.

"Just a shame Sydney couldn't have gone to Texas to visit."

"That would have blown her cover. She's never been a target, and we're not even certain anyone is aware that she's your sister.

"Cassandra's years of searching for you and your dad, combined with her very public presence while searching for other missing persons, put her identity out there, and brought her to the attention of the Minnows."

"If she was under the protection of Meyers, how the hell did the Minnows get their hands on her?"

"That, my friend, is a long story, and one you'll have to hear from her. She's a tough cookie, Matt, and doesn't back down or give in without a fight."

"She was always feisty. Wanted to do everything I did, go where I went. Taught herself to ride a bike so she could go with me when I did my paper route." He smiled. "Yeah, not surprising she can handle herself. She was a fun kid. Disconcerting to think of her as a mother of twins. Syd, yes, she was all about her dolls. Cass had a thing for animals. I was always bringing some critter home, and she'd end up helping me hide them."

"Yeah, she loves her cats. Swears one of them talks to her. You guys had lots of pets growing up?"

"None, actually. They were always sent back. Do we have the dates of Cass's trip for the timeline?"

"Give me a minute and I'll ask Julia."

Matt studied the data they'd accumulated, and spotted several points of interest where there were quite a number of entries. He'd go over those for correlation later. First, he had to be absolutely certain every iota of data had been visited, only then could his plan be initiated.

CHAPTER 12

Angie's heart warmed while she watched Dhillon. He was sitting cross-legged, syringe-feeding a black kitten snuggled in a towel on his lap. Chance leaned against the boy's leg and studied the small creature.

"I'm keeping him you know," Dhillon said without looking up.

"Are you?" She knelt beside him and sat back on her heels.

"Please, Mom, he even looks like me." He touched a fingertip to the white strip on the tiny face.

She'd grown used to the thin white streak in her son's black hair and rarely gave it any thought. It had appeared in the weeks after his heart stopped and Quinn's wife Rachel used her gift of healing to bring him back to life. Then she'd disappeared.

Dhillon stirred more of the kitten food and warm water to create a soupy mixture he could suck up into the syringe. "They searched for more, you know, but there was only him, and no mother. He needs a family, and that should be us."

Rachel had called Angie and asked if she should bring the kitten to the house for Dhillon to look after. Something for him to focus on while they were all on lockdown.

"I suppose you've already named him."

He glanced at her with a hint of a smile. "Christopher."

"What?" She couldn't let him name the poor thing after Kelton, a man who'd gone from mentor to monster at warp speed in the eyes of the boy's father. But how could she explain? And why should a boy have to be afraid of people he used to trust? It wasn't as if he'd ever see the man again. Or would he? And there it was. She'd have to tell her son in order for him to be safe. But what if it turned out differently, and by some miracle Matt was mistaken?

"Why Christopher?"

"Christopher Columbus because this guy's an adventurer, an explorer of new territory. Rachel found him trekking across the parking lot at Haven, and she says he's only about five or six weeks old. A long journey—well, at least for him—to an unknown place, but he's too little to handle a big long name, so I'll call him Chris for short."

"Works for me." And heck, she'd never heard anyone call Kelton Chris. "How often does he need feeding? And shouldn't he still be getting milk?"

"Rachel says he's old enough for this stuff. I make it extra-mushy, and he takes it from the syringe for now, but I can put some on a plate too and see if he can figure it out." He demonstrated, but the kitten didn't seem interested in the food in front of him.

"I'm supposed to fill him up with as much as

he'll eat, every three hours. I've already set my watch and see," he held up a notebook, "I'm keeping a log of intake, and Consuelo gave me a kitchen scale to weigh him before and after every meal. That way I can be sure he's okay. According to my research, he should gain at least ten grams a day, twenty is better."

God, she loved this kid. Instantly wishing she could share the moment with Matt, she was reminded that Dhillon had stopped asking about his dad, shortly after...

"Are you ever curious about your father?" What the hell was she thinking? Exactly, there'd been no thought. The words had fallen out on their own. She watched for a reaction.

Dhillon stroked the kitten. "I used to think about what it would be like if I had a dad."

"And what did you come up with?"

"It would be fun if he lived with us, because then when you went on an op I'd get to stay home."

"What's wrong with staying at the big house?"

"Nothin', but home's better. I can keep working on my stuff, and nobody's riding me to make sure I'm looked after." He glanced up. "Does this mean you're ready to tell me?"

"Tell you?" Well, that sounded stupid.

"Who my dad is."

Angie's heart thumped. Should she? Matt wanted him to know. Or had before he found out Kelton was one of the people from the murder scene years earlier. How did that change things?

"I might be. Are you ready?"

"I might be." His eyes were steady and a smile hovered.

She sat cross-legged beside him on the floor.

"It's not going to be simple. There are complications. Things that will account for him not being around, even after I tell you who he is."

"Will he visit at least?" He tucked the now-sleepy kitten into the blanket-lined box and snuggled him up to the hot water bottle wrapped in fleece.

"Someday." She'd make sure of it, even if she had to hog-tie the man. "Do you have any ideas, I mean, about what you hope he's like?"

Dhillon smiled. "The uncles, only better," he said with a grin.

"Better?"

"Sure, so I could say stuff like, 'Oh, yeah? Well my dad is faster than you, or stronger, or smarter.' That would be great."

Was there something she was missing? "Why do you want that? Are they hard on you?" She'd put a stop to *that* in a New York minute.

"Naw, but they *are* better than me at everything, just 'cause they're old. I'm catching up. Just not fast enough."

"You create better codes than all your uncles combined."

"Yeah, but that's not as cool as sinking baskets and target shooting, or holding your breath underwater the longest."

Angie clamped her jaw on the laughter trying to escape. "What if your dad isn't better at stuff like that?"

"He's a weenie? Dang."

No, he's a nerd. A gorgeous, brilliant, soft-hearted nerd. "His only athletic talent is mountain biking." Looked good in the gear, too. She forced the image away.

"I guess that's better than nothing. So I get to meet him soon? That's what you're leading up to, isn't it?"

Too smart for his britches, her kid. But how could he help it considering the environment he was being raised in? "Maybe soon, maybe not. Depends on a lot of things that—"

"That you can't tell me about. Yeah, I know the drill."

"You're getting a smart mouth you're gonna have to watch." She drilled him with her best stern mother look.

"Sorry."

"That's good. And I'm sorry too...that I can't tell you much about your dad."

He put his arm around the dog and they leaned into each other. "Can I ask one thing?"

"Sure. I hope I can answer."

"I obviously don't look like you, so do I look like him?"

She battled back the lump in her throat. "Yeah, you do. More and more every day."

"So he has blue eyes and black hair, and he must be tall, 'cuz I've been able to see over your head since I was ten."

"Careful."

"No offense, Mom, but you are, um, vertically challenged."

"You think going PC makes it okay to diss my height?"

"You're a giant to me," he grinned. "Especially when you're makin' pizza. And when you get in the Steed, you turn into a superhero."

"Very nice save, young man. You could have a

future in politics…over my dead body." Pushing up to her feet she ruffled his hair.

"If you can't tell me stuff, how about something general about him, like is he in law enforcement, or aviation, or medicine, or marketing, or engineering? Just general, Mom, give me something I can think about."

The kid may not look like her, but she recognized her own persistence and creativity in him. Tenacity counted, too, and sometimes you just had to throw your kid a bone. "He's in medicine, which is why I seemed startled the other day when you said you wanted to be a doctor."

"Wow. Cool. My dad's a doctor."

"And you have to keep that to yourself."

He rolled his eyes. "I know the drill."

"Good. Now clean up this mess and head for bed. And yes, I know you were going to *ask* if you could take Chris up with you, so I'll say yes now, and save you the question."

"You're the best." He jumped up and threw his arms around her.

It was disconcerting to be looking her son in the Adam's apple. When the hell had he grown so tall?

"Take his supplies with you. No point coming back here for feedings. Hot water from the bathroom tap will warm the food just fine." Angie would make sure he was fed, even if the kid slept through his alarm.

While she watched Dhillon get everything gathered up, she thought about Matt. Wished he could be there with them, sharing these moments. Their son was growing up so damn fast.

***

Before answering Logan's question, Matt shoved away from the huge boardroom table and went to the window. At least here he could do that. Clouds had filled the sky since this morning as the predicted storm moved in. The one preventing them from leaving for the Texas ranch. A small reprieve for Matt, because he thought the trip was a bad idea, and, although he'd likely give in, he still hadn't agreed to going.

He'd never questioned Logan's judgement before. But, as the saying went, there was a first time for everything.

If Matt was at the ranch, the Minnows would try even harder to break through their security, and that would put everyone, especially the children, at greater risk.

When Logan and Grace disagreed, he'd countered with a different idea. "Why not use me as bait? Lead them on a journey around the country until they get dizzy enough to make some stupid moves and then law enforcement can take over."

"And charge them with what? Stupidity?" Grace's chair squeaked when she leaned back. "Or do we let them get their hands on you so we've got something to charge them with?"

"Let's not forget about Rollins," added Logan.

Matt hadn't forgotten. "And Kelton. We need to find out for sure about Kelton. Maybe it was just a case of similar appearance." He held up a hand. "I know, wishful thinking."

Grace was typing on a laptop. "Actually, there isn't enough information about his background to draw any conclusions one way or another."

"Guess this must be hard for you."

"While it's a difficult position, it's somewhat familiar. When I had issues with Kelton years ago, I did some investigation into his background."

"And?"

Her expression was closed, unreadable. Not uncommon for Grace. "My conclusion was that no matter how it looked, or sounded, he never meant any harm. That said, he can be highly insensitive, and self-absorbed to the point that harm often does come from his actions." She reached for the water jug in the middle of the table, filled a glass and took a swallow, looking lost in thought, her actions appearing by rote. Matt was surprised when she suddenly continued.

"I was out of touch with my sister when she became involved with him. It was a shock to me, and I used my Interpol connections to dig even deeper than I had previously. The research was extensive, and there was not so much as a shadow to be found. And he's an only child of only children, so there's no chance the guy in the photo is just a relative, so we have to speculate that the missing person report was a ruse to get him clear of the Minnows."

Matt sat down so he was at eye-level with his friends. "You two are about as close to family as I've had in my life." He used to include Kelton in that very small group. "And I never want to do or say something that could jeopardize that."

Grace's smile had a hint of sadness. "But you have to ask."

He wished he didn't, but she hadn't offered. "Is there *anything* in your history with Kelton that I should know?"

Her gaze met Logan's, then she nodded. "He had some questionable practices when it came to recruiting. Nothing illegal, but he knew how to apply pressure. He was also known to work with other agencies who had less stellar reputations than ETC, and I believe it was for data he couldn't get without crossing lines himself. I've questioned his morality and integrity several times, and he has always had a *suitable* response."

She sighed. "Do I think he could have stood in that doorway and calmly watched an execution? The man he is today? No. A much younger version, however, might have been able to justify not making an attempt to intervene, based on sheer numbers."

Meeting Matt's steady gaze, she said, "But that's pure speculation, because I didn't know him then."

"Thank you for your honesty. And, for the record," he glanced back and forth between the two of them, "I feel almost the same way. I don't think the man I know could witness a cold-blooded murder without attempting to stop it. But at the same time, there is something about him. An edge of secrecy or something that goes along with his worldliness and—"

"Self-importance," Grace finished. "As I've probably said before, he's not someone I see myself ever trusting, yet I don't distrust him."

Logan put his hand over hers. "My feeling exactly."

Matt understood. He'd seen Kelton in action. He was very much a commander, focused on the goal, and not the obstacles on the journey.

"Okay. On that note, if he's involved in this current threat, what would his goal be? Why would he be acting with the Minnows to get to Cass's children? Wouldn't that screw up having me as an ETC asset? A term," Matt added, "that he's used to my face more than once."

"Trying to get to the girls will keep the Minnows away from you, and out of Kelton's way," offered Logan. "And, since he would certainly consider the Minnows inept, he wouldn't think they'd have any shot at gaining access to the ranch. Therefore, no risk to anyone, and ETC's world stays intact."

"What about Rollins?"

"Now, him I distrust," said Grace. "And our research shows that there have been several men and women under his command who walked away from promising careers to take up vastly different lifestyles. Currently, he has a very solid group around him, *men* who've been with him for years."

"Faithful." Matt was a scientist. He saw patterns. "No women."

"Exactly," said Logan. "Which is why we're trying to find some of those who left law enforcement while under his leadership."

Grace turned her screen so Matt could see their photos. "These are the ones who quit him. Seven women, four black men, two gay men. His inner circle contains, as you probably guessed, only white, hetero men. And of the thirteen in these photographs, up until they encountered Rollins, every single one had exemplary records, with six to eight years in the FBI. Now, of the group, there are three farmers, two fishermen, and a couple of full-time moms."

"That's only seven." Matt didn't think he was going to like hearing about the other six.

"Can't find any information on them. At all. Oh

and of the previous, five of them reside in Alaska, the others are location unknown." Grace closed the laptop.

"Logan and I want you at the Meyers ranch, because then we'll be working together, with no fragmentation of resources."

"Rollins," said Logan, "has a long reach, and if he's feeding information to the Minnows, he's too invested not to want to show off by plucking you out of thin air. If you're in the same place they're focused on, the Minnows will be in Rollins' way."

It made good sense, except… "Why hasn't he taken me out before now?"

"Logan and I don't think he knew where you were. Maybe he still doesn't."

"So I'd be safer staying at ETC."

"Except for the Kelton question," said Grace. "And one more note for the record—I don't think my sister would be with a man capable of handing you over to the enemy. But stranger things have happened. Maybe he accidently let something slip, and Rollins is cashing in."

"Without a certainty that Christopher *was* the man you saw the day of the murder, we can't know if there's a connection between the two."

Again, they were back to that question. "I should have confronted him instead of calling you and running away like I was still ten."

"Don't second-guess yourself. Your gut said to call me and get out. I think it was a smart move. Grace and I both, even with our extra senses, depend on gut reaction. It's your brain at its most primitive level acting to keep you safe. Plus, you have Dhillon to worry about as well."

Matt agreed with that assessment, and reminded himself that he *wanted* to go to the ranch, but was resisting because he thought it would increase risk for others. Grace and Logan had sound reasoning why it would be the complete opposite. "I'll go."

"Great. I'll contact Julia." Without using modern technology of course.

Matt worried that Kelton could pick up telepathic communication the same way cell phone signals could be intercepted.

Logan placed his hand on the table between them. "Relax. They use code and their own version of mental imaging."

"Good. That's good. Because ETC is constantly developing stuff, and people, with amazing skills."

Logan grinned. "It's always pissed Kelton off that he couldn't keep Grace under his net. She's done work with him and for him, but she'd never sign on the dotted line."

"I refused to be owned," said Grace, leaning forward to rejoin the conversation. "We're set for whenever the weather lets up. Meantime, I think we should keep working the Rollins angle by backtracking to find out how he got to where he is."

CHAPTER 13

Angie landed the Steed at Paradise with her heart pounding as hard and fast as it had on her first solo flight. And wasn't that just ridiculous?

She'd had far less visceral response to the many hair-raising situations she'd encountered as a member of Meyers. Of course, they hadn't involved the man she loved, the father of her son. Today it was her job to get Matt to the safety of her family's ranch, and there could be any number of unfriendlies watching, locking on, and firing high-powered weapons.

The Steed had great armor, but it also had some weak spots. Not unlike her. It sucked to admit to weakness of any kind, especially for someone surrounded by alpha males. She snorted. And females.

Was that the problem? Or was this about taking Matt home to face that family of hers? Dhillon already knew him, but he'd be confused by Quinn and Gage's reactions. Sure, she'd threaten them, but would they be able to maintain? Yeah, they would. She needed to chill. The long flight had given her too much time to think. To borrow trouble.

Safely on the ground and about to shut down, she was surprised when Logan stepped into her line of sight and whirled a finger in the air. Oh, hell, something was way off if Grace was willing to let Matt load hot.

She hit the door releases and gave him a thumbs-up. Scanned the area for trouble.

Instead of just Matt, Grace and Logan also climbed on board, all reaching for and donning the sound reduction communication helmets before they closed the doors.

She was ready to lift off the moment Matt, in the seat beside her, said, "All secure."

"Copy, secure." Angie gave her full attention to her craft, the ground they were skimming over, and the sky around them.

Once at a comfortable cruising altitude, she was able to ask questions. "Why the last-minute change of plans?"

Grace replied, "We'd always intended to join you, just didn't want to put that information out there."

Made sense. "Then why load hot?"

"Unidentified foreign energy," Logan said. "We couldn't even pinpoint a direction, which is beyond odd."

Grace and Logan's extra-sensory perception was legendary, and they were a force to reckon with when working together. If the pair of them sensed something off, it was off. "Do you think anyone would try using a drone here?"

"Entirely possible, but nothing has registered yet on the sensors. Could be fun, though. We left Sergei on duty. Anyone dares to send a drone into our airspace, he'll pick it off like a clay pigeon at the shooting range." There was laughter in Grace's voice, which Angie loved to hear. If Grace was laughing, all was well with the world.

"Do you have any guests in residence?"

"No. Sergei and Caroline have the place to themselves, which is nice, because he's coming off a long op." Sergei was a career sharpshooter, and his wife ran Paradise, a position which included mentoring the girls and women. Helping them adjust to rejoining society.

"Any new developments at the ranch?" asked Logan.

"Nothing. Anything more on Kelton?" She glanced over at Matt and found him staring forward, as though not even listening to the conversation, so she wasn't surprised when Logan finally answered.

"We've done several deep searches and found the numerous roadblocks we'd expected."

Silence hung until Grace spoke. "How's Cass holding up?"

"She was spooked at first, but now she's just pissed. Doesn't like that a bunch of idiotic guppies are fucking with her life—her words. And that was before she learned about their connections to the FBI and ETC. She appears to be calm, but you can see the fire flash in her eyes once in a while.

"The girls are happy to be camping out at the big house, as that just multiplies the number of people available to dote on them. And Gage is resigned to keeping things calm."

"I don't envy Gage his position," said Logan. "Must suck to be running an op that involves his own children and his wife."

"Actually, Julia's taken the helm on this one. She wants Gage to be able to focus on Cass and the girls."

"What about Dhillon?" asked Matt. Angie glanced his way and found him watching her.

"Dhillon doesn't know his connection yet, so he's pretty laid back. Playing with his animals and helping run herd on the twins."

"Are you going to tell him?"

"Yes. He needs to know, and finding out you're his father will be part of that, but I thought you should be there for the explanations." She almost held her breath while she waited for his reaction.

"You don't think it's too soon? Too sudden?"

She snorted. "No. I think it's about thirteen years too late, and sudden is the only option." The fact that Grace and Logan were listening made no difference; she needed Matt to understand what to expect *before* they arrived.

"We had a talk last night. I told him he might get to meet his dad soon, that his father is a doctor. He wanted to know if he looked like you and I told him the truth. I'm betting that our extremely bright child is going to connect the dots the minute he sees you."

His hand came up as though to rub his face, but the helmet was in his way.

"You know him, Matt, he's a cool kid. My best advice is to simply follow his lead. Leave control in his court, and, for the record, he already likes you, so don't look for trouble. At least not there."

"Meaning?"

Logan laughed. "She has two older brothers who owe you a beating."

"Logan, be kind," said Grace.

"They don't owe him any—"

"Yeah, they do. Their fifteen-year-old sister turns up pregnant, they need to do something to right the wrong."

Angie was annoyed enough to want to stomp her foot, but that wouldn't be a healthy move at the moment. "It was my choice."

"But on their watch. Both Quinn and Gage have told me your dad left them in charge," said Logan.

"And I was able to sneak away."

"They'll see it as me luring you away."

"Oh, for heaven's sake, I wasn't twelve. I made my choice. Now, back to business. What kind of dirt did you find on Rollins?"

"Besides him being sexist, racist, and likely homophobic?" asked Grace. "A few tidbits he'll have a very, very hard time talking his way out of."

***

Once on the ground, Grace and Logan took one of the four-wheelers and headed for the main house, leaving the other two on the helipad beside Angie's home.

Matt sucked in Texas air for the first time in more than fifteen years and was surprised by the humidity, and the rich scent of the trees. He'd been expecting something much different. A unique blend of dust, mesquite, and freshly cut hay to stir old memories of when he and his dad—

"Matt?" Angie's voice dragged him back to the present. Standing beside the Steed, she looked deceptively tiny, when in reality she was as big and as fierce as the helo she commanded.

"You okay?"

Just like her to be worried about him when she should be concerned about how bringing him home would affect her family dynamics, her world. Would their son hold it against her that she'd kept his father's identity a secret?

"You're sure you're ready for this?" He'd hate it if she changed her mind, but he'd hate himself if he didn't give her the option.

"Don't even think about backing out on me, cowboy." She slid her arms around his waist. "It's gonna be okay. Dhillon already wants to be you when he grows up. Sure, there might be some less than comfortable adjustment time, but we'll get through it. Somehow, some way. It's what family does."

No freaking wonder he loved her. *Had* loved her, almost since the day they met. "How long will it take Dhillon to get here?"

"Grace will send him back with the quad as soon as they get to the house, and he'll ride like somebody left the gate open, right up until the last curve in the road. Then he'll throttle back to an acceptable pace before he comes into sight. You want to do this inside or out?"

"Where's he most comfortable?"

Angie shook her head. "He's not a stranger to you, Matt." Then she grinned. "And here he comes, so unless you plan on running indoors, the decision has been made for you." She moved to face her son, with one arm loosely draped behind Matt, her thumb hooked in a belt loop.

The four-wheeler slowed as it came around the curve of the road, but was still clipping along at a brisk pace. The best part was the look on the face of the dog perched behind the boy. Apparently the canine didn't feel any more secure when the machine slowed, and when it came to a stop, he happily jumped off and shook himself.

"Poor Chance," said Angie. The gangly greyhound began hopping up and down with his thin tail whipping wildly, as though to encourage his master to abandon the machine immediately.

Dhillon didn't move. Just sat there staring at Matt, eyes wide, mouth slack, his expression, in a word, shocked. Oh, hell, looked like Angie was wrong.

When Matt shifted his feet, Angie's hand moved to grip his side. "Give him a minute," she whispered.

Dhillon finally shut down the machine and climbed off. Walked slowly toward them.

"Hey, Doc."

"Hey, Dhillon."

The boy's gaze was locked on where his mother's hand rested at Matt's waist. "What are you doing?"

Again, Angie's grip tightened. Her tone was soft, yet firm. Unapologetic. "You've known for some time that I was seeing someone, and I told you I'd bring him here to meet you."

"But *him*? He's my... How can you go out with my doctor?" He frowned. "Isn't that, like, unethical or something?"

"Actually," said Matt, "The ethics thing is sort of covered, because I've known your mom since before you were even born."

Dhillon turned his attention back to his mother. "Why didn't you tell me?" The dog shoved his head up under the kid's hand.

"Because it was none of your business." She let go of Matt. "I don't know about you two, but I'm going to turn into a puddle on the pavement if we stay out here any longer. I'm going in for AC and fluids." And she left the two of them standing there.

"Coming?" Matt asked Dhillon his patient, not Dhillon his son. That made it easier to get the words out of his dry throat.

"I guess." He fell into step, the dog glued to his side. "S'pose this'll be okay," he said, "As long as you don't get like my uncles and do suck-face all the time."

"I promise to try not to embarrass you."

"Sounds good."

Matt held the door open, and Dhillon hesitated for a split second, then went in, muttering, "Ya don't have to do that, I'm not a girl."

Reminded how much he liked this kid, Matt grinned. Angie watched them come inside, but quickly turned her back and dug a carton of orange juice and a large bottle of soda water out of the fridge. "You okay with orange fizz, Doc?"

"Never had it that I know of, but I like orange juice, so I'm game."

"It's Mom's idea of keeping me away from drinking a bunch of sugary sodas. Half orange juice, half fizzy water. Consuelo called it a virgin Mimosa when my aunts had to switch off champagne because they were pregnant." Dhillon dragged out a tall stool and sat up to the long counter.

Angie placed frosted glasses on two coasters, then took one for herself. "Sit," she said, and Matt did.

Tension crawled up his spine. Was this the

moment? What the hell was he supposed to say?

"So, Doc, you into horses? We could grab a couple and go for a ride if you're going to be here for the day." Dhillon gulped down three-quarters of his juice and wiped his mouth with his sleeve. "Or we could go four-wheeling." His eyes lit. "I could get another machine for us. Trent's got a new one and it's freakin'-awesome-fast. How long you here for?"

"Ah—"

"Matt's going to stay until the lockdown is over."

"Why?"

Oh, hell. This is the stuff they should have talked about on the flight in. Matt's gaze swung to Angie, and thankfully, she supplied the answer. "He's going to be helping out because he's had some experience with the Minnows. And you know this stuff is classified, right?"

He shrugged. "Sure. So how about a ride? Or do you guys have to go up to the war room for a consult or debrief or whatever?" Pushing back his chair, Dhillon took his empty glass to the sink, rinsed it and put it in the dishwasher.

"Well," said Angie, struggling to keep the nonchalance in her voice. "There is a bunch of that *whatever* to be done, but first the three of us need to have a serious talk."

Just look at the two of them, she thought, when they both gulped visibly, and she stifled a grin. If their basic physical resemblance wasn't enough to give away their relationship, their personalities would certainly seal it. Neither one wanted to deal with serious stuff. Matt, with fallout from a parentage announcement, and Dhillon who'd be anticipating a talk about Matt's relationship with her.

She strolled over to the doorway, watching to make sure they both shifted to look her way. Now she needed to make sure they noticed the mirrored wall to her right, so she turned as though to check herself out. Fluffed a hand through her hair, then said, "Hang on. I forgot something."

Using her cell to call up to the house, she talked to Julia. "Hey, Mom, how's everything going?" She nodded. "No, I just wanted to see what the plans were for dinner tonight, and you know, catching up."

Julia was quick. "You needed a distraction did you?"

"Yes. I had a brilliant idea. I'll tell you all about it later." She glanced at the mirror and her heart did a quick double thump. Matt was watching her, but Dhillon was studying *him*. And judging by the wide-eyed look on their son's face, she was next to certain he'd seen the likeness.

"How's it going so far?"

"As expected."

And being part of the big group at the house tonight would give Dhillon some time to adjust. To sit back and observe. No doubt it would be harder on Matt that way, but Dhillon came first. He was the one getting news dumped on him. He'd handle whatever came his way, because he was that kind of kid. But no point in making it harder on him.

"You still want me to send Cass over?"

"Yes." She deserved private time with her brother. "Now'd be good."

When she clicked off from her call, she turned to study the reflections of father and son. "What are you thinking, Dhillon?"

"It's him." His gaze bounced back and forth

between his own image and Matt's. "I look like him. And you said I looked like my dad." Chance moved from his bed in the corner to lean on the boy's legs where they dangled from the tall stool.

"Yeah," she said, going to the fridge. She popped the top off a container of cut veggies, and opened another filled with yogurt dip. Put them on the counter between her two guys. "That gonna be a problem?" She dipped a chunk of cauliflower. Crunched.

Dhillon, without looking, reached in and grabbed a handful of carrot sticks. "Dunno. All this time, you both knew, but I didn't. Means you were lying to me."

Matt's gaze swung to her, and she nodded. It was only right that she lead. "You know how it is with the business, that the truth often has to be protected, right?"

"Sure, but—"

"There's a good reason for protecting Matt's identity and his connection to you for so long."

Matt sent a quick glance toward her, then added, "And I always wanted you to know me."

Dhillon continued to stare at the mirror instead of at the man. Seeing, Angie was sure, the likeness between them, and a sort of relationship between their two images. It was time to move on. "The latest development has put you at as much risk as the twins." Dhillon finally swung around to stare at his mother.

"The Minnows?"

"I love that I have a smart kid. How much backstory do you know about Cass?"

He opened his mouth and closed it again.

"Never mind if it's information you weren't

supposed to have access to. You have extraordinary hearing, and a penchant for eavesdropping. So let's just keep it real."

His mouth twisted in a half-smile. "Cass's brother saw a guy get murdered so their whole family had to make a run for it. Then the Minnows kidnapped Cass a few years ago because they thought they could use her to get to him. That's about when she met Gage, and escaped from the Minnows, but they've found out about the twins and know they're here on the ranch"

"I'm Cass's brother," Matt said quietly.

"But his name is Dean." Dhillon shook his head. "And her name isn't Cass either." He stared at Matt. "You've been in hiding all this time? That's why you could never be my dad?"

"Exactly," said Angie, diving in before Matt could give him a long, complicated answer. That could come later. For now, Dhillon had enough to digest, and Angie heard a vehicle approaching.

CHAPTER 14

After a cursory knock, the door swung open, and in marched a tall, thin, attractive woman wearing jeans, a flannel shirt, and a wide smile. "Hey, Angie, Julia said you needed…" Her voice trailed off when she spotted him and she froze. "Dean."

Matt hadn't seen her since she was five, but Angie had shown him recent pictures of his sisters. His voice was suddenly trapped in his throat, and the silence hung heavy while her glance travelled over the three of them.

"Dhillon and I," said Angie, "are going to make ourselves scarce for a while." She slung an arm around her son's shoulders and nearly dragged him from the room.

"Such a long time," murmured Cassandra. Not the name she'd had back then, but he'd grown used to it when Angie had talked about her. He was glad her voice sounded stronger when she continued. "You said you'd come back for me, and I hung onto that promise for years. It kept me going sometimes when things weren't great."

"I'm sorry I reneged, but I couldn't come back for you. Dad said it would endanger your life. But I thought about it a lot. Even tried to set up a safe meet through Meyers, but they swore it would put both you and Sydney at risk." He shook his head. "I guess you know that part."

"I'd already figured out you were Dhillon's father, and when Angie confessed, told us the whole story just the other day, it all fell into place." She shook her head and stepped closer. "You're really here. And you look different, yet familiar. You don't look like Dad at all. He came to meet with me after I escaped the Minnows the last time. Thirty minutes. That's all we had, but I cherish it." Her eyes filled with tears. "How long? When do you have to go?"

"I'm staying." He held out a hand and she stepped into his arms. Strangers, they were total strangers who'd happened to share the first five years of her life, and it felt so right to hold onto her. Have her hanging onto him, digging her fingers into his back as though afraid he'd vanish.

She sniffed mightily and pulled away. "I don't do weak and blubbery. Honest." She swiped at her tears. "But, holy hell, you caught me off guard."

"If it's any consolation, I didn't know you were about to walk through the door. Figured I was meeting you later."

"Angie's tricky that way." She smiled.

"Apparently."

"I can't wait for you to meet my babies. And Gage." Her smiled widened. "Um, so. Are you prepared to meet the wrath of Angie's brothers?"

Nope. "Not like I have any options. Will they

swing first and ask questions later?" She laughed, and he suddenly saw the little sister he'd loved.

"I am so freaking glad you're here."

***

Angie gave them about twenty minutes. Sent Dhillon up to wash and change his shirt, then went into the kitchen. Matt and Cass were sitting at the counter. "Time to join the others at the big house."

"The part I wasn't looking forward to," said Matt, his face grim.

"How about I introduce you first, then just take things as they come," offered Cass.

He looked at Angie. "Works for me."

On the walk over, Dhillon was his usual self, apparently comfortable with the surprises of the day, and for that Angie was grateful.

She felt the tension in Matt when Cass stopped in the doorway of the enormous living room. His back was poker straight while he surveyed the setting and the people. Probably felt like a worm being dropped into a pond full of trout. Added to that, his arguments against Christmas with her family came back to her. He'd said he lacked social skills, didn't do crowds, or small talk, had nothing in common with people who weren't like him—living in a glorified bunker surrounded by secrecy and security. He hadn't sat down for a family meal since he was ten.

"Helloooh," Cass called out, and one by one, they focused on her. "I'd like you all to meet my brother, Dean. Aka, Dr. Matthias Alejandro Martinez."

Gage was first to offer his hand to Matt. "Damn

glad you finally made it. She's never stopped looking for you." He glanced at Dhillon, then Angie, obviously uncertain if the boy knew yet.

As voices rose and others approached Matt, Angie, and Dhillon stepped past them. "You or me?" she asked him.

Dhillon stuck two fingers in his mouth and blasted the room with a whistle, then with nothing more than a grin for preamble, he announced, "Dr. Matt is my dad."

Silence.

Matt touched Dhillon's shoulder and cleared his throat. "I'm sorry I missed out on so much of my son's life, but I'm hoping to make up for it. Dhillon and I met several years ago when Angie signed him on for my research project at ETC, but he only found out today that we share a great deal of DNA."

Quinn's approach was slow. Measured. He stopped in front of Matt. "You're lucky the kid likes you. I'm Quinn," he said, holding out his hand. Angie thought she detected just the faintest wince from Matt. Ouch, she thought, knowing how strong Quinn's grip could be. "We'll talk later."

When Angie took a step toward them, Matt's glance stopped her while he replied to Quinn, "We will, I'm sure."

"Come on," said Angie and led him to the far side of the room, where three women sat in oversized wingback chairs. "My mother, Julia, my sister, Eve, and Rachel, who has the distinction of being married to Quinn. But we love her anyway."

"Angie." Julia's tone held just enough censure to have Angie nodding.

"Mother, I'd like you to meet Dhillon's father,

Matthias Alejandro Martinez, also known as Cass's brother Dean."

Julia rose, slowly smoothing a hand down her dark brown jeans as if they might be wrinkled—which was laughable because, well, starch—and straightened to her full height. At more than a head taller than her daughter, she was nearly eye to eye with Matt. They studied each other for a couple of beats, and then, reminding Angie what a gracious woman her mother was, Julia took both of Matt's hands in hers.

"I've been *aware* of your presence for many years. I'm glad you've finally joined us. Your son needs his father. Welcome."

"Thank you. I hope I don't bring trouble in my wake."

"The trouble was already here, young man. No point avoiding what needs to be done. James, my husband, isn't here tonight, but will meet with you tomorrow." She turned to the group. "If we don't sit to eat soon, Consuelo will start packing things away."

"Great. Straight to dessert," said Dhillon, and there was laughter.

"Excuse me?" Angie used her best mom voice.

He shrugged. "Worth a try. But it's okay, Doc, dinner will be good. Consuelo's the best cook ever."

Matt, remembering Angie's frustrations in the kitchen when they'd been on the ranch, leaned over and whispered in her ear, "Bet she can't fly a helo." And Angie's sudden smile loosened something inside of him.

There was laughter, and the temperature in the room had warmed considerably. But he wouldn't be tricked into thinking all was well. Not yet. Both Gage and Quinn would have a go at him, no doubt. And he'd just have to deal with them. Meantime, Logan gave him a nod, and Grace smiled. Yes, he did have people of his own here. They'd sat silently while the family introductions were taken care of, unobtrusive as always, and, of course, observant.

Matt glanced at the imposing table at the far side of the room—probably set with fancy dishes, glasses, and *silverware* like his mother's Sunday table had been. He hadn't thought about those days for a long time, but now they came rocketing back. The white cloth she'd iron, then put right onto the table—to avoid wrinkles. The cloth napkins folded to stand up in the middle of the plates, and it had been his job to put the cutlery out in the proper order, because the girls were too small to reach. Fancy crystal glasses would be half-filled with tomato juice—in the kitchen so as to not jeopardize the white cloth—and then set carefully at each place.

This incredibly long table had seven chairs on each side, and one at either end. He did a quick head count, Angie's five brothers, two sisters-in-law, one sister, plus Julia, Grace, Logan, Dhillon, Angie and himself. Fourteen. Before they sat, he was introduced to Consuelo, so that made fifteen. Julia took one end of the table, so he assumed the empty seat opposite her was her husband's.

The man he'd be meeting tomorrow. The family patriarch. The father of the fifteen-year-old girl Matt had gotten pregnant more than fourteen years ago. He pushed that concern aside, since it had no bearing on what would happen here, tonight, and judging by the keen looks, he'd need to be on his toes. This family might seem to be accepting him with open arms, but he wasn't naive enough to believe there was no underlying animosity.

Not wanting to engage with anyone, he focused on the table. Dark blue cloth with brightly colored woven mats. Knives and forks were plain in style, not fussy like his mother's, but he'd bet they were silver. Just two forks, one knife, one spoon. He could handle that.

Thick, smoky-looking glasses sat alongside heavy coffee mugs, and there was no fancy, flowery thing in the middle. Just several sets of salt and pepper, baskets of bread, butter dishes, a couple of bottles of ketchup, and some hot sauce. This table was all about eating.

Conversation swirled around him while plates filled with steaming food were brought in on a trolley and passed around. Dhillon leaned close and whispered. "If there's anything you hate, slip it to Chance, he'll get rid of the evidence." The dog's face was all innocence as he gazed up from his spot beside the boy's chair.

"Thanks," said Matt. "I'm good as long as there's no Brussels sprouts."

Dhillon snorted. "Only at Christmas, and I have to hide them in my napkin, because Chance hates them too."

"Whispering isn't polite, Dhillon," said his grandmother.

"Yes, ma'am."

Seated directly across from his sister, Matt watched her and her husband interact. He handed her a roll, she passed him the butter, and very slickly transferred her broccoli and carrots to his plate. Matt had taught her that trick when she was about three or four. She'd always hated vegetables, and he loved them, so he'd eat hers when their mom wasn't looking. "Still don't like vegetables?" he said quietly, and she met his gaze.

"Hush, or you'll get me in trouble. I only get away with it when the girls aren't here."

"Where are they?"

"Because Julia had planned a late supper, I treated them to an early picnic, and now they're tucked in." She held out her phone to show him the video stream of two small beds with tiny figures barely visible under the covers because of the large black dogs. "Puck and Stick are on duty." She set the phone back down in front of her.

"Puck and Stick."

Dhillon pipped up, "I named them for my uncles because they were away when the puppies got here. They're Black Russian Terriers.

Nathan, one of Angie's younger brothers nodded. "Yep, by the time we got back from our mission, the names had stuck."

"What would you have called them instead?" asked Matt.

Nathan waved his fork while he chewed and quickly swallowed. "Not sure, but it would have been something regal, for sure. Notice the kid gave his own dog a good name."

Dhillon shook his head. "Rachel named Chance. He was her dog before…"

Silence slipped over the group, and Matt waited, watching his son, and wondering how they handled the past and what had happened to him.

"I rescued the mutt from a dismal racing career, so I thought his name should be Chance, since he was getting a second one," Rachel said.

"Like Rachel gave me when my heart stopped," said Dhillon.

Matt knew the story of how Quinn's wife had used her very special gift to save his son's life. "Thank you seems enormously inadequate, but it's all I have."

"You're very welcome. I'm glad I was able to make a difference. And thank you. Because of your research, our son was tested as soon as he was born, and we don't have to be concerned that he could have the same thing happen. We'll be able to let him play and have fun like any other child."

"You should have heard the belch Jamie let out today when I was helping Rachel," Dhillon said.

Laughter filled the room and difficult subjects were left behind.

Everyone passed empty plates around until they were stacked and taken to the kitchen. By the time ice cream and chocolate sauce were set in front of him, he'd almost grown comfortable with the group.

Almost.

CHAPTER 15

Angie dug in her heels when Matt balked at the sleeping arrangements. They were alone in the kitchen, but she kept her voice low. "You have to stay in the main house. We're all under one roof to make it easier on security."

"I understand the reasoning, but why make it easy to get us all at once? It's a better tactical move for me to stay in your house instead, with Logan and Grace."

She concentrated on relaxing her jaw, and flexing her fingers. He was right, and she'd just have to get over it.

"With Logan's extra security gadgets, we'll be perfectly safe, and won't be spreading the family security resources thin. Your people will continue to concentrate on this house and Cass's girls."

"Sucks that you'll be sleeping in my bed without me."

He leaned his forehead against hers. "Believe me, you won't be suffering alone. Olfactory memory will have me twisted up half the night, I'm sure." He leaned down and brushed his mouth across hers just before the door opened.

"Gross." Dhillon slapped his hands over his eyes. "Do you guys have to do that in here?" He heaved a huge sigh. "I knew it," he scowled at Matt. "You're going to be swapping spit all the time, just like my uncles."

"Hey, kiddo, mind your mouth." Angie shot him a heavy-duty Mom look. "You may be bigger than me, but I'm still the one in charge."

"Sorry." He scuffed the toe of his runner against the floor to make a squeaking sound.

"Good. I guess since it's past your bedtime, you were looking for us so you could say good-night?"

"Yeah. Sure." He grinned and glanced at the cookie jar.

"And you figured a bedtime snack was in order?" She couldn't seem to fill the kid up anymore. When he nodded, she said, "Two cookies, and milk."

"Can I take them up with me?"

"Yeah, and take an apple too. Just in case you're still hungry."

He grabbed his supplies and hesitated on his way out. "I'm glad you're here, Doc, and that Mom's boyfriend isn't some loser. C'mon, Chance." And without a word about Matt being his dad, he was gone.

***

Grace perched on a tall chair alongside the counter in Angie's kitchen while Logan made them breakfast and Matt prowled from one window to the

169

next.

"Anything you guys want to talk about before we join the others?"

Good thinking, Logan's sidelong glance and small smile warmed her as much as his internal voice did.

Matt picked up a blue and silver ball cap from a shelf. "Kid's into sports. Can spout off names of all the big teams, players, positions. And I have no clue about that stuff."

Grace was stumped for a response, but Logan apparently had this one. Without looking up from the toast he was buttering, he said, "Ask him to teach you. No better way to connect."

Matt nodded. "That could work as long as he doesn't think I'm an idiot because I don't know the kinds of things his uncles do."

"Oh, hey," said Grace. "Be yourself and do *not* try competing with them."

"No shot but to come out the loser?"

"Don't be an idiot."

Logan laughed. "You're you, man. The uncles just have different strengths and weaknesses. Something for everyone. Mostly, stay open to the kid. Available. Not much else you can do but try to find some common ground. Something you can enjoy together."

"That's what Angie said."

"Then listen to her," said Grace. "Now, on another front, I had a call from my sister this morning. Kelton's worried about you not returning last night."

"Why would he ask his wife to check up on me through you? That's way out of character."

"For one, he knew you left with Logan. But she

contacted me without him asking, or knowing."

"More plausible. But aren't they like you and Logan? Living in each other's minds? Hearing each other's thoughts?"

Grace tilted her head. "Even though the capability is there, it doesn't mean there is no privacy. Logan and I actually tend to have conversations out loud, as opposed to tripping around perusing each other's thoughts and ideas. That said, I'm sure Sarah and Christopher have their own set of boundaries." She picked at the omelet Logan set in front of her. "She assured me he didn't know she was contacting me, and I believed her. Had no reason not to."

Standing across the bar from her, apparently too restless to park, Matt set down his fork. "Apologies, Grace. I didn't mean to come off as doubting you."

She hesitated. "You're going to be up against this kind of thing a lot in the next while. The Meyers are a tight-knit family, and there will be times you'll have to trust each person's integrity. Not going to be comfortable. But you need to find a way through it without alienating anyone. They're likely to be impatient with defensiveness as well."

He set his knife and fork across his plate still filled with food.

"Ah, one more thing? Your whole life is going to be in turmoil for hours, days, maybe weeks, therefore, appetite or not, you need to eat. You can't work out the family dynamics or fight the Minnows without fuel." And that was way more lecture than she was used to delivering, so it was time to shut up.

Do as I say, she thought, not as I do. *You want this?*

Sure.

She pushed her food onto Logan's plate, then put hers in the dishwasher. "I'll meet you guys back here in forty minutes so we can go up to the meeting together." She slipped out the door.

***

Matt plucked a slice of bacon off his plate. "I know she's right about everything," he said, watching Logan refill his coffee cup.

"Usually is." He smiled. "But she makes mistakes, too. Although in this case, she's dead on. Things aren't going to be easy, for a day or two at least."

"Them against me?"

"No, not that bad, or at least not such a distinct line."

That was hopeful.

"What you need to do is relate to each member of the family separately. Learn a bit about them. Find some common ground if possible."

"Who will be the toughest to deal with?" Information was as good as ammunition. "Don't answer that, because I already know. Quinn and Gage, the big brothers looking out for Angie."

"You're forgetting her father."

The cold toast became hard to swallow, so he chased it with coffee. How would he feel if he had a daughter and some guy got her knocked up when she was well below the age of consent? Hell, judging by the way he already felt about Dhillon, he could only imagine the level of rage he'd experience if anyone messed with his kid.

"Do I need armor?"

"Depends. I've only met James a few times and

always found him pleasant."

"How does the PTSD work into it?"

Logan shook his head. "It's not like a label stamped on his forehead. Sure, he has some issues, but his symptoms are invisible." He ran hot water into the cast iron pan and steam billowed up to fog the window over the sink.

Matt adjusted his position, unwilling to give up the view. Outdoors was a novelty that wouldn't wear off quickly. Distance was something he didn't get to see a lot of. From one wall to another was his norm. Even the big areas and hallways at ETC topped out at about fifty feet. And while the vast, mountainous landscape visible from the bike trails in Whistler had been magnificent, the normal, everyday sight of a yard with a fence and fields and trees beyond it created a peculiar ache around his heart. He forced himself to tune back in to Logan's voice.

"When the kids were growing up, James spent quality time with them when he could, but he was Special Forces, and on several other distinctive teams at the highest levels of security. He was away more than he was home."

"Which is why Julia became the functioning head of the family, according to Angie."

"Exactly."

"She also said that's why it was easier for him to be close to them as adults, because he hadn't known them that well as kids." And speaking of role reversals, Logan was very much at home cooking and cleaning up, while Grace looked more comfortable outdoors, or in a boardroom setting.

"If James's PTSD isn't such a big deal, why does the family wave it like a banner?"

"For one, because it *is* invisible. And none of them had any idea what he was going through until he was in trouble so deep they feared he'd never find his way out. He ended up on the street, virtually lost to the family, but eventually found the help he needed to fight his way back.

"It's like a marker to them. Life before they lost him, and life after he came back. Harder still since Quinn's a psychologist specializing in PTSD treatment, but he couldn't reach his own father." Logan concentrated on one final wipe of the counter and then tossed the cloth into the sink.

"I wonder," said Matt, "if there's any such thing as a normal family." His had been anything but— even before they'd split in half and gone into hiding.

"Until kids grow up and see things as an adult from the outside looking in, very few even realize their family is dysfunctional. They think everyone lives the same way they do."

***

Angie paced to the window to stare in the direction of her house, hoping to see Matt approaching. She'd wanted to go over and meet the three of them at her place, but her mother had been adamant that she was to stay put. If it had been personal, she'd have damn well done as she pleased. But this was an op, and Julia was in charge. Oh, what she'd give to be trekking around in the mountains with Matt again.

Whining and wishing certainly wouldn't get them there, but hard work might. She checked the clock for about the fiftieth time. Where was everyone? The briefing should be underway in just ten minutes.

When the door opened, Angie spun around and was surprised to see Cassandra alone. "Where's your sidekick?"

"Off somewhere with Quinn. Said he'd meet me here. We're the first?"

"Yep." She nodded at Eve and Rachel when they entered. "Looks like an all-female cast. Makes me wonder what the guys are up to."

Were they lying in wait for Matt? To get all possessive, thump their chests and threaten, or worse? If they dared, she'd hurt them. Every one of them.

"If they ambush Matt, I'll get even."

Rachel and Cass exchanged looks.

"You two know something. Spill."

Cass folded first. "There is a quick meeting in the kitchen before—"

Angie was gone before she finished. She'd damn well stop their heavy-handed brothering right here and now. About to shove open the kitchen door, she heard Dhillon's voice and stopped in her tracks. Leaned closer to hear what he was saying.

"I heard you guys talking about my dad last night."

"You mean when you were supposed to be in bed asleep?"

"Yeah. I just wanted a couple of cookies. Didn't know you were in here, but you were. And you were saying stuff."

Angie leaned back against the wall. Shit.

"And?" prompted Gage.

"And, well, I just want to ask you for a favor. I don't ask for much, but this is important, because

Matt's my dad. Gramps might not have been around a lot when you guys were kids, but you still had a dad. I want mine, and I don't want you to mess it up because of something that happened like a hundred years ago."

Oh man, her kid was good at this. No doubt a product of being surrounded by nothing but adults since the day he was born. But on top of that, he'd always had an innate sense of fairness with a healthy dose of smarts. She wished Matt could hear this.

"Seems to me," said Gage, "that's a reasonable request."

"Thanks." She could almost hear Dhillon's grin.

"Not so fast." Angie nearly groaned at Quinn's comment. "You don't think he should be punished for his, uh, mistake?" Now it was a snort she was forced to muffle. Yeah, Quinn, how did you talk to a kid about his mother having sex and getting pregnant—with that kid? Oh, to be a fly on the wall. Too bad video cameras weren't allowed *inside* the house.

"I think he's been punished enough. It's not like you guys never had sex before you were married." She shot a fist into the air, barely able to contain a shout of *Yes!*

"First of all, I'd like to thank you, Dhillon, for calling this meeting, and for sticking up for me." Her jaw dropped open. Matt was in there? "But now that you've had your turn, I'd like to say something."

She covered her mouth and closed her eyes.

"While I appreciate Dhillon's defense, and also the position you two were in as Angie's older brothers, this whole issue is part of our history, not our present. I regret nothing, because what happened was not only a memory that kept me going for years, but gave me a son to be extremely proud of. On that note, I know that you both served as great role models for him, and I cannot thank you enough."

Angie's throat closed, and she heard a sigh, Quinn probably. "You're welcome. Not much else we could do with the rug-rat underfoot."

"So are you guys going to leave my dad alone now?"

"Well," said Gage. "We won't beat him up, if that's what you mean."

"Good."

"And we're late for the meeting," Logan added.

Angie scrambled to get out of sight before the door opened, and ended up in a closet, holding her breath while they passed.

Logan opened the door and grinned at her. "You can come out now, they're gone."

"How—" She shook her head. "You were in my head weren't you?"

"Guilty as charged. And I commend you for your restraint."

"It *was* pretty amazing."

"Yeah. Come on, the rest of the day isn't going to be anywhere near as rewarding, so we'd best get in there and try to make sense of this mess."

"Mess?"

"Seems like."

As with most Meyers meetings, they weren't slow to get underway. Julia began with a quick overview. "Analysis on the drone that crash landed on the property has been completed, and no active devices were found on board."

Julia frowned at Dhillon when he muttered,

"Knew it." And Angie kicked him under the table. It wasn't the first time he'd been allowed to sit in on a briefing, and he'd been admitted to this one on the strict condition that he remain silent unless spoken to.

"Investigation into the FBI connection has been tedious. Rollins was very careful early on in his career. Covered his tracks well, and had elaborate alibis for times that could come into question." Julia tipped her chin toward Gage, one of her silent and well-recognized signals.

He took over. "Fortunately, we're better than he is, in a variety of ways. The most important being our ability to find that which appears to be invisible."

"You've got him," said Angie, resisting a gleeful rubbing together of her hands.

"We do, indeed, have enough evidence to open an investigation that will have federal powers reaching for a bucket of commercial strength antacid. The trick will be to keep them unaware and digesting happily until we have everything we need to make an accusation that will stick, no matter what he uses to counter it. And he will counter."

"Agreed," said Julia. "Rollins will, if nothing else, sacrifice his team members. People whom he's carefully set up to take his falls for him. Agents with no idea what is about to hit them, and they'll be too stunned in the beginning, and feel too isolated, to defend themselves." She nodded toward the door, and everyone stared when James stepped into the room, his service dog Swagger at his side.

"Rollins and I have a personal history," said James. "Very early in my career, I took a hit for something I hadn't done, and Rollins—at that time a total stranger from the Federal Bureau—went to bat for me. Swore it was his man who'd made the mistake. Believe me, he's very, very, good at what he does."

"You'd been set up, and he threw one of his own under the bus to save you?" asked Logan. The implications were ugly, but not unexpected, considering Rollins.

"Exactly. At the time I remember thinking what a bad leader he was because he didn't stand behind his own man. Just cut him loose. When the guy came to me and swore it hadn't been him, I tried to help him out, but he disappeared, and before I could do anything about it, I was sent on a mission that kept me off the continent for the better part of a year." James went to the coffee maker, and poured himself a cup. Slipped a biscuit from his pocket to his dog.

That would have been the mission that crippled him emotionally, chipped away at his psyche for years before he finally came undone.

"May I ask a question?" asked Matt.

James nodded.

"Where does this event fit into the timeline of my witnessing the execution, and your family protecting us?"

"It was shortly after we met with you in Vegas."

Matt smiled at Dhillon. "Roughly fourteen years ago."

"Yes. I was overseas when Dhillon was born."

"So," said Gage. "You have no doubt Rollins is corrupt. What about the team he's built? Are they all dirty?"

"From what I've seen of this kind of thing, there has to be some balance, or it's a setup for mutiny. The difficult task will be trying to figure out who we can trust within his ranks, because they'll be the key to taking him down." James remained standing near the head of the table. "It's been awhile, but I'd like to take the lead on this portion of the investigation if that works for everyone."

Angie wasn't used to this kind of visceral response. For the third time in just a few hours, a lump formed in her throat and she was unable to speak. Matt met her glance from across the table.

"I, for one, would be honored, sir. I've brought a mess to your family, and would appreciate your expertise in cleaning it up."

James suddenly smiled. "So long as that's the one and only time I hear even a hint of suck-up from you."

A flush showed at Matt's collar. "Agreed."

"As for the structure of the investigation, Julia will stay as lead, with three departments below her. I'll take the FBI portion, Gage the Minnows, and," he glanced at Logan, "I'd appreciate if you and Grace would handle the Kelton piece."

Logan nodded. "Just one thing." His gaze moved around the table. "Kelton left ETC headquarters about an hour ago, and told no one of his destination. Didn't file a flight plan." He waited a beat. "He'll be here by noon…if he's given permission to land."

CHAPTER 16

Questions bounced around in Matt's head. Would they allow Kelton to land? And why was he coming here? How did he *know* to come here?

Matt wished he, Logan, and Grace hadn't agreed they wouldn't carry on telepathic conversations in the presence of the others. Sure, it was the polite thing to do, but, dammit, he wanted answers. The private kind. But there was no choice now.

He glanced across at his friend. "Not a social call."

Logan shook his head. "No. And he had a message for you. He apologizes for breaking a confidence and accessing your computer records."

Matt wasn't the least bit surprised by the breach of trust. It had been expected. And Kelton being at the top of the food chain meant that everything Matt did went through him anyway.

Logan then addressed James and Julia. "He's requesting permission to land, and an opportunity to explain Matt's findings. He swears he has no connections with the Minnows."

"Do you believe him?" asked Julia.

"I don't disbelieve him."

She nodded. "Your opinion, James?"

"The man has rubbed me the wrong way more often than not, but I think we should hear him out." His dog stuffed its nose into his hand, and he absently rubbed the animal's head. "The question is, where do we have the meet, and who attends?"

Angie tapped the table. "We could do it at the hangar, not let him get any closer to the kids than that."

"But," said Quinn, "if some of us go to the airstrip, then we're leaving less protection here at the house."

"Is he alone?" asked Matt.

Logan nodded. "Just him and Galen, his pilot."

"I'd trust Galen with my life, and my kid's." said Angie. "He's solid. How about leaving security with the plane and bringing both Kelton and Galen in here?"

"No." All eyes swung to Matt. "He's too proficient at mining information. If it was up to me, the meet would be outdoors, and in a reasonably neutral spot, like at the end of the runway. My gut says don't let him close." His mentor. A man he'd trusted for the past twelve years. Aside from Logan, the closest thing he had to a friend.

James was studying him. "We'll go with that, then. Do you want to be part of the meet?"

"I think I have to be." Like it or not. "I also think Grace and Logan need to be there to make sure we keep his power and abilities under control."

"Agreed. That's three, Quinn and I make five.

Anyone else think they should be a part of this?"

Cass was frowning. "Having my children threatened by the Minnows, the same idiots who tried to kill me a few years ago, I'm torn. I want a chance to look Kelton in the eye and find out if he's connected to them, but I want to stay in the house and protect my babies."

Angie reached out and touched her hand. "Since the kids should be together for the duration of his visit, I'll step into whichever role you say. I'll either go meet him and stare him down for you, or stay with the kids. You deserve to make this call."

Cass's smile bloomed. "You should definitely go, because I can depend on you to make him feel like pond scum. Dhillon will stay with us."

"With that settled, we'll continue," said Julia.

***

Angie watched the small jet come in smooth as silk, with barely a chirp of tires when it touched down. Galen was a fine pilot, one she'd known for a long time, and had always respected.

But this meeting wasn't about him. It was about his passenger, Dr. Christopher Kelton. Cofounder of ETC, and head of both the Medical and Psychic Divisions. A man she'd admired and been completely intimidated by. But that was in the past. Now she was furious that he might have been using and manipulating both her and her family. And the thought that he might have betrayed Matt gutted her.

When she and Matt were together for that week, finding out about each other's pasts among other things, he'd spoken of Kelton with respect and affection. Had opened up about how he felt Kelton had saved him, given him a purpose. And now it was possible the whole thing had been a ruse, a way to control Matt.

She didn't bother to try and shake off the anger. She'd need it in a minute.

The plane taxied to the end of the runway, where Kelton's interrogators waited in the large passenger van used to ferry workers around the ranch. A perfect choice, since it wasn't something any of them had regular contact with, and, once they were done with it today, would be parked in a remote location on the property, and left until there was some resolution of this crisis. James was taking no chances.

From the moment Christopher Kelton, an accomplished strategist, pushed open the plane's door, he never broke eye contact with Matt. Descended the few steps and with hand held out, approached the man he'd betrayed.

Angie almost grinned when her father slipped between them and took the visitor's hand. "It's been a while."

"Good to see you." Kelton's face remained passive as he shifted his gaze to James.

"I hope I'll feel the same by the time you leave." James scored another point, and Kelton nodded, making no further comment or move. Apparently conceding control.

Thinking he looked pale when he got off the plane, Angie revised her initial assessment to gray.

They loaded into the van, Kelton choosing to have his pilot join them—which the family had expected and were in favor of, because Galen deserved to know what he was in the middle of.

James had chosen a picnic area at the lake for the meeting. "As I'm sure you'd expect, we are under video and audio surveillance here. And we won't scan you for devices, because we know it would be pointless." ETC had the best, most cutting-edge and impossible to detect technology.

They sat around a low wooden table with matching deck-style chairs.

"You're obviously well aware of the information Matthias uncovered, so I'm giving you the floor to tell your side of the story," said James.

Angie had forgotten how her father cut to the chase when he was on an op. His silent stare being a favorite tool.

Bonus points to Kelton for not wilting under the pressure. He took his time, which reminded Angie he'd had hours to plan and rehearse what to say when he met with Meyers.

He paused. "I had a twin brother." A scenario they'd already considered and come close to rejecting. "We were seventeen when our parents sent us to America to live with an aunt in New Jersey."

When sorrow flickered across Kelton's features, surprise coursed through Angie. It was the first time she'd ever seen emotion on the man's face.

"I lost track of my brother for a period of time prior to when he contacted me on the day he realized the extent of the trouble he was in. He was terrified." He shifted in his seat, another unusual sign of emotional discomfort from the king of stoic.

This is a real live being, thought Angie, unlike the automaton she'd grown used to when she dealt with him.

"He'd been enlisted to assist in what he was told

was a decontamination process." He rubbed his hands over his face.

"He didn't know that was code for extinguishing the life of an informer. The person in charge had told him he needed to know what happened to snitches. He needed to see firsthand, before he became a full member of the Minnows." Kelton's expression was bleak. "My brother was smart enough to understand that he was in a dire situation. Not only would he be unable to change the outcome, but, because they were exposing him to this experience, they'd never release him. He begged me to help. He had no money, and wanted to go home to Sweden, where the Minnows wouldn't find him."

That sounded like a good plan to Angie. She glanced around the group and saw faint nods as others obviously agreed with her.

"They put him on the door to wait for the cop— a guy they referred to as Bender—the one who'd squealed on the snitch. Once he arrived, the execution happened quickly, and Tim was forced to help transfer the body to a waiting car. Then they instructed him to sit in the backseat and wait while they had a word with Bender.

"He watched, and when all three turned to focus their attention on him, he knew he was in trouble and decided to make a run for it, but the doors wouldn't open." Kelton got up and paced.

He cleared his throat. "Neither of us doubted that my brother's life was about to end, and nothing we did or said would change the expected outcome." His shoulders sagged. "All I could do was keep our telepathic link open and gather as much detailed information as possible about the men involved. I promised him his legacy would be their demise." He sat again.

"I stayed with him to the end, which was blessedly quick, but not before an hour-long drive to the kill site."

He looked at Matt. "When Logan told me your story, I admit, I thought, why? Why had you survived when Tim hadn't? What made your life more important than his? If you'd been discovered in that loft, Tim could have gotten away."

Matt's gaze never wavered. "Then why help me?"

Angie thought, seriously? How could he not see, not get why?

"Because I couldn't help him. Because by forcing myself to give you a chance at a future—something more than living on the run—I was making up for not being enough for my brother." He shrugged.

"You can't put that on me," said Matt.

"I'm not. That was the reason in the beginning, but then I met you and I was okay. You're not Tim's replacement in my life. ETCETERA is."

Color seemed to be returning to the man's face.

"Tell us," said Quinn in his low, compelling counselor voice.

Kelton flicked him a look that said he fully understood what Quinn was up to, and of course, being a psychiatrist, he would. "It grew slowly from the frustration of having Tim's voice in my head, but not being able to see what he saw so I could at least find his killers." He looked at his hands where they gripped the arms of the chair, loosened his hold.

"His remains were discovered six months later, and I couldn't claim them. Didn't dare let the

Minnows know about me."

"But you were identical twins." Matt's voice was level and his expression gave away nothing of his thought process.

"Our appearances were dissimilar. He'd spent a couple of years adorning himself with tattoos and piercings, allowed his hair to grow long, and wore leathers. I on the other hand could be described as scholarly. I also wore a full beard until I was challenged to remove it not all that long ago."

"And you live in hiding at ETC, the same way Matt does. Did." Angie wasn't letting him off easy. She wanted everything on the table, important or not.

"I chose to live that way until I married Sarah. Then I offered to move to a traditional house, but it was her choice to stay underground."

That gave Angie a pause. Would she be willing to live that way for Matt? If it was just her, perhaps. But Dhillon was already feeling the pinch of living isolated at the ranch. Was ready to spread his wings.

Logan spoke for the first time. "What did you do with the information Tim gave you before he died?"

"I called one of those anonymous hotlines and gave the names of the Minnows involved. Two months later I found out the case had already been relegated to the cold file due to no leads and no evidence."

Angie had to ask, "What about the cop?"

"Tim's description was exceedingly general, and I never discovered anyone who matched in even the slightest manner." He glanced at Matt. "I've been through your computer records since you left."

"Rollins." Matt left it at one word.

"Thank God I've never cared for the man, nor

was he ever cleared to set foot inside ETC. But I was still shocked to realize I've dined at the same table as the felon who ordered my sibling's execution."

"Your story," said James, "is completely believable. And although I'm not saying I'm entirely sold yet, I *will* invite you to contribute to our investigation into the threats against my grandchildren."

Kelton nodded. "Thank you. I in turn will offer any and all of ETC's resources."

"Appreciated."

That was it? Angie stared at her father long enough for him to raise an eyebrow. Close enough to an invitation for her. "What would you like to see happen, Dr. Kelton? How would you be applying your resources if we weren't willing to take you on board? And will you be working *with* us? Or taking a different path for your own version of revenge?"

She gave him credit—grudgingly— for not backing down. Nor losing sight of his own agenda. He met Matt's gaze. "Rollins is the reason your son has been growing up without the benefit of a father."

Once again playing the role of devil's advocate, Angie said, "Let's not forget that without Rollins, Dhillon would not have been born."

Matt slid his hand over to touch hers.

"If Meyers is amenable," said Kelton, "I would appreciate an opportunity to work side by side with you. No separate agenda."

"What about the Minnows?" asked James.

"I have no doubt Rollins is the head of that snake. Eliminate him, and the remainder will crumble."

"I hate to be the wet blanket here, but we need

more than desire for success and retribution."
Dhillon's future was Angie's driving force. "Will ETC
stand behind you? Actually give us the resources
you're offering?"

Color rushed back into Kelton's face. "You're
asking if, in fact, I have the power to make that kind
of a commitment?"

"Yes."

"As your father is aware, I founded ETC."

Evasiveness annoyed her and she wouldn't be
sidetracked by a non-answer. "And?"

"Yes. I have that power."

James took over again, asking each person for
their opinion on whether to let Kelton stay.

***

Matt watched Kelton while everyone gave a yea
or nay—plus their reasoning behind the decision.
He'd been the second person Matt learned to trust on
his own, without the influence of his father or the
security experts helping to keep them safe. And it
hadn't happened overnight. He'd maintained careful
distance. The kind his father and the situation had
engraved deeply into his psyche.

And Kelton had been smart. Hadn't pushed
himself on Matt. Had allowed the young and
distrustful teenager room, space to breathe, where he
could learn to feel safe again as he hadn't since he was
a boy.

Throughout Matt's education, Christopher had
been there for him if he needed a hand, help with his
classes, the middle man delivering lessons back and
forth between student and professors. He'd allowed

Matt to use the ETC laboratories. Hell, Matt was given carte blanche of the facility, a room of his own, and anything else he needed.

Where would I be, Matt wondered, if Logan hadn't taken me to Kelton? His gaze traveled out across the scrub and dust. Out there, likely, a working cowboy on a ranch, up at dawn, and, if he was lucky, a hot meal and shower at nightfall. It was a simple life, but not an easy one. Weather could create havoc and destroy everything from the landscape to a day's plans. And the ripeness of cow shit would always linger on a man's clothes, live embedded in his nostrils.

Not much chance he'd have ever learned about Dhillon. His father wouldn't have told him. Hell, hadn't told him. Not that they saw each other more than once every few years.

"Matt?"

He blinked, turned to Angie. "Lost in thought for a minute there."

"It's your turn."

James said, "You get the final say, whether he stays here, or goes back to ETC to work from his end."

James Meyers was exactly as Matt remembered him. He might have been a just kid when they met, but right up to that last meeting before he disappeared as a teenager, he'd been treated with compassion, and the facts were always laid on the table and never glossed over. Now the man was waiting for his answer.

"I think it would be wise to have everyone here working together, so there is no need to relay information back and forth." He turned his attention to Kelton. "That said, should we be concerned that your absence will send up flags elsewhere and create a problem?"

"When I left this morning, it was understood that my return date was unknown, and that isn't unusual. Also Sarah is aware of the situation."

"Then you'll stay," said James. "You'll stay in a guest house within the main compound and be free to move about." He turned his attention to Kelton's pilot.

"I've known you long enough to trust you, Galen, so you're free to go. It would be best if the aircraft wasn't here forcing us to do full scans on the electronics to clear it. We'd rather not waste the man hours."

He nodded. "If you need me, or Liz and her skills, at any time, please don't hesitate."

"Appreciated," said James.

Half an hour later, Matt stood with Angie, watching Galen take off. The others had headed for the war room, where Kelton would be brought up to speed on the investigation, and there'd be a progress briefing for all members in two hours.

"Let's go to my place for a bit," said Angie while they made their way to where the golf carts, a muscular jeep, and a couple of SUVs were parked.

He slung an arm around her shoulders, and feeling her tension, he drew her closer and pressed his lips to her temple.

She sighed. "It felt so wrong."

"What did?"

"Questioning my dad's judgement. But it was like I had no choice. I couldn't help it, but it hurt."

He stopped and turned her to face him. "You are

a ferocious mother. Your instincts are to protect Dhillon, no matter what the cost to yourself or those around you."

She frowned. "I guess you're right. But it's not easy to question the man who taught me how to be a warrior. The man I've looked up to all my life."

"You did what you had to do. And I think he respects your position and doesn't expect you to blindly accept his opinion, or decision."

"He taught us to always trust and respect our leader, and I couldn't do that."

"I'm betting your dad has never been in command of a mother defending her child before. New ground for both of you, so you'll have to cut each other some slack, or better still, talk about it with him."

She nodded. "You're good for me, you know that? Your perspective broadens my thinking." She rose to her tiptoes, brushed a kiss across his lips. "I'm glad you're here."

Another fleeting glimpse, he thought, of the kind of life he'd always believed he couldn't have.

CHAPTER 17

Angie's house felt smaller with Matt in it, and it wasn't just his size. Everything was the same, but different. Kind of like rearranging the furniture, or painting the walls. But more. Much, much, more.

The air was charged with more than sexual tension, although that was a major player. His presence filling the air with electricity, and a scent she couldn't describe. It was just his. Him. She'd resisted the urge to join him in the shower, instead burying her face in his pillow. Waited until he was done before taking her own. Now she watched him prowl her living room. Restless.

"What is it?"

He glanced over. "Hmm?"

"You're stewing over something."

"Hah. Everything maybe?" He shrugged. "The world as I knew it has, once again, disintegrated. I just need a bit of time to fit everything back into appropriate slots."

"What's the most troublesome?"

"Muddy feet."

She fought the urge to do a curious pup head tilt. Then the light bulb went on and she grinned. "Feet of clay."

He smiled. "See, you get me."

"Apparently I do."

His smile faded. "Not only has Christopher fallen off his pedestal, but I'm forced to acknowledge that I put him on one."

"Why wouldn't you?" She sat cross-legged on the couch. "He saved you from a life of uncertainty, of running from people who wanted you dead. Gave you an opportunity to get an education, and facilitated a career far, far beyond your reality—"

"I hadn't even dreamed it."

"Exactly."

"He made me forget about you."

"Ouch, I'll have to hurt him for that." She smiled to buffer the impact. No point adding her emotional load to his. "It was what you needed at the time. He believed we could never be together, which made it apropos to wipe me from your mind."

"Was it?" He sat beside her, hauled her into his lap, and wrapped her up in his arms. "You'll never be anything but a bright, bold presence now." The look on his face undid her, made her heart thump against her ribs. She couldn't speak, so instead put her lips against his throat where his pulse beat.

He'd have more to work through about Kelton, but no way was Angie going to ruin this moment by asking him, prodding him, to talk about it. Instead they stayed snuggled together for a few precious minutes before they had to leave.

Halfway up to the main house, Matt said, "It's

odd to realize everything that happened, everything Christopher did for me, was because his brother was murdered, more or less while he was watching."

"Direct hit to the ego for sure, if you choose not to believe what he said, that it became about you after a while."

He tugged her closer to plant a quick kiss on the top of her head. "I love your attitude."

She shrugged. "No point living as though being followed by a dark rain cloud. I prefer to find the good in everything. Negative breeds negative, and I just refuse to go there."

"Dhillon thinks that way too."

She laughed. "He absolutely doesn't get negativity. And having nearly a dozen adults catering to his every need kept him from even understanding that negative was possible."

He glanced at her. "His cardiac event changed that in him."

"Not to the naked eye." But she'd seen it. Minute hesitations, furtively seeking confirmation. Not quite trusting himself or what was going on around him. "Getting into your program made a huge difference. Understanding what had happened to him, and why, gave him back the freedom of self-confidence."

When Angie and Matt joined the group in the war room, it was obvious that Christopher Kelton's presence added another level of tension to the already supercharged atmosphere. Residual relaxation from her time alone with Matt evaporated.

Since Angie was the only female among the five men in the room, testosterone was one more layer, and, oddly enough, she found it comfortable. Not odd really, though, because she'd grown up as one of three females in a family with six males. Then there were the uncles and male cousins who also worked for Meyers. Add in her career choice, and she was definitely used to being the token female.

James, appearing comfortable with command—a position he hadn't held for over five years—used nothing more than a small hand gesture to get everyone to their seats. "Dr. Kelton is now a contributing participant, and has been updated on our end of the investigation. Questions for the Meyers team?"

"No."

"Questions from my team?"

Angie held up a finger, and when James nodded, she asked, "What happened to the Minnows responsible for the executions? The two actually discharging their weapons."

"They're dead."

"When and how?" No way was he getting off that easy.

"Both ate their guns within two weeks of my brother's death."

"Were you responsible?"

"No."

"Do you wish you had been?"

"Yes."

"One would wonder," said Matt, "if Rollins was involved."

"One certainly would," Christopher agreed.

James shifted in his seat for about the third time, and Angie tried not to watch him, but couldn't seem to look away. His dog shuffled under the table and when James finally stood, Swagger leaned against his leg, and the tension she'd seen building eased. He was once again in command. "We'll investigate that avenue, although it will be difficult, considering how much time has passed. If nothing else, we can use what we find when it comes time to build a case. And if we're really lucky, we can find early connections to Rollins who wouldn't be unhappy about having him put away."

He flipped over a paper in front of him. "Further to the drone incident. As far as we can tell, it was dispatched as a distraction, and to strengthen the threat against the twins by showing they could get through our front lines of defense."

"What they didn't anticipate," said Gage, "is that it would seriously piss us off, and we wouldn't rest until we had them by their slimy throats. Nobody threatens my children."

Kelton held up a hand. "I am partial to the theory that Rollins was behind the drone launch, with the objective of drawing attention away from himself, and returning it firmly back to the Minnows."

Angie shook her head. "There was no heat on him."

"That you know of."

James rubbed his dog's head. "I'm thinking distraction. Rollins may be up to something and needed us to be preoccupied by the Minnows' security breach."

Matt, Gage, and Quinn were all nodding.

Angie's gut twisted and goose bumps covered her flesh like a blanket of ice. This was about more than stupid fish. "How secure is Haven, Quinn?"

"It has its weak spots, because not everyone on-site is family. But we're as secure as possible."

"Could Rollins infiltrate? Use a plant? Someone new coming in for treatment?"

"It's possible. We run full backgrounds on everyone, but in his position, he can create completely believable records, so we're not impenetrable. That said, between family, staff, and service animals on the property, we have enough extra senses and gut instinct specialists to keep tabs on everyone." He shook his head. "But I won't take any chances with my family. Rachel and Jamie and I will stay here until Rollins has been dealt with."

James nodded. "No one currently on these premises will leave, unless under my orders, until this situation is resolved. Any and all movement through the gates is prohibited. There are no exceptions." His eyes were sharp as he scanned the group. "I expect this process to take less than fourteen days."

And the ranch had a thirty-day rule. Always stocked with enough supplies for a minimum of a month. There'd be no need for even a supply truck to pass through the gates.

Being locked down was a normal state for Matt, but what didn't sit well was the expectation they'd take Rollins down in under two weeks. That just didn't seem realistic.

And he had no doubt that Rollins was aware of what was going on inside Meyers Security. In fact, hadn't he orchestrated the entire situation?

Matt wasn't a seasoned special security agent like Angie's family members, but he had to speak up. "Couldn't Rollins be playing with us? Am I crazy to suspect he's behind everything, and knows exactly what's going on here?"

James was frowning while his hand moved

steadily back and forth on the dog's head. Kelton's face had the pinched appearance he often wore when puzzling over something, and Angie's eyebrows had shot up.

James was the first to speak. "You really feel this?"

Matt nodded.

"Then we find another perspective or two, and see if we can ferret out what's got hold of your gut."

Kelton opened his mouth, then closed it again, and Matt found himself wishing he dared communicate telepathically with Logan. But with Christopher in the room, and possibly able to intercept, he stuck to verbal communications.

"It occurs to me," he said, "that it was too easy for me to find the information about Rollins. Even with the ETC equipment and exclusive access, it should have been harder for me to dig out."

All eyes went to Christopher, and credit to him, he never flinched, but answered carefully. "What are you suspecting?"

"That Rollins made the information reachable. The question is, was it to draw me out? Or was it for another reason altogether?"

Kelton's shoulders lowered and Matt nearly smiled. Christopher had been afraid Matt was going to lay the blame on him.

Maybe later.

***

Angie wiped the counter for about the fifth time. Rearranged the daisies she'd stuck in a shiny orange vase a few days earlier. Added a bit more water. And glanced at Matt yet again.

What was he thinking about? Standing alongside the kitchen window, he was uncannily still, and appeared to be staring out at the landscape, but his eyes never moved. Didn't blink. She'd seen mannequins with more expression.

Everyone processed things differently. She got that. But dammit, she wanted him to talk to her, tell her what was going on inside his head. She wanted to be able to help him deal with the effect of having his perception of the world turned on its head.

She grabbed the damp dishcloth and headed for the laundry room. When you had a son, there was always plenty of wash to be done. She filled the machine and turned it on.

"You're frustrated with me."

Shit. She slapped a hand to her chest while her heart slammed against her ribs. "Dammit, don't sneak up on me like that!"

"Sorry."

"Me too. I don't want to sound like a nag, but you scare me when you retreat inside yourself that way. How can I understand or help you if I don't have any clue what you're thinking or feeling? Some people put up walls, but not you. You turn into a garden statue. It's freaky." She resisted the urge to touch him. "You barely breathe."

"I learned to become invisible by blending into the background and becoming unnoticeable. It kept me alive the first time, and became a useful habit while I was on the run.

With one hand on his cheek she said, "Let me go on record by saying I'm glad you have great life-preserving skills and instincts. But—"

"I hate that word."

"Don't we all? What you need to understand about *me*, then, is that I come from a family filled with problem-solvers. We rarely accept things as they are. Instead, we study and roll stuff around, share with each other, and brainstorm. The people I'm closest to are the ones I share everything with."

"Yet you kept me secret from them."

"If you recall, I didn't have much choice. I was young and in love, and when you asked me to promise to keep our relationship a secret, I wasn't about to argue or do anything to jeopardize our future."

His eyebrows went up.

"Yes, at fifteen, I decided we'd have a future. You'd come to the ranch and carry me off into the sunset."

"Instead, you were pregnant, and I was nowhere to be found. I guess that screwed up your fairy tale ending."

She scooped the clothes she'd stuffed in the dryer several hours earlier, nudged him out of the way, and headed to Dhillon's room. Matt followed, and studied the books on the kid's shelf while she folded and hung.

"I loved reading when I was his age. Loved sliding into an alternate world where no one was chasing after me, trying to kill me."

His childhood had ended abruptly, but it was nice to know something had given him a break from that reality. "Do you still read?"

"Off and on. But research data occupies most of my reading hours now."

"What do you do for pleasure? You can't

possibly work eighteen hours a day."

"Research is very absorbing. There's always something new to read and learn about."

He was serious. "So the time we spent together when I came to your place at ETC, those were hours taken away from the job. If I hadn't been there, you wouldn't have been watching a movie, or television, or playing video games." His face said it all. "You don't do any of those things. But you mountain bike in a simulator. Does that at least take your mind away from work?"

"It does. Rather like meditation."

"You meditate?"

He shrugged. "Those of us living at ETC are encouraged to participate in yoga and meditation to keep our minds in peak working order. Likewise, we're expected to exercise our bodies. Christopher calls it a holistic approach. He wants his people to be the best they can be."

"And he's been lying to you for years. How does that make you feel?"

"Pissed. Betrayed. But he had good reason."

"Do you think he's been lying about other things?"

"Perhaps."

"Will you go back to work at ETC when this is over, even if you won't need to hide anymore?"

He cupped her face. "You're still looking for your fairy tale ending."

"Damn straight."

"I can't make promises."

"Cop-out, Matt. You *won't*, and that's completely different."

His hands dropped. "You're right."

When he turned away, she said, "Don't." She stopped. Worked on reducing the sharpness in her voice. She'd plead if she had to. "Please don't shut me out."

She grabbed his hand, brought him around to face her. "I want a life with you and Dhillon. Color me bold to ask, but it's what I need, and I'm not afraid to fight for it. When this is over, will you stay with me?"

"And do what? I'm a research scientist."

"So's my sister, Eve. She has a fully tricked-out lab right here on the property." She placed two fingers against his lips. "Don't say anything. Just think about it. Visit the possibilities before you write off a future with us. Dhillon needs his dad, and I need you." She rose to her toes and brushed a kiss across his lips. "And you, Matthias Alejandro Martinez? I think you need us."

***

Had he been asked a few weeks ago, Matthias would have said his life was just fine the way it was. Would he have opted to spend more time with Angie and Dhillon if it had been possible? Sure. But he knew it wasn't possible, so he'd given it no more thought. He learned long ago that dreaming was a monumental waste of time, and besides, it messed with his head.

He'd learned how to live in the moment. And now that his moments had changed drastically, he had to consider the future. Would he like to become a part of this family? A father? Sure. But if he was truly free, the whole world would be there for him to explore without fear for his life. He could attend conferences, travel, or sit and stare at an ocean if that's what he felt like doing.

And there it was. What would he do if the choices were unlimited? Who would he be as a free man?

The woman at his side was a powerful entity. He loved her, but could he fall into the kind of life she dreamed of? And what was that life, exactly?

She tugged on his hand. "You've disappeared again."

Her eyebrows were drawn together, her eyes worried, and he hated that he was the cause. But he couldn't fix it. "Introspection is a part of who I am. Not something I can easily change. I'm sorry if my silence has a detrimental effect."

"Was that your polite way of telling me to get over it?" She grinned. "Likewise, you'll have to live with my need to understand what's going on in your head."

"Point taken." He couldn't resist. Leaned down for a quick taste of her smile.

She wrapped her arms around his neck and held him there while she deepened the kiss. She was warm under his hands, a perfect mix of muscle and softness that stirred him. Made him want to drag her to the floor and cover her body with his. Instead, he pulled away.

"We need to get back." The one-hour break had passed quickly.

The tone in the war room was somber, with a thin layer of anticipation. Looking at the three men positioned at the far end of the long table, it occurred to Matt that they'd all served important roles in his life.

James saved his life when he was ten. Kelton gave him a safe haven and a career. Gage was his sister's husband, the man who kept her safe.

And now he'd been given the opportunity to work alongside them, to help change their lives. The universe worked in remarkable ways.

James was watching him. "You have something to say?"

He didn't hesitate. "If we don't appear to be going after the Minnows, Rollins will know he's made. I think we need to pursue the Minnow leads he's put in front of us. Track the drone through the manufacturer in order to identify the owner. Pull that person in for questioning, and let them lead us astray."

"In what way?" asked Gage.

"When they give us some story about just playing with a new toy, meaning no harm, lost control of the dang thing, or anything along those lines, the interrogator has to stay tough, but eventually buy into their story. Grudgingly."

Everyone was nodding. "Then we keep things open by running the buyer, his family, and any acquaintances we can tie to him. Or her."

"A full investigation makes good sense," said James. "While at the same time we dig and find a way to nail Rollins for everything, past and present."

"Exactly." Matt turned to Christopher, who hadn't said a word. "Comments?"

"A very solid plan," he replied.

Angie added, "To lend strength to the demonstration, we make it look like there are several of us working together on the drone incident. Even if it's just to make a phone call. That way it will appear that the whole team is focused on them."

Her tone was all business, as was the glance she sent his way. Not the kind of direct look he'd grown used to. Was she still pissed at him for earlier? Should he have shared this with her first?

"Agreed," said James. "Virtual fingerprints from at least four team members should be enough to make our point."

Gage spoke directly to his father. "I don't think you should be one of them. You're in a good position to stay under the radar, and be our secret weapon."

James smiled wickedly. "Won't Rollins be surprised to find out the Chameleon's back at work?"

CHAPTER 18

Julia's heart ached while she watched Angie prowl the office, apparently struggling for words. The pre-dawn call for help—although a huge step for Julia's most stubborn and self-sufficient daughter—hadn't been unexpected. "Whatever it is, honey, just blurt it out, and we'll go from there."

Angie stopped in the middle of the room. "I didn't speak up yesterday. Didn't voice my concerns to the team." She held out her hands, palm up. "I've lost my objectivity, and it's scaring hell out of me."

"Ah, well, welcome to my world." It had been a long night without knowing where James was, if he'd even stayed on the property. That in itself wasn't new, but it seemed bigger with the Minnow threat hanging over them.

"I didn't expect this. The insecurity, the doubt and confusion."

But Julia had. "I considered warning you, but believed it was better you go through the experience, then work on getting your equilibrium back. If you hadn't called me this morning, I would have called you." Julia opened her day-planner and deleted ANGIE CONSULT, an entry she'd made yesterday.

Angie grimaced. "Besides being an emotional wreck, it scares me that I'm censoring myself. I don't want to hurt Matt. It took him years to learn to trust Kelton, and having that implode sucked sideways. Which means when I continue to voice my opinion and doubts about his mentor's motives and honesty, it has to twist the knife."

"You don't have the option of remaining silent in this situation. The team needs to know what you've come up with regarding a suspect."

"I know that, but I need your help, Mom. Tell me how to do this. How to be a good team member, share openly, without confusing my son, or hurting the man I love."

Julia shook her head. "Honesty, consideration, and respect. They're all you have to work with. Keep both your men in the loop. And whenever possible, give them a heads-up before you drop a bombshell."

Angie threw herself into a huge white leather chair and covered her face with her hands. "I am a kickass, shit-together woman. I'm a damn good single mom. I believe in myself. I'm smart—"

"And you're hopelessly in love."

She dropped her hands to her lap. "Why should that change anything? Why do I have to become what I see in other women? I don't want to be dependent. I don't want to make decisions based on how someone else *feels*, for God's sake. I want my decisions to be smart, not emotional. I don't want to care that what's *right* is going to make someone else miserable."

Julia didn't bother trying to suppress her smile.

"So, how do you like your personal dose of reality now? Are you having regrets about judging those whose shoes you'd never walked in?"

Her frustrated daughter tipped her head back against the chair and stared up at the ceiling. "Fuck."

"Yes, my dear, you had it coming."

"I'm not a bad person. I'm not insensitive."

"I'm not saying you are. However." Julia waited for Angie's bright green eyes to focus on hers. "Your perspective has never allowed for consideration of the experiences of others. You've naturally had difficulties accepting what you didn't, and *couldn't possibly* understand."

"I owe Rachel and Cass apologies. I was hard on them both while they were going through rocky times in their relationships. I just didn't understand. I said things…"

"Tell me. If someone rode you hard about how you're feeling about this op and Matt right now, would you hold it against them? Expect them to apologize?"

"No."

"Then before you beg forgiveness, think instead about sharing your new perspective with them, and asking for help. It would mean more."

"Like when both of them asked me about childbirth. I'd been there, walked the walk. I get it."

"Good. Now put it aside. The family briefing's in an hour."

"First I have to talk to Matt about what I'll present to the team."

"I'm sure you'll find everyone else was having similar doubts about Kelton. You opening the door will make the team more comfortable with the discussion."

Angie stood. "I'll get out of here now."

Julia held her arms out for a hug, something she rarely did, and Angie stepped into them. It felt good to hold her daughter, to be needed as a mother. It didn't happen often anymore. "It will take some time to get the kinks worked out, but things will be okay for the three of you."

Angie pulled away. "Having Matt here, watching Dhillon with him, it makes my heart ache, but in a good way. Like the pain of a good massage. Hurts, but feels good."

Julia smiled, and as Angie closed the door behind her she thought, yes, love is a complicated bitch, but so worth the aggravation. Who knows better than I?

***

Matthias swallowed hard and stepped back to let the man and his dog into Angie's house.

"Good to see you, sir."

James walked through the kitchen to stand at the sliding glass door. "You can drop the sir. I meant what I said about not wanting to hear suck-up from you."

"A leftover from our days on the run. You were the person of power, always able to get us to safety." Besides that, he was unsure how to address the man.

"Fine. We need to clear the air. No room for unsaid words between team members, or between leaders and their men. Our situation here falls within those parameters." James stuffed his hands in the pockets of his black cargoes, and stood with his feet spread—looking anything but relaxed—but the dog lay down and rested his head on the man's boot.

"You're the father of my grandson, a gifted doctor, and apparently the man my daughter is in love with. You are also responsible for my daughter giving birth at the age of fifteen."

Matt thought there was a possibility he might simply vaporize under the man's deadly gaze. Fought the urge to say sir.

"If I'd managed to get my hands on you all those years ago, I would have hurt you for daring to touch her. For taking the safety I made sure you had and repaying me by seducing a child. *My* child. I would have sent your ass to jail—if you'd survived the beating." And there was no doubt in Matt's mind that there would have been one.

"But none of that would have done either of us any good. And, luckily for both of us, Angie refused to name the culprit. She protected you, even though you hadn't protected her. Made me fucking crazy."

Yeah, now that Matt was a father himself, he could imagine the crazy part.

"I no longer have the burning need to beat some sense into you." Words at odds with his icy-blue stare.

Matthias didn't so much as blink. The man might be saying he wasn't going to get physical, but—holy shit, he was intense.

"My son Quinn is a psychologist, and, according to him, you're going through hell right now because of Kelton's betrayal. I got that already. But what I hope you'll remember is that this family has never let you down. We were there for you and your father in the early years, and we had your back for as long as you allowed us to do it. Meyers is still that family. You can still depend on us. Logan and Grace will never let you down, either."

Not the direction Matt thought this was going. "Thank you."

"You're welcome." The dog stood. "Are we good here?"

Should he apologize? What was expected of him? Going with the honesty theme, he said, "Thank you for not beating the shit out of me. I can't say I regret being with Angie in Vegas, because, for one thing, her memory kept me alive for years, and two, I have an incredible son."

For the first time, the expression on James face softened. "He's a great kid. His uncles have been important role models for him, but I'm glad he finally has a dad. Someone of his own." He slid the glass door open. "Briefing in thirty."

***

Angie spotted her father marching along one of the paths leading from her backyard to the main house. "Oh, hell."

She went through the door at a run...and found Matt sitting at the breakfast bar with a bowl of cereal in front of him.

"Was James here?"

"Yep, you just missed him."

"What did he want?"

"He came to have a father of the pregnant daughter talk." He continued to spoon up cereal.

She clenched her fists. "And?"

"And." He set the spoon on the paper towel beside the bowl. "First off, let me say that your dad can be a very scary man."

She rolled her eyes. "Duh, like that's news. What happened?"

"Nothing. Well nothing, aside from him talking, me listening, and him reminding me there's a briefing shortly."

"Don't play dumb with me, Matthias, or I'll be forced to hurt you."

He held his hand out to her. "Come sit. It was all good, and I get the Chameleon tag. He can turn scary on and off impressively. Bottom line, he's glad his grandson has a father, so he's not likely to beat me to death anytime soon."

She sagged. "Thank God that's over with."

"You thought he'd do me harm?"

"No. But then I kept remembering the freaking testosterone and threats when they—my dad and brothers—discovered I was pregnant. If they'd been able to get their hands on you then, they'd have torn you apart and fought over who got to stuff the pieces in a wood-chipper."

"Ouch. Thanks for not giving me up. Not that they'd have found me, but still. Thanks."

"We have to talk."

"We are." He resumed eating.

"I mean about the case. Kelton. My suspicious mind has come up with some stuff I'm going to share with the team, but I want you to know beforehand, because you don't deserve to be blindsided again."

"Angie, you don't have to take care of me. I can handle whatever comes."

"It hurts you." When he started to shake his head she put a hand on his arm. "Don't even think of bullshitting me. You feel betrayed by Christopher, and I don't want to make that any worse, but I've got more than a niggling feeling that he's got even more up his sleeve."

"Like what?"

"Like why would you be the only one? The only person from back then that he's brought into ETC. Weren't there others? Or connections to others? And what was his original motive? Was it revenge? Was it using you and whoever else for a specific mission?"

"All good questions, but what makes you think you can get answers out of him?"

"I don't. But I think we need to be looking at other people within ETC."

"For connections to the Minnows? Or to Rollins? Or is there more?" Matt drizzled a drip of green dishwashing liquid into his bowl, swished it around with hot water and the spoon, rinsed and dried, then put them away.

"I'm looking at the broad picture for now. His story about the brother going bad. There could be other people possibly tied to losing his brother. Other cops who didn't follow the case afterwards. What about the two shooters committing suicide. Why? Or was it murder? Again, why?"

"I confess to having many of the same thoughts and questions in my head last night."

"Seriously? Were you going to tell me?"

"Probably."

"Just probably? Dammit, Matt—"

"Hold it. Before you get all twisted up, I hadn't gotten that far yet. I was just sitting here thinking it through when your father walked in, which kind of brought my thought processes to a screeching halt. And then you."

"Okay." She sighed and glanced at the clock.

"We'll get this communication thing figured out eventually.

***

Angie felt a new energy in the war room when James addressed the group.

"Christopher Kelton has been left out of this meeting because he's the subject. All team members are expected to speak freely."

He looked at Angie. "You've had a hard time accepting Kelton's position from the moment he arrived. I trust your instincts, but we need to know more. What is it that's jumping out at you?" Obviously Julia had updated him.

When Angie hesitated, Gage spoke instead. "I also question his honesty and integrity. I think there's a whole lot more to him and his story than he's telling us."

"Ditto from me," said Quinn.

"Specifics, people?"

Angie held up a finger. "I think it's highly unlikely that Matt is the only one at ETC connected to the death of Kelton's brother."

"There's our starting point, then, and we'll move on from there."

The discussion wound around to the suicides, the police directly and indirectly involved, and every other detail that had niggled at Angie, and she was delighted to discover that her sibs, her dad, *and* Matt, all had similar thoughts and feelings.

"How much of this discussion will we share with Kelton?" asked Grace.

Angie looked at her dad. "Your call, of course,

but I think the more he knows, the more he can counter and block."

"Agreed," said James. "Anyone have argument for otherwise?"

His gaze moved around the table, waiting for each person to shake their head before he continued. "We will keep him apprised of the Minnow-related investigation only. He will be aware that we're keeping things from him, but it's exactly what he'll expect.

He held up a hand. "Going a layer deeper. If and when we discover other ETC members connected to our investigation, where do we suspect their involvement?"

"Someone opened the pathways for me to get the info on Rollins," said Matt.

"Agreed," said James. "We look for tech skills, and FBI access or connections. Anything else?"

"Are they working for or against him?" Grace's question had eyebrows going up. "There's a chance someone discovered Kelton was using them due to their connection to his brother's murder, and didn't like it."

"Convoluted, but possible," said Quinn.

Grace nodded. "Very possible. And not dissimilar to when he was trying to recruit me. Because my father stood between me and ETC, I suspected Kelton could have been involved in his murder."

"But that turned out not to be the case." Quinn was watching Grace like one of his patients.

"As far as I know, he wasn't directly involved."

Holy cow. Did that mean she wasn't sure? Hadn't she found the culprit a few years ago, when she met Logan? The Meyers family had been unaware of Grace's existence at the time, so her history was still somewhat vague.

Julia only met her niece the year after Isaac—the half-brother Julia had never known—was murdered.

Kelton, a man who some surely believed was worthy of a halo, was now in jeopardy of being choked by it.

But she was forgetting. His brother had been murdered by the Minnows, at the order of a man high up in the FBI. That's what had started everything. Was he driven by revenge? Or was he a good and honest man, trying to do right by everyone? She was afraid the answers were behind door number one.

***

Christopher Kelton was unused to being held prisoner. Not that this room was anything like a jail, but he wasn't free to leave.

He had to grudgingly give the Meyers family credit for a smart setup. While he was being excluded from a meeting in the war room, Julia had escorted him to her office, a room with a force-field similar to that inside ETC. An electronic scrambling which prevented interception of thought waves or even detection of patterns.

Luckily he'd been able to plant a device in the war room, so everything being said there would be available to him whenever he wanted it.

But it would have to wait until the matriarch and her grandson were finished grilling him.

"When exactly did you start ETC?" asked Dhillon.

"ETCETERA didn't begin. It evolved."

"Explain the process," said Julia.

They kept him talking for more than an hour, and he wasn't pleased. Hadn't picked up any information from them except that the pair were adept at asking open-ended questions with never a yes or no option.

And the kid had a brilliant mind. Was quick to catch directional nuances, and was possibly communicating telepathically with his grandmother. And, dammit, Christopher just couldn't get tapped in. Picked up nothing but a toneless hum.

He narrowed his field of vision, just taking in Julia, and saw that clearly, in spite of her and Grace having no contact until a few years ago, there were very similar mannerisms, the kind one often assumed were learned, but might, in fact, be genetically hardwired. And really, wasn't everything?

Genetics. His secret passion. When you're a twin, it's in your face from the day you're born. And when you go a completely different direction from someone who is supposed to be a carbon copy of yourself, it raises questions. He had questions. Always had questions. And he also had something no one—not even his wife—knew about.

He studied the boy sitting across from him and wondered if he was aware of all his gifts yet. Abilities handed down through generations unaware of what they were sharing with their offspring. Dhillon's cardiac anomaly was there in his DNA. Good fortune put him into Kelton's legitimate database, and, as the cliché went, the rest was history.

He switched his attention to Julia, and was surprised by the threatening look on her face. Had she picked up some of his thoughts? Impossible. He schooled his expression and her eyes narrowed. He'd need to be careful with this one. She was too much like Grace. "Could you repeat the question?"

"You've said your parents sent you and your brother to America when you were teens. Why?"

"For an education."

"Sweden has some of the best schools in the world."

He sighed. "Timothy had been a problem for a while, had dropped out of school."

"Still doesn't tell me anything."

"He was to attend a special school. He'd be fast-tracked from there for college admission."

"And what about you?"

"My grades were such that I could choose where to attend."

"It's unusual for identical twins to exhibit such differences academically."

"Timothy was lured by drugs at a young age, a victim of his surroundings. Influenced by the friends he'd chosen."

"Prior to shipping him across the Atlantic, how did your parents handle the problem?"

"He spent time in the best of inpatient facilities, but when he came out of the programs, his old friends would find him and take him back down the wrong path. That's why we were sent away. To give him a chance to stay clean."

"Did he?"

"No."

"That must have been a huge disappointment to you. Did you try to intervene?"

"There was no point. He didn't want to be well.

Nothing could make him be well. He liked being my opposite. Having, as he put it, his own identity." He shook his head. "He had a brilliant mind, and others used him because of it."

"So," said Julia. "You've excused his bad decisions by making them someone else's fault."

"No I—"

The woman's raised eyebrow stopped him. She was right, and that irked him. "I was in his mind when he was murdered."

"That must have been awful for you. I can't imagine the horror of it."

"He wasn't a bad person."

"I believe you."

He sighed. "He made mistakes."

"We all do." She wasn't going to let him off.

"He was given many chances to turn it around, and I couldn't understand why he threw them all away. He said he was sorry." He folded his hands in his lap. "The last thing he said to me was, 'I'm sorry I couldn't be as good as you.'"

He dug his nails into his palms. "I tried to help him study, but he'd blow me off. Said he had better things to do, but then he got mad at me when he didn't get a passing grade. He'd grab my test papers and lay them alongside his, then laugh and say there wasn't much identical about us after all."

"That your brother didn't own his behavior is not on you."

He didn't need this woman's pity. Relaxed his hands and leaned deeper into the chair. "I've always wondered if I could have changed the way he was. Made a real difference in his life."

"And you're still trying to change people, aren't

you, Christopher?"

CHAPTER 19

Angie was in her element, flying the Steed on a mission to locate, interview, and possibly retrieve a witness James had identified through one of his connections.

Unknown and possibly hostile territory was nothing new for Angie, but having Matthias at her side was a game changer. And dammit, she didn't like it. He wasn't trained, and therefore a liability. However, she had to admit that, as much as she didn't want him in danger, she also wanted him with her.

She squelched a sigh. Contradictions seemed to be the norm in her life lately.

Even this op made no sense. But it made perfect sense. They needed to have a chat with Broughton. He was one of the few who'd left Rollins and the FBI, but stayed in the lower forty-eight. He'd moved from Philadelphia to New Mexico when others had opted for Alaska, Hawaii, and other countries, even continents.

Living off the grid on the outer edge of

Reservation land was apparently Broughton's way of staying below the radar.

The Meyers contact who'd set up their meet gave them very detailed instructions about where to land the Steed, and to stay put until contacted by Broughton.

So here they sat. Engine shut down and defenseless, in the middle of nowhere, waiting for a man who might or might not be one of the good guys.

And the first glimpse wasn't exactly promising. Fortyish, tall and rangy, dressed in desert-brown camo, and surrounded by large, scruffy-looking dogs positioned as sentinels. Oh, yeah, he looked like a man who trusted no one.

He stared through the windscreen, then waved them out.

"Remember," she said to Matt, "I make the decisions, and if I give you the signal, get your ass back in the Steed."

Instead of acknowledging her, he hopped out of the craft and left his helmet on the seat, even though the plan had been to hang onto them. Not a good beginning.

Angie scooted to catch up.

"That's far enough." Broughton's voice was low.

Matt stopped. "Thanks for meeting with us."

Angie stepped between the two men. "Meyers wants to thank—"

"Jake said you could be trusted." Jake was former FBI, Angie's cousin, and a member of Meyers Security. "If he was wrong," he shrugged, "the dogs are hungry."

Angie gave them a glance. Seven canines, and

not a happy grin or wagging tail among them. She cut right to the chase. "We have reason to believe Rollins is in bed with the Minnows."

Broughton's deadpan expression gave way to slow smile. "So Jake told me. And while that was nice work, you're only getting warmed up. Rollins is the backbone of the Minnows. Without him they would collapse and fade away."

"We intend to put him behind bars."

He shook his head. "I don't like your chances."

"Why not?" asked Matthias.

"He's so fucking well-insulated, nobody can get near him. He's built himself a solid team of no-gooders, and he has several of his federal superiors by the short hairs."

"Meyers expected no less, and we're prepared to put an end to it all," said Angie. "We're willing to negate his hold on them by exposing the secrets."

His gaze bored into her. "That's a big undertaking, with repercussions your family might not want to tackle."

"We know what we're doing. Tell us what Rollins has on them, and we'll make sure there's nothing left to hide. Then they can roll on him."

"Come." He turned and walked toward a mass of scrubby bushes, never looking back to make sure they were behind him. Hiked for what Angie estimated at close to a mile, zigging and zagging between bushes and rocks, changing directions so many times Angie guessed they'd traveled in a circle, but couldn't be sure. The dark, cloudy sky gave her no point of reference.

Their destination was an old wooden shack camouflaged by branches and patches of dried mud.

Angie was surprised to find it clean and tidy inside. A single room, with a scarred table and four sturdy chairs, a narrow bed, and shelves filled with books. Without windows, the interior light was provided by a trio of battery-powered lanterns.

"Sit."

Once they had, the dogs sprawled on the floor around them. Watchful, but non-threatening—so far.

"Jake," he said, "filled me in on your reason for wanting to put a stop to Rollins and the Minnows, so I understand what's driving you. But I don't believe you can make a difference." With his chair shoved back from the table, he had room to stretch out his legs and cross them at the ankle.

"Rollins hasn't been able to stay out of trouble all these years by accident. He's smarter than most, and sees everything from three or four angles. Always. It's what's made him phenomenally successful. He's brilliantly twisted. Plays the ends against the middle. And pulls it off by making other people believe they're in control."

"He's good, we're better," said Angie. "Our team is filled with some of the best of Special Forces and every other elite group you can think of."

"Yet Rollins has been playing all of you for years. What makes you think he's not pulling the strings right now, making you follow the exact path he's dictating?"

Matthias held up a hand. "What makes you think he could be doing that?"

"It's what he does."

"Okay, let's consider a different angle." Angie wasn't about to fold her tent and go home. "What if we've got a wild card he doesn't know about?"

"Like what?"

She smiled. "If I tell you, it's no longer a wild card." Jake had only told Broughton about the Minnows breaching the ranch security and threatening Gage's children. He hadn't shared anything about Matthias or Kelton.

"If you don't tell me, I can't help you take the bastard down."

Exactly the reaction she'd hoped for. "We know the whereabouts of Dean Lewis. The uncle of the children Rollins is threatening to harm. He was the boy who witnessed a Minnows execution attended by Rollins years before he was FBI."

"And does Dean Lewis have enough information to get a conviction?"

"Nope. But Rollins obviously thinks he does, and that's what matters."

Broughton turned his attention to Matthias. "And why have you come out of hiding now?"

***

Matthias wasn't surprised the man had figured out who he was. And he'd been prepared to tell him anyway, but Angie had stiffened like someone put a gun between her shoulder blades.

"I'm tired of hiding. What about you? Do you want to spend the rest of your life living this way?"

Broughton nodded. "I'll work with you, not because I don't like living here, but because I wouldn't mind having options."

Angie didn't waste time. "Will you come with us? Back to the ranch to work with the team?"

"My dogs."

"I only have room to transport three of them, or maybe four if they're okay being squeezed together in a crate."

"Only two are mine. The others are borrowed. Never hurts to look like you have lots of firepower." Getting to his feet, he snapped his fingers and the dogs went to him. "Take the trail leading away from the back of the cabin. It'll take you to your craft, and I'll meet you there in about fifteen minutes."

Angie looked like she didn't want to let him out of her sight, but she got up and followed Matt to the door. "You'll come for sure?" she asked.

"My word is good."

Walking a straight line, they came upon the Steed in less than five minutes. "Smart man. Circled us around instead of taking us directly to his home," said Matt.

"I was pretty sure we'd done a full three-sixty on the way in."

Sixteen minutes later, when Broughton showed up, he wasn't alone. The three men with him weren't huge, but their presence was. Golden skin, straight black hair, and an athletic ease of movement that screamed power and agility.

Each drew Broughton's outstretched hand between both of theirs and spoke words Angie didn't understand. Then, with dogs at their sides, they walked—more like glided, or drifted—out of sight.

Once Broughton's dogs were secured in the insulated hold, where they'd be safe from the Steed's internalized engine noise, he climbed in, donned a helmet, and Matt slid the door shut.

"You need to get airborne quickly, and head east immediately," Broughton told Angie.

Not one to argue when she heard urgency in a voice, Angie did as instructed, and when he asked her to circle left, she did. A solid plume of black smoke dirtied the desert sky above where his cabin had been.

She glanced over her shoulder. "A bit dramatic, don't you think?"

"Probably, but I couldn't risk leaving any evidence there to endanger the good people who've had my back for so many years."

Angie nodded, and Matt held his fist back for the other man to bump it.

Once at the ranch, Matt was impressed by how seamlessly Broughton fit into the team, and within hours they were making plans to visit with a senator and a very important person in the FBI. A man and a woman whose lives would never be the same. Who'd have no choice but to go along with the program and help protect the Meyers children.

Kelton looked relieved, no doubt glad the focus was no longer on him and ETC. But he had to know he was still a bug under glass, and his agency had not been removed from the spotlight.

In fact, Angie's sister Eve was ensconced in her lab, meticulously going through ETC records Logan had been able to access the night before. She'd be doing deep background searches on ETC, as well as the agents and employees Matt had pointed out—those like him, who rarely went topside, staying instead within the safety of the underground metropolis.

It was odd to sit in the midst of the group without Angie. He missed her vibrant presence. The room lacked something without her. And he'd grown accustomed to things like the touch of her hand or a quick glance that made him feel, oddly, as though he was home.

But after their morning flight to and from the northern tip of New Mexico, she'd had to step away for mandatory downtime. The family had strict rules about logged hours, something they rarely deviated from because of the crash that had happened way back when he and Angie were in that camper in Vegas.

***

Angie was usually good at falling asleep when she needed to, but thoughts were swirling and sleep wasn't happening.

Eve had updated her on the team's progress, and told her they'd soon have enough information from ETC's confidential databases to either hang Kelton or clear him of all suspicion.

Was he the victim he tried to portray? A man simply wanting to make up for not being able to save his brother? Was he more?

Angie replayed every encounter she could remember having with him. Tried to view each from more than one perspective. And kept circling back to the same one.

Years ago, when Eve had been researching the anomaly that caused Dhillon's heart failure, she discovered ETC had just launched a new research project on pediatric cardiac events. She'd contacted Kelton, and he'd flown to the ranch to interview Angie and Dhillon before accepting him into the program, and he'd asked for blood and DNA samples from both of them.

At the time, desperate, and still reeling from her son's heart failure, she hadn't questioned his request. She'd do anything to help find out why it had happened, and to prevent another occurrence. Dhillon's life was all that mattered to her.

But thinking back to that day, Kelton had been the most animated she could ever recall. As though he was barely containing his excitement.

It had only been two weeks later that she walked into the office of the doctor leading the project and found herself face-to-face with the father of her son. The only man she'd ever been with. Ever wanted to be with. And wasn't that the most wonderful coincidence?

Dense. She'd been completely dense. Blinded by the relief of Dhillon's diagnosis, plus her own heart and various other body parts had taken over her brain. Yeah. Fucking stupid. She'd never even considered the possibilities.

Kelton had probably orchestrated the entire thing. Didn't Matt tell her he'd been lucky to be guided toward the perfect type of research to be able to help his own son?

Suddenly sitting up, she slapped her hand over her mouth. She had an analytical mind, was highly trained to recognize subterfuge, and never believed in coincidence. Yet here she was, looking back and seeing how easily she'd been duped and put her whole family in jeopardy by naively going along with Kelton's plans.

She flung the blanket aside and surged to her feet. Grabbed her clothes off the floor and dragged them on while racing through hallways. Barreled into the war room and there he was. Surrounded by her family.

She froze. *Think!* Kick him out so she could talk to her family first? Or blurt everything now, like an angry, undisciplined child.

"Angie?" her mother's voice was low.

Angie backed toward the door she'd left open, reaching for the handle. "Sorry. Confused. Must have been a nightmare. Need food. Coffee."

Her mother caught up to her quickly, motioned for her to keep walking, but didn't speak until they were inside the bright, spacious kitchen. "What is it?"

"I've been duped. We all have. For years. I need to tell everyone. Except Kelton and Broughton."

Julia didn't say a word, just filled a glass with chocolate milk and handed it to Angie.

She chugged it down. Took a deep breath. "Okay. I'm okay, but I need them out of there."

"Go find a mirror, then join us. I'll get the two of them tucked away."

Mirror? Angie went into the powder room just off the kitchen and surprised herself by laughing. Her shirt was on inside out, and her hair standing on end. "Yikes." She fixed the shirt and wet her hair, then finger-combed it into place. The joy of short.

The team members were all seated when she returned, and stayed that way while she filled them in.

Eve was the first to comment. "Since we accessed his comp system in the wee hours this morning, I've been able to cruise through a DNA database that goes back years before DNA testing was recognized by law enforcement. I'm sorry to say it contains an up-to-date file on our entire family. No exceptions."

Everyone's attention automatically swung to

James, and he held up one hand while the other rested on Swagger. "I expected no less."

Eve continued. "Dhillon's information was input to the system the day he was born. However, the other grandchildren were born here on the property, and their data was input about six months ago. I see nothing on our computers to suggest we were hacked, but I see no other way he could have obtained the information."

Angie frowned. "You planted the seed in my mind this morning when you told me to think about all my interactions with Kelton. To look for what was out of place."

"True. And if you hadn't come up with anything, I'd have shared my findings at the next briefing." She turned her watch hand. "Which would have been an hour from now, and none of this was time-sensitive."

Matthias held up his hand. "You're saying that Kelton might have known I had a son, right from the time he was born?"

"Affirmative. Dhillon's DNA was filed in ETC's system, with both your name and Angie's as his parents. Kelton knew from the outset."

James, in that quietly lethal tone that made everyone sit up just a bit straighter said, "Then he knew about you and your connection to Meyers long before you met. Before you met Logan."

Logan frowned. "Good chance that was orchestrated as well."

Eve cleared her throat. "I can confirm some of this, Matthias. You were fourteen when your DNA went into his records."

"He knew about me. He *found* me, but did nothing." Matt scraped his hair back. "I just don't fucking get it." He glanced at Julia. "Sorry." His hands dropped to his lap. "Have I ever had a thought or an idea of my own? Or have I been manipulated forever?"

"More to the point, why? What was his purpose?" Julia touched Matt's hand. "Not to negate what you're going through, but we need to understand where he's coming from in order for any of this to make sense, and to stop the Minnows. Yes. I think it all ties back to the original incident you witnessed."

"Rollins." said Gage, who'd stayed silent until now.

Quinn also weighed in. "Correct, as long as Rollins *is* the Minnows, as we've been told."

"Where is Broughton?" asked Angie.

"He's in the security room with Lance." Julia smiled. "We put Christopher in the kitchen with Consuelo and Dhillon."

"I don't want—"

"Dhillon is safe, because he doesn't trust Christopher at all, and with Consuelo there, the man won't dare to have so much as a wrong thought. Cass and Rachel are in the playroom with the little ones."

Angie sighed. "Okay, what's our next move?"

James stood. "We proceed with even more caution, but the goal remains: take down Rollins and the Minnows. Part of that will require profiling as many ETC agents as we can."

Grace joined in the conversation then. "Here's something from left field to consider. If Kelton has had all this information and done all this manipulation, why? What has he to gain? Why would he want this family's DNA? Is it related to Matt and the Minnows? Or is it something else altogether? Could it be that he's actually mining for information about extra-sensory perception? Could everything connected to Matt be merely a by-product of something else altogether?"

She stopped then and smiled. "This being said by someone who's never trusted the man, but feels obliged to play devil's advocate. And for the record? I'm pissed we can't find the bug we know he has in here."

Logan placed his hand over hers where it lay on the table.

James nodded. "Good points, and all worth consideration." But his expression never changed. "It's time to put it away, and resume operations. Everyone continues with what you were working on. Matt and Angie will join Eve in the lab.

They detoured through the kitchen, where Consuelo was chopping vegetables and Chance was stretched out on the big dog bed with Dhillon at his side stroking the sleeping kitten in his lap. For a boy who played rough-and-tumble on a regular basis with his uncles, the kid had kind and gentle hands. Like his father.

"How's Chris doing?" asked Angie.

"Okay. But there's too much confusion if there's a person with the same name, so I'm calling him Santa."

Angie's eyebrows went up before she could school her expression. "As in Claus?"

He gave her an exaggerated eye roll. "Get real. As in the Santa Maria, one of Christopher Columbus's ships."

"Of course. I guess you'll have to explain that to

the twins."

"Oh, yeah." He frowned. "My other idea was Roger. For the black flag pirates flew when they were going to attack. The Jolly Roger is black with a skull and crossbones."

Matt smiled. "I think it's an excellent choice, so you can still honor his toughness."

"Great." Dhillon grinned, then lifted the sleepy kitten up so they were face to face. I hereby dub thee...Sir Roger of Jolliness."

"Looks like you've worn him out," said Matt.

"He ate lots, so needs to sleep for a while." Roger was gently tucked in beside the hot water bottle with a blanket draped half over him before Dhillon glanced up. "You guys still working, or you wanna go for a ride?"

"Sorry, pal, duty calls."

He shrugged. "Figured as much."

Bugger it, thought Angie. "Hey, how about I cover for Matt for an hour or so and you two could sneak away."

Dhillon hopped up. "Awesome!" And Matt's hand tightened on her shoulder.

Angie laid hers over it. "But you have to take a shadow with you." No way the two could go off without an armed guard watching over them.

"Yeah, I know the drill," Dhillon said.

CHAPTER 20

Matt rode beside his son on a trail winding along the edge of a skinny creek. And it felt damn good.

"What's it like for you to suddenly have a kid?" asked Dhillon.

"Complicated." Very freaking complicated.

Dhillon snorted. "My mom would call that a cop-out kinda answer."

Point to Angie. "Let me think about a better one."

"Why, so you can word things the right way? Decide how exactly to say something? Mom says that's a good plan when you don't *know* the people you're talking to, but you're my dad. You should be able to tell me stuff straight up, shouldn't you?"

Crap. How was he supposed to deal with this man-child? "You have to remember that I've been guarding my words and my identity for such a long time, just spilling out information doesn't come naturally."

Dhillon was nodding, with his chin stuck out like

a serious old man. "I get that. But as Mom would say, ya gotta get over the old shit and get on with the new."

He delivered a mock-serious sideways glance. "I'm betting that's not quite how she put it."

Dhillon opened his mouth to answer, then closed it.

"I knew you were my son before we met the first time, so I had lots of time to prepare myself. It was still a crazy half hour for me. I had to keep to the interview for the project when I wanted to ask you all kinds of other things, to find out about you."

"You asked me lots of stuff when we had our consults."

"Yeah, after that first time, once you were comfortable with me and the program, I indulged myself and got to know you."

He had the boy's attention now, and as intimidating as that serious young face was, he let himself just talk.

"When you said how much you liked sports, and wished you could go to real school so you could play on teams, it hit me in the gut. I was the same. I couldn't go to school because we were on the run. I understood how you felt, and that was the first time it seemed like you were my son. Because we shared something, a common wish or longing for something we couldn't ever have."

Dhillon stopped his horse and Matt reined his mount in. "How old were you when you saw the murder?"

"Ten."

"What was it like?"

Oh, not going there. "It was awful, but even

though it affected my whole life, I don't let the memory of those ten minutes get any traction."

"But it changed your life and mine too. I hate the Minnows."

Matt leaned forward, resting a forearm on the saddle horn. "Number one, hate's not worth the wasted energy. And for two, I'da never met your mom, and Gage would never have met Cass if it wasn't for them. You and the girls wouldn't be here. Because of that, I'm grateful for the route my life took."

The horse under him was fussing, having trouble standing still. Matt glanced at the open trail in front of them. "This guy needs to stretch his legs. How about a good lope up to that big rock? Come on." The horse bounced into a lope and Matt nearly laughed out loud at the joy of wind in his hair and a powerful beast reaching for ground under him.

Dhillon's mount came alongside, and the two horses picked up speed.

"Race ya!" Dhillon shouted and took the lead easily.

Matt stayed just behind until the kid finally brought his horse back to an easy jog and swung around with a grin on his face that made Matt's heart suddenly too big for his chest.

"You win," he managed.

"Ha, ha, nobody can outrun Max. He's the best. He used to be a race horse until Uncle Quinn gave him to me last year."

"I thought he looked like a Thoroughbred." The horses walked side by side, content to cool down after their short gallop.

"Yep. Kentucky bred, too. Won a bunch of races

when he was young, but he'd become a cheap claimer and mean as a snake. Rachel spotted him and made Quinn claim him. Took a long time to make him happy again, but he loves it here with us. Doesn't mind packing a western saddle, either. Yours was a racehorse, too, or tried to be, but he wasn't fast enough. Rachel found him at an auction. Quinn says she's a soft touch. Can't resist a sad story."

"Sounds to me like she has a big heart."

"Yep, that's why Quinn loves her. She gave me Chance when she took off before. Said he needed somebody he could depend on, and she was going to be on the move. I was worried a bit when she came back to live here again, thought I might have to give up my dog. But Rachel said Chance and I owned each other, and she'd never break us up."

"You're lucky to have great aunts and uncles."

"Yeah, but it's better to have a dad too."

How was he supposed to respond when his voice was trapped behind the lump in his throat? Lucky for him the trail narrowed and Dhillon took the lead, as well as taking over the conversation with a constant barrage of information about their surroundings until they came out of the trees.

"Mom's gone."

"What?" Matt urged his horse up to see what the boy was seeing. The airfield spread out before them. Empty but for a blue helo parked outside the cavernous building.

"Bluebelle's out."

Matt caught himself before asking. It was obvious. A blue-colored Bell helicopter. But he needed the details. "Explain."

"When the Steed's not home, they pull Bluebelle

out. She has to be ready to go just in case. Otherwise she's kept in the hangar."

"Maybe Trent has the Steed."

"Nope, he only flies it if Mom's grounded." The kid's shoulders had sagged. Having a dad might be a great novelty, but it was his mom he wanted at home with him.

"No point speculating. Might as well wait until we get back before you start worrying about her."

He glanced over at Matt. "S'pose you're right. Geez, doesn't seem fair, though. First time she's gone, and I've got you so I don't have to hang at the big house, but we're under lockdown, so I have to be there anyway."

"All part of the adventure. Besides, Chance and Roger are there waiting for you. Are you really just looking after the kitten for Rachel, or are you planning to keep him?"

His smile came like a flash. "Hey, you can help me negotiate terms with Mom." He shot a fist in the air. "Ha, ha, I have backup!"

"Don't get your hopes up, kid. I never managed to convince my own mother to let me keep a cat." And why the hell had he said that out loud?

"No? Well, shit."

"Ah, and just so you know, I'm not going to nail you on your language, but if you get comfortable using words that aren't allowed at home, you'll start slipping."

"And then I'll be in shit." He grinned.

"We both will. So knock it off."

Dhillon laughed, reminding Matt how easy it was for a child—even one over five feet tall—to shake off one mood and move on to another. Had he ever been as lighthearted as his son? Maybe before the barn, but not after. He'd do his damnedest to make sure Dhillon never felt that kind of uncertainty.

"So you never had a pet?"

"No."

"But you wanted one?" They'd completed the loop and were back at the barn where they took the tack off their horses.

"Oh, yeah."

Dhillon swung each saddle onto the long low rack and flipped the saddle pads upside down over them. "Sucks for you. But you got to work on ranches at least, and you rode bulls."

"Yep." Matt gently curried each horse's back, then picked their feet while Dhillon hung the bridles on the wall with dozens of others, stuck the helmets in a cupboard.

"What was the best part about bull riding?"

"Winning. Nothing like it. All that adrenaline pumping, watching the bull trot out, and seeing an eighty-plus score on the board."

"Did you get in any wrecks?"

"Yeah."

The kid's eyes lit. "You get gored? Ya got scars?"

"Nope and nope. I quit rodeo when I was eighteen, so I got away without much more than a few broken ribs, a couple of broken fingers, and a dislocated shoulder."

Once the horses were released in their pens, Matt and Dhillon hopped on four-wheelers and headed for the big house. Matt was just as anxious as Dhillon was to find out where Angie had gone. He didn't like it one bit that she was probably doing something dangerous.

Liked it even less when he found out exactly what she was up to.

***

It had been a long time since Angie'd been on a mission with her dad, and apparently, she'd forgotten how intense he got. Not that intense was a big enough word for the persona he donned as easily as his flight suit.

And nothing, not a single word was spoken between James, Gage, and Logan for the entire flight. She'd been the only one to speak, and that was just to give them the official "twenty minutes out," so they'd be prepared when she began descending to their target.

Everyone had an assignment. Each knew his job. And something that blew Angie away? They'd be communicating telepathically. Everyone but her— she'd discovered in their last briefing—was adept. She knew about Logan, and suspected her father and mother communicated that way. But Gage's abilities had been a complete surprise.

Angie's training wasn't advanced enough for use in the field, but she might be able to receive if they targeted her.

In the meantime, she *could* scan for energy fields. Upon landing, she identified two humans in the building, held up fingers to the others and they silently nodded.

Now she waited. Alone in the Steed while they did the extraction.

The two FBI special agents were expecting to be met at an exclusive hunting lodge by an assistant to the director. But Meyers had other plans for them.

Angie watched the digital timer while it ticked off tenths of a second. James had decreed they'd be in and out in less than three minutes, and they'd already used up two.

When double swaths of energy swooshed toward her, she braced, hoping everything was unfolding according to plan. Because the three men wore blackout suits, their energy fields only registered as faint blotches. Angie could only hope they *were* with the entities coming toward her.

As soon as the group materialized from the dense bush, she disengaged the exterior locks. Placed her finger over the single button that would have the Steed started and airworthy in less than thirty seconds. Angie hated starting up this way, but the system was there for just this kind of mission. One where they needed off the ground immediately, and didn't dare to load hot because their unconscious guests were slung over the shoulders of Gage and James.

Logan closed the door, and dragged a helmet onto each before they were strapped to immobilization stretchers.

With one hand on the timer button and the other on the starter, Angie monitored the sensors, and their surroundings visible through the windscreen, while she waited for clearance.

Upon a single tap to the shoulder, she stopped the timer and started the Steed in a single move, got airborne, then glanced at the red numbers on the screen and grinned. Two minutes, fifty-seven and a half seconds.

Silence reigned for the entire two-hour flight.

James had slipped into the seat beside her and given her a thumbs up, but nothing more, leaving her lots of time to think instead. Think about Matt. And their future as a family. Time they'd spend together. Normal time, with breakfasts and suppers, laundry and adventures. He could join Eve in her lab and continue his research with plenty of time to lose himself in the work when she was on missions.

Maybe he'd become part of the team. Of course he would. He had a brilliant mind, an asset for the planning and research areas if nothing else. What a joy it would be to work with him, and have him at home with her and Dhillon every day.

She watched them on the stable cams this morning while they prepped a couple of horses for a ride. They were already visibly connected. One holding a horse while the other tacked, Matt steadying the pad so it wouldn't shift when Dhillon hefted the saddle into place, all with a similarity of body language, gestures, movements.

When Dhillon said something to make Matt flash a grin at him, her son cracked up laughing, and the lump in Angie's throat kept her from answering when someone spoke to her.

She shook off the memories. Prepared to do a precise pass over their landing zone at exactly the right height to activate the sensors already primed for their arrival. The camouflage would draw back then, and expose the LZ for only thirty seconds. Located close to the forty-ninth parallel, this safe house was their most remote, and most secure, buried in wilderness, miles and miles from the nearest road.

She slipped the Steed in before the cover was halfway off, and it immediately slid back into place, hiding them completely from satellite cameras.

Once the men offloaded their guests, Angie used the hidden controls to lower the Steed into the underground hangar alongside the small, bug-like two-person helo already stored there. Then she trekked through a series of halls and up dozens of stairs to finally end up inside the house. A fantastic place. A massive country lodge-style log structure, with floor to ceiling windows and an enormous stone fireplace in the center of the great room.

It reminded her of the ranch where she and Matt stayed for that glorious week—but ten times bigger. This place could sleep twenty comfortably. More, in a pinch. She hadn't been here since Gage and Cass met. *And now I'm here in a bid to protect their children. How appropriate.*

"Angie." Lissa came to her from the kitchen area, arms open wide, and Angie met her halfway.

Then she grinned at her cousin's wife. "You've let your hair grow." What had always been worn ultra-short and nearly snow white was now falling softly around her face.

She laughed. "It's been months since we've left here, and I won't let Kyle cut it for me."

Lissa's husband, Kyle, was Angie's cousin. "Well it definitely suits you this way."

"Thanks. According to James, our guests will be waking up in about an hour. You want to catch a shower or grab a bite while we wait?"

"Shower sounds good. It's been a long day."

"Use either apple green or apricot." The bedrooms were color-themed.

"I'm feeling orange today. I'll take apricot, and I'll be back in ten." She had to set herself a time limit or she'd never get out from under the pounding spray. And water, although plentiful from an underground spring, was a luxury, and not to be wasted. As it was the shower water would go back through the treatment system and sent to a holding tank for future use as unpotable.

When she emerged, in precisely ten minutes, James, Gage, and Logan were at the long, rough-hewn table with steaming bowls of food in front of them.

Angie lifted the lids from two slow cookers. Passed on the chili and filled a bowl with chicken stew instead. "This is the worst part for me," she said.

"Are you nuts? Lissa's cooking is to die for," said Gage.

"Idiot. Not the food, the waiting. Downtime when we can't do a damn thing but wait." They wouldn't be interviewing the women they'd picked up until the next morning.

"Rest is an essential component in any mission. And this time it's especially important for you, since there's another cross-country flight tomorrow." Her father pinned her with a look, and she experienced something she hadn't in a while. Uncertainty. James hadn't brought Swagger on this mission. Would his judgement be impaired? Would he be able to sleep tonight?

Back in her room, Angie stripped down, put on a long T-shirt she found in the cupboard, and crawled under the soft duvet, hoping sleep would come—but knowing she wasn't close to resting yet. She wished she could try connecting with Matt, but everyone at the ranch was shut down telepathically because of Kelton. Instead, she thought about Dhillon and Matt, imagined how they'd spent the rest of their day.

She wished she'd had a chance to let them know she was taking off, but the op came together rapidly, and there was nothing she could do but pull out the card and leave it on the table. She made it for Dhillon years before, when he told her he hated walking into the house when she was away unless she'd left him some kind of a message.

She made a sturdy card and always set it on the counter before she left. It was simply a piece of white cardboard folded over to make it stand up, with four words printed on it. "Back sometime, love ya."

When she got home, the note went back into the drawer for the next time.

How would Matt feel about her sudden departure? Would he be pissed at not being in the loop? Because she didn't tell him she was leaving? Or would he even care?

What if he didn't? What if he'd had enough of her and her family and just wanted to take off and find a nice quiet place to live. What if he didn't want to make a life with her and Dhillon? Sure, he said he wanted to be a father to his son, but did that mean he wanted to live with them?

She lay on her back staring at the ceiling. She wanted to get married. Be a family. And she'd expected him to want the same thing. He'd said he loved her. Shown his love for her. But had he ever once said anything about marriage? Or even about living together?

She groaned and pulled a pillow over her face. As was her new norm, she'd gotten way ahead of herself. Made assumptions. Drawn conclusions. And none of them were based on solid information. No, dammit, all she was working with were feelings. Her own.

She tossed off the pillow, and the cover, hit the floor with both feet and marched across to the window to drag the curtain aside and see nothing but blackness.

The faux window had been programed for nighttime. She could hit the override and choose something more interesting, but that was pointless. She didn't want to look at anything. But she longed for a distraction from her thoughts.

She huffed out a breath and threw herself into an oversized armchair in the same pale orange as the duvet cover.

That last time they discussed Christmas, he'd been adamant. But wouldn't that have changed now, since he was already there on the ranch? Or would he leave after this mission ended?

He'd been dead serious when they were alone for that week, telling her they couldn't have a future. But since then everything had changed.

Her guts churned when she again saw herself in the same way she did so many other women, trying to change the man they loved. Taking what they could get until they could fix him. Make him into what they wanted.

Had she been doing that? Just going along while expecting things to work out the way *she* wanted?

"Fuck." She sucked in air long and hard. Exhaled slowly. She needed to put this away so she could rest. None of her questions could be answered tonight anyway. She slid out of the chair and onto the floor. Crossed her legs and rested her hands, palm up, on her knees. Began her mantra.

CHAPTER 21

Dhillon had become distant after seeing his mom's note, and when they got to the main house, he asked his grandmother when Angie would be back, but asked nothing about the mission. Which made sense, of course, because the boy had lived this way for his entire life.

But he didn't look happy about it. They headed for the kitchen to take care of his responsibilities before supper.

Consuelo studied the boy. "Not looking for a snack?"

"Nah. I know it's too late for one."

She tipped her chin toward the big ceramic containers on the counter. "One cookie won't put you off your grub. But only one, mind." She watched him, and sent Matt a look he couldn't interpret. Then turned her back on them while she tended the food on the stove.

Dhillon shoved the whole cookie in his mouth, sat in the middle of the dog bed to give Chance a big hug, and then he got busy weighing and feeding the kitten, making notes on the chart.

"How do the numbers look?" Matt asked.

"Okay."

"Just okay?"

He shrugged. "Yeah."

Matt toyed with the idea of leaving him alone, but decided against it. "How much does he weigh?"

"Four hundred and eighteen grams."

"Grams? Not ounces?"

"Eve says if I want to be a doctor I have to understand the metric system, so I never use ounces anymore."

Doctor. That landed a funny feeling in his gut. "What did he weigh before his last feeding?"

"Four twelve."

"Okay, if a six-gram gain is only okay, how much more would tip the scale at good?"

He glanced up. "You trying to take my mind off my mom?"

"I guess. Mostly I'm thinking you won't worry as much if there's something else to concentrate on."

He snorted. "You sound like my uncle Quinn. He's a shrink."

"Yeah, and damn good at it, I hear. I bet he'd ask you how you feel about your mom heading off on a mission and leaving you with me."

He offered Roger another half a syringe full of food, but the kitten turned his face away, obviously full. Dhillon leaned back against the wall and stuck his legs out straight in front of him. "Guess I'd tell him it always feels weird, because she's out there doing team stuff and not even thinking about me, but I'm sitting around thinking about her the whole time she's gone."

"You sure you're not on her mind?"

"Positive. Ops require total concentration. She can't let her mind wander, or she could make a mistake, and hers isn't the only life she'd put in jeopardy."

"That sounds like a line from a training manual."

Dhillon said nothing, just watched the kitten trek across the thick fabric.

When it reached the edge, Matt scooped it up and it hissed at him. He cupped it between his hands. "You my friend, are definitely adventuresome. And well named." He crouched and held Roger out to Dhillon. "Your runaway."

"I wonder how far he'd go?"

"You'll have to test him somewhere safe without a slippery floor and a constant parade of people to step on him. Want to watch a movie after supper?"

"S'pose."

"Anything else I can do to help you pass the time?"

"The movie idea works."

"Good. I'm new to this stuff."

"Yeah, me too."

"What do you usually do when she's away?"

"Hang out here with my grandmother and whoever's home. I'm not allowed off the property while an op is live, which means I can't go over to Haven, and that sucks. But I can go to our own stables, so that makes it suck less…but usually nobody wants to go riding with me, and I'm not allowed to go alone."

"Well, I can help there at least. We can ride again tomorrow, and you can show me another trail, a different part of the ranch."

Dhillon looked up at him and this time a smile threatened. "We'd have to pack."

"Pack?"

Dhillon's expression was dead serious. "A gun. We'll be in snake territory."

Matt was glad he had years of practice at not showing his emotions. No point letting the kid know he had a snake phobia. He fought back a shudder and hoped like hell Angie would be home in the morning so he wouldn't have to go on the ride.

Surprised when the door swung open and Kelton strode in, Matt wondered why he was free to move about the house. Kelton tapped what looked like an old-fashioned red button on his lapel. "I agreed to wear a monitor so they'll always know where I am."

But couldn't he just take it off, then go where he pleased?

"It transmits pulse and respiratory rate, therefore, no, I cannot simply remove it. And no, I am not trespassing in your mind. I'm anticipating the reaction of a mind I know well due to years of interaction and study. There is a distinct difference, and your privacy remains intact."

Kelton eyed the boy and his pets. "Our society commonly frowns upon the presence of animals in an area where food is being prepared or consumed. Companion animals have unhygienic grooming habits, and are host to microorganisms, parasites, and communicable diseases which are not only transferable to human beings, but inherently life-threatening."

He pinned Dhillon with a look. "I have seen that

canine outdoors, and considering the proximity of defecating farm animals, there is an extreme risk of it transmitting E. coli." His gaze flicked to the kitten. "That feline looks awfully young to be away from its mother."

"She's dead."

"Oh, well, then its chances for survival have been seriously compromised and euthanasia should be considered."

Dhillon stuffed Roger under his shirt and scrambled to his feet. "He'll not only live, but he'll thrive. I'm very good with animals, and I know what I'm doing." He took a step closer to Kelton. "And I'm not stupid, so don't think you can talk over my head. As for my dog being unsanitary because he licks his own dick, I bet you never wash your hands after you pee, so you're doing the same thing." With that, he and his dog marched out of the room, leaving the door swinging in his wake.

Consuelo's shoulders shook, but she kept her back to the room.

Matt's anger at Kelton had dissolved along with the need to defend Dhillon and his pets. Instead, stifling a laugh, he said, "Catch you later." And followed his son. His freaking amazing son, who in that moment in the kitchen had sounded just like his mother. No bloody wonder he loved the two of them.

Guessing the boy's destination, Matt headed for the war room and grinned when he found Dhillon there telling the group what he'd said to Kelton.

"Rude," said Julia.

"I was polite! I never even swore."

"I meant your adversary. He was rude. And although your reaction was a bit over the top, I commend you for standing up for yourself and your charges. Now. If we could get back to business here?"

Quinn and Trent exchanged fist bumps with the kid before he took a seat, and Matt slid into the one beside him. Listened to Julia outlining the plan for the next day.

***

There'd been a change of plans. Instead of prepping for a morning flight home, Angie was busy setting up unnecessary recording equipment on a plain wooden table in the middle of a windowless room. Video cameras and audio receivers were already mounted in every corner of the room and hidden by sinister-looking black fabric draped floor to ceiling.

The two witnesses had been informed three hours earlier about why they'd been picked up, and told to prepare their statements. This was a one-time-only opportunity for them to save their own necks before they were either placed in a witness protection program, or, if they opted out of that, returned to where they'd been picked up.

There'd be no option for a last-minute change of heart, because what they didn't know was they'd be leaving here as unconscious as they were when they arrived, and would wake up in Meyers custody.

Gage and James brought in Special Agent Felicity Bellows. Shoulders back and head high, she led with her impressive chest, as though it would protect her from what was to come. She'd also made good use of the generous guest supplies. Lips painted well past their natural edges, eyeliner applied with a heavy hand, and hair pulled back into a fancy knot distracted from the fact she hadn't bothered to use the room's iron on her rumpled navy blue skirt and jacket. She'd also chosen not to wear the shirt she arrived in. The look in her eyes was razor sharp, and her hands were steady on the table when she sat across from Angie.

James remained on his feet and in command of the room. Gage stepped out, closed the door.

Once Angie had covered the "state your name and position with the FBI" part, James took over the interview.

"We're aware that although you knew Rollins was a key member of the Minnows, you chose to keep that information to yourself."

The expression on Bellows' face didn't so much as flicker, and she was obviously not going to respond. James pressed on.

"Is that a correct statement, Ms. Bellows?"

"You haven't Mirandized me, and I don't have to answer your questions without counsel present."

The smile James flashed sent a chill through Angie.

"Ms. Bellows," he said. "You *have* no rights here. Consider this a type of purgatory. You're being given an opportunity to redeem yourself, to make a choice between upstairs or down. You have the option of giving us a comprehensive statement and then vanishing into a witness protection program or another avenue of your choosing. Or. You will be handed over to the director. There you *will* have rights, such as counsel. But I assure you, you'll live in fear, not knowing who you can trust."

"Fuck you."

His smile widened as he pointed a remote to make the door swing open, and nodded to Gage. "Ms. Bellows doesn't wish to make a statement. Please return her to her room."

The woman stayed seated. Her face expressionless, but her eyes held a glimmer of indecision.

"Ms. Bellows?" Angie kept her voice neutral. "You'd be stupid not to take the opportunity we're giving you. And you didn't get this far by being stupid."

One at a time, she grazed the tip of her thumb with the ends of her long red nails. "I'll need time to think."

James shook his head. "You had several hours prior to this interview to make up your mind one way or another." Placing his hands on the table, he leaned down, pinned her with his laser gaze. "Make a decision and live with it."

She didn't flinch. Didn't even blink.

"We're done." James straightened, headed for the door.

With a lightning fast move, Bellows heaved the table up and sent it and the equipment careening toward Angie, who blocked neatly just as James spun and caught the woman launching herself at him.

Finding herself face down on the floor with a foot in the middle of her back apparently—judging by the growls—hadn't been her plan.

They hauled her to her feet. "I gave you credit for brains you just don't have," said James.

Gage gripped one of her wrists behind her back while James held the other. "You done with her?"

"Affirmative. Get her out of my sight before I

change my mind and leave a mark I'll have to explain."

She twisted around with a snarl. "Mother fucker." She spat. "You have no idea who you're dealing with. You'll pay. You'll all pay in the end, and I'll be getting the last *fucking* laugh."

James shook his head. "You got her?" he asked Gage.

"Yeah."

James stepped back. "Drop her."

"Happy to." With three well-placed fingers at the back of her neck, Gage knocked her out cold, then slung her over his shoulder and marched off. And that, thought Angie, was just one more psychic power she hadn't known about. In her father? Yes. But not Gage.

The next interview was with Special Agent Danica Price, and before she even sat down, she said, "I've been thinking about it, and I'm going to accept your offer of protection. I'll tell you everything if you can help me get started in a new life." Unlike Bellows, she was pale, her hands shook, and her pupils were dilated to the point her eyes appeared to be black instead of blue. She sat, then said, "Even if all you do is let me go to find my own way, I'm coming clean."

James pulled the chair beside Angie back in order to sit away from the table with his feet spread, elbows on his knees and hands steepled under his chin. "Why don't you explain your connection to Rollins, and why you've never come forward about him being corrupt. Being part of the Minnows."

He held up a hand when she was about to speak. "In detail, Agent Price, so we completely understand your position."

She drew her shoulders back, her spine straightened and her chin came up. "S.W.A.T. handed me over to Child Protection when I was five. My parents—" She huffed out a breath that might have been a half-laugh. "I was living in a drug house. My mom and everyone else was arrested. But I was hiding, and watched it all. Up until the police dog found me."

She tucked her long black hair behind her ears. "I loved dogs, but wasn't allowed to play with the pit bulls chained up out back. They used them for fighting, and I remember crying when they'd bring them back with blood all over them."

When no one spoke, she continued. "Anyway, when they found me, the police were nice. They stopped yelling at everyone, and took me outside to a car. It was nighttime, and cold, but they wrapped me in a blanket, gave me a toy—a stuffy—and I sat in a warm car with a nice female officer who talked to me until CPS came." She glanced up. "I never forgot that instant island of calm in the middle of chaos. I grew up wanting to be like those cops."

Angie glanced at James when the silence stretched and when he nodded, she prompted with, "What happened then?"

"The usual. I bounced around in the system. Foster care, back with my mom when she wasn't in jail." She sighed. "Long story short, at fifteen I met a guy, got involved, and went where he led. His dad was a Minnow. I spent a great deal of time at their house, and I saw stuff. People. Men." A shudder ran through her, but she pressed on.

"Took me a couple of years to get smart enough to care about what I was involved in, but once we broke up, I took off." She lifted her gaze to James. "I hitched my way across the country, waited tables, worked hard and saved money. I wanted to be a police officer. It took me ten years."

Angie was skeptical. "All the background checks, and they never found your connection to the Minnows?"

"Nope. I was a runaway from the foster system and using a phony name when I met Josh. The hardest part of getting into the academy was my parents being convicted felons. But I made it. Finally. And graduated top of my class."

"Why move on to the FBI?" asked James.

Shifting her attention to him she replied, "Why not? It seemed to me an even better place to make a difference, and as one of the only women on my town's police force, I'd handled enough rape and battered women cases to last me a lifetime."

"What's your connection to Rollins?" Angie asked.

"We bumped into each other. I was on loan to another field office for a kidnapping case, and when I was introduced to my temporary commander I recognized him. My shock must have been visible. He cornered me later. Told me my life was worth shit if I so much as breathed the wrong word. Said he'd see to it that I was tortured for a week or two before I was allowed to die." She swallowed hard.

"He reminded me he had people on the inside, *and* in the Minnows, who'd be happy to do his bidding."

James addressed what was rattling around in Angie's brain too. "I'm surprised he recognized you so many years later."

"I'd met him several times when he was at Josh's house, and he gave me the creeps."

Her glance met Angie's. "I used to keep my hair short like yours—as a kid because of head lice, and later in law enforcement it was a rule for a while." She gathered her almost-waist-length hair and lifted it to expose the back of her neck, to show them a star-shaped birthmark nearly an inch wide. "He said he recognized this."

James pulled the interview back to the present. "How long has it been since he recognized you?"

"Five years. Five long, fucking years since I found out he was FBI. I'm glad to finally be able to do something about it."

"Even though it will cost you your career?"

"He'll be in jail, and I'll be alive." She rolled her shoulders. "I kept trying to find a way to make it work, but figured that one day he'd kill me even if I didn't expose him. I went to an attorney and had him create documents to be released if I turned up dead."

"How did you decide who to trust with the information?"

She smiled. "We figured the best way to deal with the possibility of it landing in the wrong hands was to send out copies to the Attorney General, the FBI Director, head of Homeland Security, the New York Times, USA today, CNN, the major wire services like AP and Reuters, plus a handful of other news agencies and reporters. Hard copies are in safe boxes in ten major cities in the US, and there are files on secure computers around the world. It's taken me a few years to get it all in place, but I figure if I die, the information won't disappear with me."

Angie nearly rubbed her hands together. What

Price had put in place could be used to blow the Rollins thing out of the water with very minimal Meyers involvement necessary. All they'd have to do is keep Price safe.

"What will you do once you leave here?" asked James.

"I'm not sure. I guess it depends on where you or the marshals put me. But I can handle whatever comes my way. Wait tables or clean toilets for a while if I have to."

James was nodding. "What can you tell us about Special Agent Bellows?"

Angie was surprised at how quickly Price responded. "Word is she's dirty, and a snitch."

"That's why she won't talk to us or consider going for a deal?"

"She's something of a femme fatale, and I'd be shocked if she didn't have compromising videos on people at every level of the organization. She hates men and loves to manipulate them. Does nothing to hide or even camouflage that she's living far beyond her means. I'm surprised she's yet to vanish or die a mysterious death."

James crossed his arms. "Interesting idea."

CHAPTER 22

Matt was enjoying the pre-dawn solitude of the kitchen when Kelton arrived, poured himself coffee, then skirted Swagger to sit at the table.

Christopher looked uncomfortable, making Matt wonder which bothered him most, the dog's presence, being persona non grata at the ranch, or sitting beside the man he'd been lying to and manipulating for over ten years.

"Sarah has informed me that you and I need to have a conversation about our history, and that you will require an opportunity to verbalize your concerns. Personally, I don't see the point. But my wife says I need to pursue this line with you, and because the troubled psyche is her area of expertise, I shall concede to her wishes." He sipped at his coffee, then pushed it away as though to let it cool. "Go ahead."

"I do have things to say to you, questions I'd appreciate getting answers to, but considering that you've been lying to me since the day we met—hell, even before that—why should I expect that anything has changed?" He held up his hand. "In case you didn't understand, that was only a rhetorical question." Swagger laid his head in Matt's lap, and he stroked the soft, black ears.

"Yes, there are things I think I would like to know, but in reality, the past is what it is. It can't be altered without changing where we are now, so what's the point? For now I can live with knowing you will always have an ulterior motive."

Kelton blinked a few times. "To have action without motive is a waste of energy. I do nothing without a purpose. Why would I?"

"Exactly." Matt pushed away from the table. "Enjoy your coffee." Swagger followed while he went in search of Dhillon. He glanced at his watch. Seven, and the kid was usually scarfing down cereal by six-thirty.

Matt stayed in Angie's room last night—to feel close to her in her absence, and to be there for their son—and had checked on Dhillon before heading for the kitchen at five…but something was niggling at his gut now as he shoved through the door.

Unsurprised to find the room empty, he spun and took off for the security room. Swagger was stuck to him like glue as he burst in asking, "Where's Dhi—"

The kid was sitting cross-legged in one of the big office chairs, with Chance next to him on the floor and the kitten nosing at the empty cereal bowl in front of him. He grinned. "Hey."

"What the hell are you doing in here?"

Dhillon hesitated. "I saw Kelton go into the kitchen, so we came here instead. Besides, they have the good stuff." He pointed at the half dozen brightly colored boxes on the counter at the side of the room. "Consuelo makes me eat healthy cereal first."

Tricky ground. "What about your mom?"

He made a face. "We bargain. Two bowls of healthy for every one of sugar-coated."

"What's the score so far today?"

He grimaced. "You gonna hold me to it?"

"You're putting me in a spot here, kid. How can I keep both you and your mom happy?" Matt held up a box of plain whole grain cereal.

"We-ell," he stretched the word into two syllables, and made a face that almost ruined Matt's attempt to look serious, but he managed to maintain. Lifted an eyebrow and outwaited his canny son.

"How about one bowl of whole wheat instead of two?" Dhillon suggested.

"Seems fair." And when he reached for the sugar, Matt turned his back. Sure it was a cop-out on parental duties, but he'd been a kid with a sweet tooth, and this was just one bad breakfast in a lifetime of good ones.

"Can't believe gramps left Swagger behind," the kid said around a mouthful. "Musta been a big op, lotsa action, maybe firepower or explosives, I guess."

Crap. Same thoughts he'd been having.

"Mom will be stoked. She always says the worse the bad guys, the more fun it is to take them down. Action. That's what she's about, and I'm going to be just like her—except for when I'm a doc, and then I'll be patching everybody up. The crazier the better, Mom says. Otherwise it's just boring."

How the hell could he have a future with her if she was constantly putting herself at risk?

And then it hit him like a brick between the eyes. What future? He didn't make plans. And even if he *did* get his freedom from the Minnows, he wouldn't tie himself down again. Well, at least not right away. He should take time first. Live in the moment. Anywhere he chose. Hell, he was financially secure enough to take a year and travel from one medical conference to the next. The world would be his to explore. The kid's voice brought him back.

"She even got shot once, but that was when I was too young to remember, and it was only a flesh wound. That's when the bullet doesn't go in."

Matt's gut roiled. Shot? There was a detail she hadn't shared. She'd told him their ops were tame. Mostly surveillance and research. But she'd been shot, dammit.

"But it bleeds a ton. Then there's the time somebody was shooting at the Steed and hit the rotor, I think, or hit something that almost brought it down. Crazy shit."

"I thought the Steed was indestructible." This was all in the past. The past was over. No point dwelling on something he couldn't change. Sure. He was good. No big deal.

"Well, it is mostly." Dhillon powered on, unfazed by his father's silence and likely the draining of color from his face. "Then there was the time in South America when she had to fly under the radar and nearly clipped the top of power lines installed by the drug cartel. They weren't on any maps, and Mom was loaded down, so she nearly lost it trying to grab altitude in a hurry. She was stoked for days after that one. Said it made her feel like a superhero."

No way he could live with her flying off on

dangerous ops like that, not knowing what could be happening to her. He couldn't protect that kind of woman.

"Hey, Doc, wanna go for another ride now? When I'm on Max and flying past the trees and stuff I feel invincible like Mom."

"Ah, sorry, I've got something I have to do right now."

Dhillon looked down at his empty bowl, stroked the kitten sitting beside it. "Yeah, okay."

Shit. "How about I meet you here at ten?"

"Sure." The smile came back, and Matt wondered if he'd just been played. Again. He needed air. Having been above ground for a while and able to get outside whenever the mood struck, it had become his go-to when things got tough, or complicated, or fucking scary.

His heart was still pounding too hard, and the dog beside him was obviously picking up his stress. Matt stopped, stroked a hand over Swagger. "You're supposed to be relaxing while James is gone, not babysitting me."

***

Angie wandered into the kitchen where Lissa was preparing lunch. "Want some help?"

"Sure." She pointed at the basket of fresh tomatoes they'd brought with them on the Steed, part of six boxes of staples and perishables to restock the safe house—standard procedure for this remote location.

"Cut some for sandwiches. And tell me about your mystery man."

Angie washed a couple of tomatoes. "Uh, he's not a mystery anymore."

"What?!" She spun away from the bread she was slicing. "I just talked to Eve yesterday and she never said a word. Wait until I get hold of her."

Angie grinned. "She couldn't tell you. Not while there was any chance of a transmission being intercepted. Short version, Matt is Dhillon's father, Cass's missing brother, and the Minnows are still after him."

"Dhillon's father?"

By the time Angie had spilled the whole story, they'd finished building a stack of sandwiches.

"So Rollins is the center of all the trouble, and has no clue Meyers is onto him," said Lissa.

"We hope."

"And you picked up these women because this Broughton fellow said they would roll over on Rollins?"

"Not exactly. Rollins had at one time said he owned Price, and offered her to Broughton as a reward for a job well done."

"That's just sick."

"Yep. Rollins claimed she'd do anything he asked. Broughton turned down the offer, but kept an eye on her. Could tell she was afraid of Rollins, and told us she might be able to help us hang him. Bellows was a different story. She'd apparently been bragging about having dirt on everyone, liked to say she could lead most of the upper-echelon around by their dicks."

"Nasty."

"Yeah. And she's refusing to talk. So she's going to be tucked away until this whole thing is over." The look on Lissa's face made Angie laugh. "No, we won't leave her here."

"Thanks. What about Price? Will she be staying?"

"Dad wants to take her to the ranch. He's maintaining his position that it's better to have everyone in one place." What Angie didn't say was that James was going to try to convince Lissa and Kyle to come back with them as well.

Lissa spread a long runner down the center of the table and set the sandwiches on it, then added jars of pickles and hot peppers. "So, wedding plans in the works?"

"Uh—" Angie rearranged the plates, forks, and napkins she'd set on the table. "Well."

Lissa laughed. "Really? You're the family go-getter. You set your sights on something and don't stop until it's yours." She tipped her head. "You told me a minute ago he was the only man you'd ever loved. Don't you intend to make a life with him once the Minnows are eliminated?"

"I do." She groaned at her choice of words. "But I'm not sure if he's on board with the idea."

"But you said he loves you and Dhillon and—"

"It's complicated. He's just discovered that Kelton's been manipulating him for years, he's uncertain about his future right now, and I don't want to push him."

Lissa leaned against the counter and folded her arms. "Interesting. Doesn't sound like you at all."

She shoved a hand through her short hair. "Yeah. I know. I thought everything was cool. I expected him to just sign on for a lifetime with us, but he's hesitating." She huffed out a breath. "I caught myself thinking that things would be great once I brought him around to my way of things. Changed him. And then I realized I was being like those women on soaps. And then everything got crazy, and thank God this op came up so I got to take off before I did or said something stupid."

Lissa was grinning. "Honey, I never thought I'd see the day. But here you are doubting yourself just like the rest of us. Welcome to reality, and to being in love." She laughed. "It gets better, really." Then a sweet softness lit her face as her gaze locked on something past Angie's shoulder. "Speaking of which."

Angie turned and the knife she'd been about to put in the sink clattered to the floor. Kyle, Lissa's husband, who'd been paralyzed from the waist down in a helo accident fourteen years earlier, was standing. Upright. Alone. And then he took a single step. Propelled it seemed by the barely visible hardware attached to his legs and torso.

Angie clapped her hand over her mouth, and a lump the size of Alaska lodged itself in her throat while he slowly walked toward her with a huge grin on his face. When he took both her hands and pulled her in for a hug, she came undone. Clung to him while her tears soaked the front of his shirt.

"Careful you don't tip me over," he said.

She backed up and studied her cousin. He was different. Even in the stand-up wheelchair, he hadn't had this look of…what was it? Accomplishment, maybe?

"Freaking cool," she said.

"Yeah. Call me robo-man. Fell on my face a couple of times when I decided to sneak more practice time in while Lissa was sleeping, but now I've mastered the balance thing, and learned the rhythm, I'm golden."

Angie couldn't tame her face-splitting grin. "Have Dad and Gage seen you yet?"

"Nope, you're the first."

"Oh, man, I can't wait to see their faces. They'll be gobsmacked. And so freaking thrilled for you."

Kyle lost the use of his legs in a helicopter crash on the ranch the same week Angie and Matt met for the first time. In Vegas. Where Dhillon had been conceived.

In the years following completion of basic rehab, he and his wife—who was a trained chef and physiotherapist—had worked for Meyers, maintaining this state-of-the-art safe house while also working on the research portion of many ops. Kyle had become a techno wizard, and for years the family had been trying to get him to come back to the ranch.

"Holy shit." Gage was standing in the doorway staring at Kyle. "About fucking time you got up off your ass." He crossed the room in two strides and they did that one-armed man-hug thing. "Happy for you, man."

"Kyle." James stepped past his son to grab his nephew's hand. "Finally. I've waited a damn long time to see this."

"Thanks for setting me up with the program. The team's been awesome, and, as you can see, the results are damn fine. I won't be running any marathons for a while, but they tell me I might one day, and that's good enough for me."

"You knew about this." Angie wasn't really surprised, because James was called the Chameleon

271

for a reason. He was everywhere, and mostly invisible. "You set it up."

James nodded. "An international group of scientists working together. They wanted subjects they could trust to keep the process and information secret until it was perfected. They felt there was too much at stake to make promises they couldn't fulfill. It's a new technology. The gear's feather-light, and the robotics are run by the wearer's own brain waves."

"Not just me strapped to a robot," said Kyle. "Without pushing any buttons, I get to decide if I want to sit, stand, walk, and, yeah, eventually run. Center of gravity is the key to everything. Well, that and my own mind. I have to be clear about what I want so I don't send mixed signals."

Angie found herself staring at Kyle while he took a seat at the table. "That really is awesome."

He glanced up at her. "You should see me on the stairs."

Lissa groaned. "Yeah, talk tough, now the bruises have faded. He was in a hurry to master that obstacle." She shook a finger at James. "I blame your side of the family for that attitude."

With a mouthful of sandwich in the way of his response, James merely shrugged, and Lissa went on. "You get the bullheadedness connection too. But what he could use is your unwavering dedication to a plan. Kyle likes to change things up and go left even though he planned to go right."

James swallowed. "Not good, pal. 'Course you need to have several contingency plans ready for just in case, but, yeah, sticking is important."

"Speaking of contingencies," said Angie. "What

are we going to do with Bellows?"

"She'll go to the ranch with us. It's the only way we can be sure to keep her out of action. I believe there's a lot more to that agent than what we know already."

Angie's eyes widened. "To Delta House?" What was also referred to as Detention House was a rarely-used set of underground cells, exactly in the middle of the vast property.

"Yeah. I think turning her loose, or even having an ally keep her for us, would backfire. I want her where I know she's secure," said James.

***

Once Angie had offloaded her passengers at the ranch, she took her time refueling and checking the entire surface of the Steed before leaving it at the hangar for maintenance—as required, due to the miles it had logged over the past few days.

Forty-five minutes later she was standing in her own kitchen, showered and ready to head for the debriefing. But instead she reached for another glass of water, and dug into the cookie jar again. Stood by the window to nibble her way through oatmeal and chocolate chips. Why was she hesitating about seeing Matt? Where was that excitement she used to feel when she was making her way through the ETC labyrinth to get to his office?

It was buried under fear. Fear because she realized he just might not want to make a life here with her and Dhillon after the Minnows were taken down. What then?

She cranked on the hot tap and waited until

steam billowed, rinsed her glass, dried it, and put it away. She wiped down the counters for the second or third time, then threw her hands in the air, kicked aside her flip-flops and stomped back upstairs. Tugged off the skinny jeans and orange T-shirt. Starting over, she went for work clothes. Khaki cargo shorts with a matching cotton shirt and lightweight vest. She dragged on woolly socks and folded them down to cover the tops of her lace-up work boots. She was going to be late now, but her dad would cut her some slack because of the long flight.

Once she washed off the mascara she'd uncharacteristically applied, she stuck her head under the tap and rinsed some of the gel out of her hair. With a quick scrub of a towel and her fingertips to put it in order, she headed out the door fifteen minutes late, but feeling much more like herself.

Until she stepped outside and found Grace waiting for her.

"You're with me. We have a problem."

CHAPTER 23

Where the hell was she? When James started the briefing, or debriefing, or whatever the hell it was, without her, Matt assumed Angie wasn't expected to be there. But why not? Everyone else was, with the exception of Kelton, Grace, and Dhillon. And Eve. Eve was a doctor. Was something wrong? His gut churned.

Matt forced himself to listen to the recap of the mission, hoping to get some clue as to where Angie was. But there was nothing. Well, nothing besides a collective indrawn breath from the others when James announced that Bellows was being held in something called Delta House.

"Due to the extra people currently on the property, from this point forward," said James, "the bunker will be referred to as DH, and the woman as BDH."

Everyone nodded.

"Agent Price will be staying here in the main house once her background has been investigated.

For the time being, Eve is processing her in the lab."

Which still didn't account for why Angie wasn't there.

When he caught an odd look passing from James to Julia, he noticed the woman was wearing a communications earbud. He checked the others in the room, and concluded it was only Julia, so he watched her and decided she was definitely listening to something besides what was going on in the briefing room.

In spite of it being forbidden while Kelton was on the property, Matt opened himself to telepathic communications by mentally sliding a door aside just a bit. Just enough to catch what might be going on around him, and Julia's power quickly became evident. She met his gaze and shook her head. He considered ignoring the silent order, but reluctantly closed the pathway.

Julia tapped the table with the white tip of an enameled fingernail, and everyone turned their attention her way. "Angie and Grace require some assistance from Matthias." She rose. "I'll take you to them."

She explained while she drove down a dirt road he hadn't been on before. "Dhillon's gotten himself into an awkward position and refuses to cooperate."

She grabbed the mic when her radio chirped, and he listened while she explained the situation to the head of security and they put a plan in motion. When she pulled up to where Angie and Grace were standing in the shadow of an enormous tree, Julia stayed in the SUV to maintain radio contact.

"Well," Matt muttered as he dropped an arm around Angie's shoulders and stared at the boy fifty-plus feet above him. "Awkward is one way to put it." Chance came over and shoved his nose into Matt's hand. Poor dog was worried about his person.

He raised his voice, staying just short of a yell. "Hey, Dhillon."

"Hey, Doc."

Matt grinned. "Okay, I'll bite," he said. "What's the deal, kid?"

"It's Roger." Even from that distance Matt heard the fear in his voice. "Whenever I got close to him he climbed higher, and now he's gone out there." He pointed. "I can't reach him and I'm *not* coming down without him."

"I get it." Matt had to squint to spot the tiny feline clinging to a skinny branch about five feet away from where Dhillon hugged the trunk of the tree.

"Stay right where you are, pal. Help's on the way, and as long as you don't move, I think Roger will stay put." He glanced at Angie and Grace. "Lance has a crew coming with a big-ass ladder, plus they're loading a trailer with hay as fast as they can."

Angie was nodding. "Perfect, it'll give us a higher base to work from, and a closer landing pad in case of a fall." She sounded calm, but the knuckles on the hand holding the corner of a plaid blanket were glowing white through the stretched skin.

"Meantime," said Grace, holding up her end of the blanket. "If the kitten happens to fall, we'll try to catch him in this."

From the looks on their faces, Matt was certain they already knew if the kitten fell that far he'd bump and bash into a dozen or more branches on the way down, and his survival would be a crap shoot.

He turned his attention back to the boy. "How

long you been up there, ace?"

"Too long."

"He started up the tree twenty minutes ago," said Grace. "Seemed safe enough at first. Roger was barely over our heads. But then the dance began, and I knew we were in trouble."

She shook her head. "When I went for Angie, Dhillon was only halfway to where he is now, because," she raised her voice for the kid's benefit, "even though he promised me he wouldn't move, he did. You and I are going to have a serious chat when your ass gets down here, Dhillon."

"You get what's left after I'm done with him," said Angie.

Matt looked up with a grin. "Geez, pal, you might want to put some thought into how you're going to talk your way out of trouble once you get down."

"Yeah."

"And I'm dying to hear how this whole mess got started," said Matt.

Grace held up a hand. "Dhillon brought me out to see the tree."

"Biggest pole oak in all of Texas," he shouted down.

"He'd set the kitten and dog together at the base so he could take their picture, and when the little devil started to climb, we both laughed. Then he started scooting higher and got spooked when Dhillon ran over to catch him." She tipped her head. "I hear a tractor."

It came into view pulling a hay wagon stacked with half-ton bales in two different levels—three high on one end, four on the other. Lance wedged the rig as far under the tree as he could without breaking the lower branches. Which was a good thing, because the sound would probably have panicked the kitten, and then of course the boy would make a dive... Matt shook off the ugly thoughts and joined Lance and Angie on the climb to the top of the giant bales.

The kid was still twenty-plus feet above them, and Matt grabbed Angie by the back of her shorts when she headed up the tree. "Hang on, hotshot, what's your plan?"

"I'm going to drag my son down from there, and then I'm going to beat him senseless."

"I like it," he said, "but how about we get Roger to safety first so the kid can't blame you for his kitten's demise?"

She stepped back. Brushed a hand through her spikey hair. "Good point."

"You okay up there, Dhillon?" he asked.

"Yeah. But Roger's not looking too good."

A security crew arrived then with a roll of garden netting, and the long pole with a large net scoop at the end. First the netting was hooked into the tree, then Lance climbed up with the scoop, and held it below the kitten. Dhillon tried to shake the frightened creature loose but Roger was a fighter, and those tiny front claws were dug in. He swung while trying to get his hind feet back up too.

Watching Dhillon trying to reach out farther was enough for Angie. "Don't even think about it!" Glad Matt hadn't tried to stop her this time, she scooted up the tree, one she'd climbed dozens of times as a kid.

When she reached her son she said, "I need you out of my way. Are you good to go up a bit further?"

"Yeah." He moved the foot he'd had hooked

beneath a branch for support. "Ouch. Pins and needles."

"Wiggle it to get the blood circulating."

He did, and nearly kicked her in the nose before climbing higher. She resisted the urge to grab his foot and place it in what she could see would be a good spot. He was doing fine without her interference.

"Okay, you got a good hold where you are, Dhillon?"

"Yeah."

She edged up until she could reach out toward where the Roger hung off a skinny branch more like a twig. From the pocket of her cargos she dug out her multi-purpose knife. "You ready down there?"

"Affirmative," said the man directly below her.

"Backup in place," said Matt, and she glanced down at where he stood with his hands under the garden netting, backup she hoped they wouldn't need.

She stretched out as far as she could, hooked the cutter around the branch. "Incoming, in three, two, one." With a quick snip, Roger and branch dropped. There was a moment of near panic when it looked like the bit of tree he was still clinging to would slide off the top edge of the catcher, but Lance's quick jiggle of the handle had everything working out perfectly. He reeled the pole in and plucked out the kitten.

"Yes!" shouted Dhillon with a daring one handed fist pump, and his dog barked in answer.

"Dammit, Dhillon, grab hold!"

He grinned down at her. "Oh, Mom, I've got a good grip with my legs, see?" He waved both hands and she had to stifle her own smile. Growing up with a houseful of brothers, she'd been a daredevil herself.

"Okay, smart-aleck, but going down is always harder than going up, and I want your attention on what you're doing. I'll be slow, so you be patient and don't crowd me. Got it?"

"Yes, ma'am."

"Nice touch, but I'm still going to hurt you when we get out of this mess."

While she eased down one branch at a time, the bark bit into her hands and bare legs, making her wince a time or two. Funny, she hadn't felt anything on the way up—while watching her kid hang out on a dangerously flimsy limb.

She glanced over her shoulder, and her worry and discomfort evaporated. Matt was staring up at them, wearing an expression she'd seen on Gage when he looked at Cass or their girls. Her heart did a slow roll in her chest.

When they were both on the ground, they were enfolded in Matt's arms until Dhillon wrenched free.

"Where's Roger?"

"Here you go." Grace released the kitten from under her sweater.

Dhillon cradled the cause of the trouble in his hands while Chance gave the squeaking ball of fluff a cursory once-over. "I've gotta get him fed. I'll catch you guys later."

Angie grabbed him by the back of the shirt. "Not so fast, bucko."

"But, Mom, he's hungry." She could tell he was struggling to keep a straight face.

"Yeah, and so are you. But look around." She waved her hand at the tractor, the crew, and the equipment. "I think you have something to say before you need to be concerned about your empty belly."

He kicked dirt with his toe. "Yeah. Thanks everyone, for rescuing Roger. He might be little, but he's a big deal to me. And thanks for not calling in the uncles. They'd have blasted me."

Angie delivered her best evil grin. "Oh, don't worry, they'll get their chance after we're done with you. Now go. Get that critter fed, and make sure Chance gets something special for being a good friend and hanging around to support you."

Without a word or a backward glance, he raced down the path, the dog loping along beside him.

By the time Angie thanked the crew and they packed up and went back to where they'd been when the call for help went out, she started to shake.

"You okay?" asked Matt.

"Yeah, just coming down off the adrenaline."

Julia called out from the SUV, where she'd remained for the entire rescue. "Briefing in the war room, stat." She tapped her earbud. "Kelton's missing."

"Dhillon." Angie took off at a dead run.

CHAPTER 24

Angie's lungs were on fire by the time she caught sight of Dhillon.

Consuelo was holding the back door open for him. Did she know? Angie fought to get a single word from her burning throat. "Kelton."

"Security's on it. He's been spotted way over in the east sector, and there's a briefing in ten. You coming in?"

She shook her head, waved, and turned back the way she'd come because she needed a minute, and there were benches along the path. She sat and put her head between her knees to get some extra blood to her brain while her breathing leveled off.

"Where's Dhillon?" Matt's hand settled on the back of her neck.

"Safe inside."

"You okay?"

"Yeah." She straightened, leaned back to look up at him. "Kid's hard on my heart sometimes."

He sat beside her, drew her against him. "Yeah,

gave mine a workout too."

With her cheek against his chest, the vibration of his voice soothed her. She tipped her head back, looked into the face of the man now sharing her son with her. Theirs. "He's not just mine anymore. He's ours finally, isn't he?"

One corner of his mouth quirked up. "Yeah. I guess he is." When she lifted up and kissed him, his response wasn't what she'd hoped for, expected. She obviously didn't have his full attention.

"Angie—"

She jerked away from him. Wasn't sure she wanted to hear whatever he was about to say. "We need to go inside."

He grabbed her arm. "What's wrong?"

"Nothing we can talk about right now, because there just isn't time."

He didn't let go, but walked beside her to the door. Stopped her before she could reach for the handle, and framed her face with his hands. "I love you."

As tears suddenly welled, she wrenched away from him and bolted inside.

The war room was filled to capacity. With the whole family crammed into a space not meant for such a use, adults filled chairs and perched on counters while kids and dogs covered most of the floor.

Matt nearly backed out when he was hit with a noise level bordering on painful. This was a different kind of reality for a man used to controlled environments and sound filters. Angie hopped up to take the last spot on the counter across the back of the room, so Matt stood, wedged in alongside, with one arm over her legs and his back against a tall cupboard door.

She paled even more after studying the room for a moment, and her shoulders were hiked up far too high. He rubbed her shin, and she rested a hand on his shoulder.

A piercing whistle brought instant silence, and when Julia stood to address the group, Matt realized James wasn't there.

"Kelton," said Julia, "somehow managed to leave his room within minutes of when Matt and I headed out to help with Dhillon. According to security, he is at the moment on foot, near the east gate. They have him on camera, and gate security is aware of his presence. We've decided to leave him be for the moment, watch and wait."

"How did he get out of his room?" asked Angie.

"Either someone let him out, or he circumvented our system, and neither of those possibilities sit well. At all."

"Didn't security see anything? Have they gone through the camera history?"

"No, and not yet. They were tied up with the boy in the tree incident. Staffing is now back to full strength, and we should have an update shortly."

On cue, the internal communications center beeped. Julia hit the speaker button. "Go ahead."

"Subject exited at thirteen hundred as though no locks were engaged. We're going over the mechanisms now."

"His timing should confirm that he has eyes and ears in here," said Matt. "Technology you can't scan for."

"Absolutely, and out of our hands, short of

drastic measures."

"What about the status of Price and Broughton? Are they at risk?" asked Angie. Matt had completely forgotten the two agents here for their own protection.

"They were relocated to Alpha and Beta as soon as Kelton's absence was discovered."

Matt could only wonder what that meant. No way he'd ask for an explanation until he and Angie were alone somewhere they couldn't be heard.

"This house," Julia's voice helped him focus on the situation at hand, "now that everyone is indoors, is officially sealed. No one in this room is to open a door to the outside. Period. No exceptions. Airing of dogs is prohibited for everyone," she pinned Dhillon with a look, "except security. Lance himself will take them out." She kept her gaze on Dhillon. "I know it's going to be a pain to stay cooped up, but there *will be no exceptions*. And you, young man, have already used up your free passes from this team, so you need to be very, very careful."

"Yes, ma'am," he said, and flicked a look towards Matt and Angie, as though looking for support. Matt kept his poker face on, even though he longed to help the kid out with a smile.

"You are now free to go with Consuelo and the girls to the kitchen. You'll be helping with meal prep. Take all the dogs, because Lance will see to them shortly."

Once they were gone and the door was closed, Julia glanced from face to face. "Due to the breakdown of security, James will be working *with* us, but will not be present for the time being."

"Is he okay?" asked Angie.

"He's been better," said Julia. "But he's been a helluva lot worse too. He has Swagger with him, and he's staying in contact with me." For the first time since he met Angie's mother, she looked her age. Up until today she'd have passed for about forty-five in both appearance and action. But now she looked like someone who'd worked hard for most of her sixty years.

"Setbacks are to be expected," said Quinn, and Matt was reminded that Angie's older brother was a therapist who dealt every day with people fighting the same issues as James. "Running the extraction op was an enormous undertaking, and not only did he pull it off, he did it without his dog for support. That had to beat the crap out of his resources, so having this breach right on the heels of the op would be a game-changer. He'll just need some time and distance to get his balance back."

"Okay," said Angie. "Meantime, what do we do about Broughton and Price?"

"My department," said Eve. "I've done the background on them, and they passed all my testing. In my opinion, they could join the family in the daytime, and return to Alpha and Beta for sleeping."

"Exactly as James predicted," said Julia. "They will be our guests until Rollins has been secured. After that, they'll be free to relocate.

"Meantime, if they wish to aid us further in building the case against Rollins, they are free to do so. James suggested one or both could be valuable additions to our team, either short- or long-term. Keep your eyes and ears open with that in mind."

Admitting them to the war room would have surprised Matt if he hadn't already witnessed the extraordinary biometric security measures. Everything from the communications and computer equipment to individual file retrieval required an iris and/or a palm scan.

When the meeting finally broke up, Quinn signaled to Angie to stay put, and she bristled instantly. "Orders like that are for the canines around here."

"Sorry," he said while crossing the room to her.

"Talk to me about Dad," she prompted, but he shook his head.

"I just want a minute of your time. It's personal."

"Anything you have to say to me can be said in front of Matt."

Quinn shook his head. "You're more than welcome to share, but I'd like to speak with you alone...no offense, Matt."

"None taken."

Angie punched Quinn in the arm after Matt left. "Why did you do that? You made him uncomfortable."

"You look like hell, and I want to know why."

She stepped back. "Geez, Quinn. So far my day hasn't been a picnic in the park. You'd think I could have a pass on looking perky."

"Things aren't going smoothly with Matthias."

"We're fine. Save the shrink analysis for your paying customers."

"Come on, Angie. You used to talk to me about everything, and I know that face. Something's eating at you, making you unhappy."

She threw up her hands in surrender and paced. There was never any point in fighting Quinn when he was dug in. "I've turned into a freaking stereotype. A pathetic female wanting to change the man she's in love with. Like a goddamn teenager. I expect him to fall at my feet and tell me he loves me and can't live without me, so we can fly off into the sunset for a happily ever after, and it's not fucking happening. I'm a mature woman with a teenage son, and I'm suddenly reduced to acting his age instead of my own. I've become needy, and it's making me crazy."

She shoved her fingers through her hair, linked them at the back of her neck. "I was fine when there was no chance at having a real relationship with Matt because he had to stay in hiding. But as soon as things changed, I started hearing damn wedding bells, and that's just not like me. I've never wanted or needed the traditional. I'm a strong woman, capable of doing what needs to be done without the help of a man. But now I've apparently changed."

"Bullshit. Didn't you go up that tree after your son today, just like the woman you've always been?"

She stuffed her hands in her pockets, leaned back against the counter. "I suppose I did."

"Was Matt there?" Quinn sat on the table.

"Yes."

"And did you wait for him to fix things or take the initiative yourself?"

She blinked. "I did what I needed to do—"

"When you needed to do it," he finished. "You haven't changed, Angie."

"But I want to be a family with him and Dhillon."

"Haven't you always wanted that?"

She nodded. "I suppose, but there's all these feelings interfering with everything."

"To be expected for a while, kiddo, because no

matter how strong and self-sufficient you are, you're emotionally immature."

Her jaw dropped, and her mouth hung open. But as though blithely unaware she was probably going to have to deck him for that comment, he went on.

"You're still fifteen. You never got to advance from there romantically, and neither did Matt, from what I understand. You're a couple of randy teenagers trying to figure out what comes after sex, because that's what you were when Dhillon was conceived. You did everything in the wrong order."

Angie's jaw snapped shut and she ground her back teeth.

"You had sex based on attraction and chemistry. Then you became a mother and had to grow up in a big hurry to be what Dhillon needed, and you did a brilliant job. But in the meantime, a part of your growing up was bypassed, and now while you and Matt are getting to know each other better, your emotional immat—"

She closed the space between them in one stride and slugged him in the shoulder. "Don't. Say that again. It's fucking insulting."

"Not my intention," he said, rubbing his arm. "The point is, you both need to work at having a relationship. Look at what Rachel and I went through before we both got on the right track, and Gage and Cass, same thing. It's not easy, but it's worth it."

Leaning back again, she crossed her arms and said, "So you're telling me not to give up. Ha ha, not like I could."

"I'm telling you to quit looking for the final score when you're only in the first quarter."

She raised her eyebrows. "A football analogy?

That's so unlike you."

He shrugged. "One of my Haven clients played at the national level, so it's in my face lately. My question is, did you get the point?"

"Yeah, got it." She grimaced. "And yeah, I'm glad you shanghaied me."

"You always used to talk to me, and I was starting to get worried. It takes a lot to scrape away your sense of humor, and it's been so thin I can see right through it."

"You keep insulting me, I won't pull my punch the next time."

He grinned. "Now I'm being threatened by a pipsqueak. That's more like the old Angie." He slung an arm around her shoulders and headed for the door. "Go talk to Matt."

"Good idea," she said. "Right after monkey sex in the shower."

"Oh man, don't put that picture in my head, or I'll have to shoot him."

***

Matt looked around his new room. He didn't much like the change, but his freedom had been once again taken away, and Angie's house was now off limits, so he did what he'd always done. Made do. Accepted what he couldn't change. But since he'd only recently gained access to the outdoors, he found it tough to give it up again.

At least Grace and Logan were in the executive guest wing with him, and there was an adult-only lounge. That's where he found Logan, at the pool table.

"Game?" he asked.

"Sure," said Logan, and he started retrieving balls from the pockets.

Matt racked them and nodded for Logan to break. "Did you notice anything odd at the briefing?"

"Besides the absence of James? Yeah. No speculation about what Kelton was up to."

"Exactly. Made me wonder why." Matt propped a shoulder against the wall while Logan continued circling the table, making shots.

"I think the family knows the answer, otherwise Angie would have been asking questions," said Logan.

"I tossed that idea around some, but I was with her most of the day, so I doubt she's heard anything I haven't."

Logan laughed. "You need to watch more closely, my friend. This group is adept at subtle signs, signals, and code. They have secondary communications going at all times."

Of course. And now he felt like an idiot. "Is James dealing with Kelton?"

"No. I suspect he's gone to do the legwork on Rollins."

Broughton and his two dogs strolled into the room, putting an abrupt end to the conversation.

He held his hand out. "I'm Broughton."

"Logan."

"Logan. Yes, the pieces are coming together. You're ETC, under Commander Platt."

"Was, but it's been awhile. What's your connection?"

"Organized crime task force. A major case some years ago. You came in at the end, helped us locate and corner the kingpin. Then the jerk shot himself."

Logan only nodded.

"ETC does the psychic stuff."

"Some, but they have many other departments and strengths," said Logan. "How long did you work with Rollins?"

"Too long." He shook his head. "Luckily I had an old injury to get me out."

"And now you hide."

"From more than him. I had a good career. There are dozens in prisons around the country who would like nothing better than to make my life hell, or better yet end it."

"If we hadn't come to you, would you have ever shared the information you have on Rollins?" asked Matt.

Broughton stared at the pool table as though setting up a shot. "I don't know. I did consider killing him. But figured that wouldn't be enough to stop the Minnows."

"You think they'll go on without him?"

"Yes."

"Which is why we're going to make sure he rolls on all of them."

"Good plan. He'd give up his own mother to save his ass."

Angie marched in. "So this is where everyone's hiding." She glanced at the pool table. "Somebody is getting their butt kicked."

"That would be me," said Matt.

"Can I play the winner?"

Logan grinned. "Sure can." He tipped his head toward Broughton. "You can play me after that."

"Thanks, but no. It's just not my game."

"Mine neither," said Matt. "I'm better at the virtual variety of most things."

Logan made the mistake of letting Angie break and the three men looked on while she sank ball after ball, calling bank and pocket of every shot until she cleared the table of solids.

"Well," said Logan. "That was fun."

"Five brothers, and I have a competitive streak."

"A mile wide. Next time, I break." He glanced at his watch. "But I have to meet Grace and Julia now, so it'll have to wait."

Angie grinned. "That's your story, you stick to it."

"Brat. We'll have a rematch later." He put his cue away and turned to Broughton. "You should come with me. Meet my wife and Julia."

CHAPTER 25

Angie didn't know where to start "Nice and quiet in here." Seriously? That's the best she could do?

"You okay?"

"Yes and no." She slid the cue ball back and forth along the edge of the cushion. "Quinn said some things I didn't really like, but he might have a point."

"About?"

Keeping her focus on the ball while she rolled it around under her palm, she said, "About us."

"He has a problem with you and me?"

"Well, me mostly, but yeah, us." She sent the ball across the table, caught it when it bounced back. Then did it again. "Our relationship…or lack thereof."

Matt grabbed the ball, dropped it in a pocket, and she glanced up to see a perfect poker face. She'd expected some anger, or defensiveness at least, but there was nothing.

Dark blue eyes she loved stayed focused on hers, but he didn't speak.

"Say something."

"I have no clue what this is about, or where it's going, so how can I respond? Tell me what Quinn said, so at least I'll have some material to work with."

"He says we're emotionally immature."

When his jaw dropped and his mouth hung open, Angie couldn't help but laugh. "My response exactly. But as always with Quinn, there was a reasonable explanation."

"I'm dying to hear it, and to hear why he felt compelled to make the comment at all."

Yeah, jumping in halfway wasn't going to make any sense, and this felt wrong. What she'd like to do is go for a long walk and talk about where they were headed, but that was off the table, thank you Kelton.

"This could take a while, and I'd hate for someone to interrupt us. Could we go to your suite?" Shit, she should have enough confidence to just take him by the hand and lead him there.

From the look on his face, she got the impression he'd had the same thought. She'd never wanted to be fifteen again, and this was why. The freaking uncertainty that came with it.

Bullshit. She pushed past the angst, grabbed him by the collar and dragged him down for a kiss. Then with his hand in hers she headed for the rooms Julia had chosen for him. And chosen well. The sitting room was at the end of the wing, with floor to ceiling windows on three sides, making it feel almost as though they were outside, a part of the natural setting.

Matt flipped the lock on the door and kissed her until she nearly forgot the conversation she wanted to have. Almost succumbed to the taste of him, the tenderness of his touch, his mouth. Planting both hands in the middle of his chest she pushed herself away. "We need to talk."

She sat cross-legged in the middle of the long sofa, patted the spot beside her and waited for him to get comfortable.

Gave him bonus points for sitting sideways to face her. Caught herself. Points were juvenile. "Do you remember the week we spent at the ranch up north?"

"Is this a trick question?"

"No. It's just that for a whole week, everything was about us. We spent time talking, sharing, really learning about each other. Something we'd never been able to do before."

She met his gaze square on. "Confession time. Prior to that week, I believed we were having," she did finger quotes, "a relationship. When, in fact, what we'd been having were fantastic booty calls."

He shook his head. "There was more than sex between us."

"Really?"

"Yeah, really, and didn't we already go over this?"

Her eyebrows went up. "You pined for me when I wasn't there?"

His gaze shifted to the windows, then back to her. "I thought about you sometimes, but my life was compartmentalized. When you were there, I was fully engaged with you. It was more than sex. I loved your sense of humor, the stories you told me about Dhillon and the rest of your family, I loved how you were interested in me and my work. It had been a very long time since I mattered to anyone."

She desperately wanted to throw her arms around him and promise he'd always matter to her, he'd never be alone again. But the woman she was trying to be elbowed her back and she made do with resting a hand on his knee. "The only experiences we had together were in the same envelope as sex. There was nothing to agree or disagree about, nothing to compromise on. No helping each other cope with daily stresses." Saying it out loud was giving her a better perspective. "I don't know what you look like when you're in a bad mood. Or sad. Or lonely."

"I tend not to show my emotions. It's part of being invisible to the people around me. A skill I learned through necessity."

She reached for his hand, and held it between her own. "Getting back to Quinn. He cornered me because he'd noticed I was unhappy and wanted to know why. I told him about my feelings for you, and about my frustration as I tried to find a way past my expectations, and the uncertainty about my future." She kept her gaze locked on his. "He said the stumbling block looming between us comes from putting the cart before the horse. We've had a sexual relationship for years, but never an emotional one." She grimaced. "And the real kicker was the fantasy I'd been feeding for years. The one about the three of us living together as a family."

Matt brought her hands to his mouth and kissed them. "You know I love you, right?"

She smiled. "Yeah, I got that." And the smile faded. "I want more, Matt. I need more."

"I'm not a normal person, Angie, I *have* nothing else."

She shook her head. "That's where you're wrong, Matthias Alejandro Martinez, that's where you're dead wrong. You have *you*—no matter what name you're using. And that's what I want. And in exchange, whether you want it or not, I intend to give you me. Bumps, scrapes, warts, and all."

"You don't have warts."

"Not lately, anyway, but I want to give you who I am in all my moods, in all my roles within this family. Does that make any sense?"

With a sigh he hoisted her onto his lap. "I think so," he said and wrapped his arms around her.

She rested her head over the beat of his heart and, for the first time in days, felt like maybe, just maybe, all would be well.

***

Leaning back in her white leather chair, Julia studied the woman on the other side of the enormous antique desk. James had said it was important for Julia and Grace to interview agent Danica Price alone. When she'd asked him why, he'd touched her cheek in that intimate way of his and said, "You'll know. Get your first impressions of her before you read this." Then he handed her an envelope and left through a secret passageway.

Her husband's comment after meeting with Price at the safe house had been that she looked like she fit her skin and her persona—all federal agent in a plain dark suit and sensible shoes. Not an image often seen in recent years.

Today she was wearing clothes provided by Meyers. Stylish jeans covered long legs, a bulky Irish sweater hung from her shoulders, and ebony hair swung loose to the middle of her back. She looked much younger than forty rather than older, yet she managed to exude an air of professionalism.

"Welcome, Agent Price, and thank you for aiding us in this investigation." She nodded toward her niece sitting in the other white wingback. "This is Grace, and I'm Julia."

Price didn't smile. "It's a pleasure to meet you both, and thank you for opening your home to me. I had expected to wake up somewhere safe, but much less…friendly. Eve was very kind and enlightening during my orientation."

Julia was picking up nothing as far as psychic abilities. "You've put your life at risk by sharing information about Rollins and his connections. How do you feel about forfeiting your career?"

Price looked down at her hands where they lay folded in her lap. "It was time. I'm glad I was given the opportunity."

Professional, polite, and hiding something. Closed up as tight as a dusty pickle jar.

Julia held up the envelope James had given her earlier. "A last minute-message, please excuse me a moment."

It took no more than that to unfold and read the words on the single sheet of paper. She laid it face down on the glossy surface, understanding why James made certain she and Grace would have time with Danica before Logan arrived with Broughton.

The original plan had been for Grace and Logan to covertly assess the two agents for the presence of psychic abilities. Apparently, there was more to investigate.

What is it? Grace's silent words slipped into Julia's mind through a special pathway they'd created years before they even met. A pathway exclusive to the two of them.

Kelton strikes again.

Why am I not surprised?

"Agent Price, are you aware of my family's connection to the Minnows?"

Her shoulders squared. "Excuse me?"

"In a previous interview, you informed my husband you had a connection to the Minnows through a boyfriend when you were in your teens. That your parents were both dead, and you had no other family. Is that true?"

"Yes."

The single word set off a hum in the back of Julia's mind, an unmistakable indicator that she was lying.

"What exactly happened to your parents?"

"My mother overdosed, and my father died on the wrong end of a shiv." Price shifted in her chair. "While incarcerated."

"And you had no one else."

"Correct."

"I understand your parents were imprisoned for a great deal of your childhood. Who cared for you during that time?"

"The government."

"There was no other family for you to go to?"

"None. This information is all in my records."

"Daniel Beardsley."

Fuck. Lockdown.

Gotcha. Julia nearly chuckled when Danica's eyes widened. "Your poker face is good, but you should shut down access to your internal voice at the beginning of an interview instead of after you've given yourself away."

"You'd think Kelton would have taught you that," Grace added.

She shrugged. "Daniel Beardsley was my mother's friend, but I called him my uncle. She used to leave me with him when she went out at night, and sometimes I stayed with him when I ran away from foster homes. He was good to me. Kind."

"And yet his name never made it into any of your records. Why is that, Danica?"

"What was the point? He was dead, and, yeah, he had a criminal record, but he was turning his life around. His parents had money. Sent him away to rehab, and when he came back he stayed clean."

"What happened to him?"

"He died."

"There's more," said Grace.

Danica's glance bounced between the two of them. "You both obviously know, so why bother?"

"We'd like to have your side of it, to compare. Don't you think your uncle deserves that much?" Grace had a way of cutting right to the heart of things. A skill Julia had always admired. But Price didn't look too happy about it. Anger, just an edge of it was starting to show through the professional mask she'd been wearing.

"Before he went to rehab, he'd been dealing to pay for his habit, and I guess he was getting the drugs from the Minnows. When he quit, they wouldn't let him go, said he owed them."

"How old were you when he told you this?"

"He never told me. I'd hear him talking to my

mom when I was supposed to be asleep in the back room." She shrugged. "Life was better when I knew what was going on. If my mom was coming back that night or not, that kind of thing. Anyway, Uncle Daniel got pissed when they tried to recruit my mom. They promised her all the drugs she wanted, that kind of deal. He started using the anonymous tip line to give information to the police. There were a few arrests, but no charges were laid. Ever."

Price crossed her legs and wrapped her arms around her middle. "He made more calls, and then a cop came to visit him. They got to be friends. My uncle trusted him, told him everything he knew about the Minnows. The cop said solid cases were being built against a dozen men, but the goal was to not arrest anyone until they had the guy in charge of it all." She let her head rest against the back of the wide chair. "I didn't understand everything at the time, but I remembered conversations and put it together years later. After.

"What happened, Danica?"

Her eyes met Julia's. "His *friend* asked him to wear a wire to a Minnows meeting to get one last bit of intel. And it must have been a setup. Uncle Daniel never came home. And my mom OD'd."

"You've worked on several special projects with ETC. Tell me how that came about." Julia waited for Danica to formulate an answer to what was clearly a question she hadn't expected. Her gaze went left, then right, then left again.

"I was on an organized crime task force and at a briefing when someone from ETCETERA heard my internal voice. Later that year, I was sent to ETC for special training."

"Did Dr. Kelton ever discuss your uncle or the Minnows with you?"

"Not that I recall."

Grace leaned forward. "I think we're past that point, Agent Price." There was no mistaking the attitude embedded in her smooth voice. "Allow me to reword the question. Regarding Dr. Kelton, did he or did he not ever discuss your uncle or the Minnows with you?"

A jaw muscle twitched, but Danica's eyes reflected nothing but calm. "Where we met, on the OC task force, the Minnows were the subject of the briefing, and would have been mentioned in many conversations."

Julia went a different direction. "You dye your hair. Why?"

"From my interview with your husband, you must know that I try to stay hidden because of my childhood connections. Being recognized by Rollins was bad enough. I don't want to repeat the experience with any of the others."

"Getting back to Rollins," said Grace, "You told James an elaborate lie about having a boyfriend whose father was a Minnow, and that's where you met Rollins. Perhaps you could share the truth with us now."

She blew out a breath. "Rollins was my uncle's trusted cop friend."

"So he knew you well."

"Actually, no. I only met him once, and didn't like him at all. After that I always stayed hidden when he was around. That's why I never bothered to change my looks when I went into law enforcement. I didn't think there was any chance he'd recognize me.

But I made a critical mistake when we met unexpectedly some years later, and my startled reaction gave me away. Then he saw the birthmark."

"Interesting he'd remember that after one brief meeting with a child. Not like it's in the middle of your forehead."

"He's got some kind of freakish memory. After that, hoping to hide from him or anyone he'd told about me, I consulted with a plastic surgeon about removing it, but was told there would still be a mark. Keeping it covered is simpler, and changing my hair was easy."

"Why did you go into law enforcement?" Julia asked.

"To get the man responsible for my uncle's death."

Grace gave her a bland stare. "Seems to me you've had more than adequate time to do that, yet Rollins, the man you believe is responsible, is still walking around, *and* a member of a federal agency's upper echelon."

Danica's nostrils flared, but again, she tamped down her anger before speaking. "The plan had been to go after a single bad cop. I only knew the name my uncle used, which of course wasn't his real name. I searched for years and came up empty. Then, when I stumbled upon him, and discovered both his position and the team he had gathered around him, I ran. Took any and every transfer offered to me, worked with ETC whenever they asked. Did whatever I could to stay off his radar. Cowardly? Sure. But he was out of my league, and so far up the freaking chain of command I had no idea who else might be working with him."

Julia pinned her with a stern look. "Did you ever speak to Kelton about Rollins?"

"No."

"Why are you willing to come forward and tell all now?"

"Your husband made me an offer I couldn't refuse. I want Rollins dead, and if I can't have that, I want him behind bars for the rest of his life. Meyers Security has promised to take him down, and all it will cost me is my identity."

"And you're willing to relocate wherever you're sent?"

"Yes. I've remade myself before, and I'm prepared to do it again."

Julia nodded. "Grace, let Logan know we're ready for him."

"More surprises?" asked Price.

"Special Agent Broughton, the man who suggested we talk to you, is here until Rollins is safely in custody. We wanted to talk to both of you about him, to help polish the file."

"Broughton's dirty. He belongs to Rollins," said Danica.

***

Angie was less than thrilled to be dragged into the interviews, but understood her mother's reasoning. Price had raised a red flag about Broughton, and Angie was the only person who'd met both of them prior to their arrival at the ranch. As a silent observer, she'd be looking for tells, inconsistencies compared to previous statements, different body language, the works.

They were already chatting in the conversation area of Julia's office when Angie got there. Apologizing for tardiness, she poured herself a cup of tea from the pot in the middle of the round coffee table and tucked her feet up under her in the only chair left.

Julia nodded and addressed Broughton. "You were on a team headed by Rollins for a number of years."

"I was a plant." He leaned forward, obviously eager to cut to the chase. "The director set things up so Rollins would recruit me onto his team. I spent four years attached to the bastard, and even though I believe down to the soles of my feet that he's a crooked mother-fu—" Although he caught himself, he made no apology. "I couldn't find any evidence. Nothing. Nada. Burned a fucking hole in my guts trying."

"What kind of evidence were you looking for?"

"Proof that he runs the organized crime group known as the Minnows. Something to tie him to them. But he's smart. And vigilant."

"And you found nothing in four years?"

"There were strings. But each one I tugged led to someone else. He was connected to nothing."

"Why did you identify Price and Bellows as agents who would potentially turn on Rollins?"

He glanced at Price and spoke to her, rather than about her. "You were at a meeting and he caught me watching you. Said he owned you, but he'd loan you to me for a while. A gift for work well done."

He shook his head and gazed up at the ceiling for a moment before continuing. "I said no thanks, and then he pushed. Told me he could order you to do anything I wanted. Repeated that he owned you, and I said I preferred to get my women the old-fashioned way. He finally laughed and let it drop. But I watched you watching him, and I saw hate." He shrugged.

"At that point I made the assumption you weren't happy about his ownership, and I filed the intel away, just in case I ever needed it."

Julia asked, "Did you ever consider intervening?"

"Considered, but kept watch from a distance instead. Always knew where she was posted. But I never made contact. "I couldn't jeopardize my cover." And from the look on his face, Angie was certain that fact hadn't sat well.

"Did you ever speak with anyone else about Agent Price's situation?"

"Never."

"Not even the director who sent you undercover?"

"Not even."

"Why not?"

"Because she'd positioned herself so far away from him I thought she was safe, and I didn't want her name on any files connected with him. There are others besides Rollins who are less than trustworthy."

"Can you name names?"

He glanced around the room. "Not under these circumstances. Neutral ground with an option to exit? Maybe."

Smart man.

Julia nodded. "How about the squeaky clean? Anyone you'd be comfortable sharing information with?"

"Yes."

"And they'd be?"

He rattled off three names everyone in the room would know well. Three power figures, who were usually grouped with a fourth—a name Broughton hadn't included.

"Have you ever worked with ETC?" Julia asked.

Broughton nodded and glanced at Logan. "I've worked with a team headed by Commander Platt, but never with the woo-woo division."

Several sets of eyebrows shot up. "Define woo-woo." said Julia.

"Psychics, mind readers, telepaths, and the like."

"May we assume you don't believe in those powers?"

Angie almost laughed out loud at the very real possibility of her mother levitating the mug on the table in front of Broughton. But it was a power Julia rarely used, and she would never do something so blatant in front of strangers. Shame, though, it would be worth the price of admission just to see his face.

"That would be an incorrect assumption," he replied. *Silent communication is one of my specialties. I also understand it may currently only be used safely in this room, and nowhere else in the house or on the property.* He glanced from one to the next, as though checking to make sure everyone was listening to him. *Now, I believe there are some strategies Chameleon wanted us to discuss.*

CHAPTER 26

This made up for being locked indoors, thought Matt as Angie burrowed her face against his throat. The pleasant smell of the leather sofa was eclipsed by the lemony scent of her hair. Wide windows and walls were obscured by the view of rolling hills and vast blue sky. His arms tightened around the woman he loved, and he thought, what more could a man want?

Freedom.

But wasn't *this* freedom, in spite of the locked doors?

What about the longing to travel? Pursuit of his vocation? Mixing with others in his field? Doing anything he—

"What are you thinking about?" Angie pushed his shirt aside to press her lips and then her tongue against his skin.

He chuckled past the groan. "Whatever it was is gone now."

"We were talking about Broughton having worked with my dad."

"Right."

"Do you ever wonder about the universe, and the way all paths seem to cross?"

"No."

"Really?" she sat up. "You don't find it interesting that," she ticked off on her fingers, "Broughton has a connection to Rollins, to Logan, *and* to my dad? Price is connected to Rollins and Kelton. Her mother and uncle were possibly killed by the Minnows. Kelton and Grace are connected through her sister and then there's my cousin Jake's link to Broughton and back to Grace's dad through his wife. It's like cobwebs."

"Family and friends deserve a better metaphor than dirt-encrusted spider webs."

"But don't you see? It's about the pattern of the threads. The thin lines connecting the people in our lives." She jumped up and rummaged around in the drawers of the desk, then sat cross-legged beside him with a pad of paper in her lap.

"Where to start?" She tapped a pencil against her mouth. "I guess with my parents." On the top left hand side of the page she wrote James and Julia, then listed their children and spouses below. Down the right side she wrote the other players, then started marking the connections with a simple line between.

He loved watching her. The concentration, the puzzling, the dogged determination. Even when frustration set in, he was mesmerized by her expressive face.

"Too many," she muttered. "How can I see with this many lines? There has to be a pattern."

"What about using colors?"

Her eyes lit. "Yes. Colors, I bet that would do

it." Then her shoulders slumped. "But I can't *get* to those colored pencils Dhillon has at home."

She hopped up and paced the room. "I hate being stuck in here." She stopped. "I don't mean in here with you, I mean in here, indoors. I don't stay in one place very well."

He grinned, enjoying the powerful, yet graceful and efficient way she moved. "No kidding."

She marched from window to window, not circling like an eagle soaring in an updraft, but more purposeful, like a hummingbird flitting from flower to flower.

"It's as though I have too much energy for my body and I need space to expand, do you know what I mean? A puppy who needs a yard to run in, or a wild horse confined to a stall. I need to smell real air."

She turned to him, raised her palms. "I know, this is air. But it's just not the same. How did you stand it for all those years at ETC? Living without even a view? I'd have ended up in a padded room before the first week was over."

"In the beginning, it *was* hard."

"Hard isn't a big enough word." Angie plunked herself into the armchair across from him and tucked her feet up under her. "Tell me about the first week."

Hell. How could he put it into words?

"What was it like when you went down the elevator the first time?"

"Damn weird. The further it went down, the more I expected the doors to open into a cave filled with shrouded cadavers. So the shiny white hallways were a pleasant surprise. But then it got spooky with the magically opening sections of walls."

He smiled. "I had a vivid imagination and began

to wonder if I'd been brought there for some macabre purpose such as organ harvesting."

Angie laughed. "Now I know where Dhillon gets it from."

Her words struck him, created a glow in his chest. "We do have a lot in common, but he's his mother's son."

"We can only hope he has the best of both of us. Go on. What happened next?"

"I was taken to a meeting room, where I met with Kelton, and we talked about my education, and then others joined us. The head of security, as well as some of the people I'd be working with in the research department when I wasn't studying. Logan had told Christopher I was good at ferreting out information." He lifted the glass of water long forgotten on the table beside him, took a swallow to soothe his suddenly dry throat.

"How did you feel?"

"Cornered."

She slapped a hand on the arm of her chair. "Exactly my point."

"But I knew there was no backing out. By that time, I understood the enormity of ETC, and knew I was in a situation I'd have to learn to live with. It was similar to my life on the run."

"That doesn't make sense."

He sat forward and rested his arms on his knees. "Before I went to ETC, I spent all my waking hours—and half of the sleeping ones—looking over my shoulder. I was never free to just *do* anything. I couldn't take a walk when or where I wanted without weighing the risks. I couldn't choose a vocation or a job, or even where to sleep, without the chance I'd have to change plans in the blink of an eye. I never got comfortable. I could never forget I'd witnessed a murder."

She straightened in her chair. "Do you get flashbacks?"

"No."

"But you remember what you saw."

"Like it was yesterday."

"Does it interfere?"

"No. I was sensitive to loud noises for a while, but that's all. So I'm lucky."

"I suppose. I wonder what it will be like for you when we put the Minnows away. Do you think the memories will finally fade?"

"Maybe, maybe not. But it doesn't really matter. They're a part of my past, not my present. And I have good memories that are far stronger. Like the day you stepped into my office and my life changed yet again."

She knelt in front of him, took his face in her hands and kissed him. Gently, softly. "You say the most perfect things sometimes."

"And now," he said, "I'm probably going to ruin the mood." She rocked back onto her heels but he caught her hands and drew her into his lap. He needed to know about some of her memories. Of events that changed *her*

"Would you share some of your history with me?"

"As in?"

"What was it like when you found out you were pregnant? How did you deal with your family, their reactions? And what happened the day Dhillon's heart stopped?" He stopped himself from blurting out any more. He needed to know about events that changed her, events that were connected to him.

"You might not like what you hear, and I don't want to scare you away."

"I don't scare easy. Show me the bridge between the teenaged girl in Vegas and the woman in my arms."

Angie stared up at him. "What about your 'living in the now' talk?" She had him there.

"You understand my foundation. I'd like to understand yours."

Hard to argue with that, thought Angie. "Being yanked away from Vegas because of Kyle's accident was crazy. I was beside myself, because I hadn't been able to say goodbye to you, set up some way to stay in touch. But I believed I was in love, and there'd be a happily ever after. Convinced myself you'd come for me.

"In the meantime, we arrived in Dallas, at the trauma center, where Kyle was still in a coma. The doctors didn't expect him to live, so my family did what they do best. They fought for what they believed in." Angie rubbed her knuckles over the ache in the middle of her chest.

"My dad had been blindsided four years earlier when his brother, Kyle's father, committed suicide, and James was determined that he wouldn't lose Kyle, too, not without a hellish and good fight."

Angie had idolized her cousin since the first time he took her for a ride in a helo. And watching him lie there in that hospital bed was the hardest thing she'd ever done. To this day, the smell of iodine took her right back to that room, and a visual of the nurses dressing his wounds.

"There was a schedule. We each spent at least thirty minutes a day with him, and we had assignments, stuff to read to him, to talk about. I'd been shadowing Kyle for years, wanted to be him when I grew up, so it was hard to watch him growing thinner, smaller by the day, with screws in his head holding the metal halo attached to his shoulders. And he had a special bed so they could turn him like a pig on a spit." She shuddered, shoved the picture from her mind.

"I walked into that room every day for two months before he started to open his eyes. It took nearly a week for him to finally wake up, and four more before he could communicate and sort of feed himself. That's when he was transported home to rehab at the ranch. Dad had the equipment set up and ready."

She stared at the button on Matt's shirt, uncertain how to continue. How much to tell him. She didn't want to censor herself, but neither did she want to make him feel worse about not being there for her.

"It was a while later, after things settled back into routine, that I realized I was pregnant. Up until then everything I thought or felt was attributed to the situation, even the weight gain. We'd stayed in an apartment in Dallas, eating fast food and packaged stuff, like muffins and donuts from the hospital cafeteria, sodas and chocolate milk, not riding and working out or swimming daily. And I'd never had any kind of a regular cycle, so I was just happy I hadn't had a period for a while."

Once reality set in, she would have gone to her brother Quinn, her closest sib, the person she could always rely on to keep her secrets, but he was a guy. Instead, she waited for Eve to come home from college at Easter. She'd gone into her sister's room, closed the door and without even a hello, said, "I think I'm pregnant."

Eve's double take would have been comical if Angie hadn't been quite so scared.

"How?"

She rolled her eyes. "You're in med school. You're supposed to know this stuff."

"Well then, who? And when the hell did you start having sex?"

"I can't tell you."

She closed the space between them and lifted Angie's shirt, stared at the small but very there baby bump. "Holy hell."

Angie jerked away. "What do I do?"

"You haven't told anyone?" She shook her head. "And nobody's noticed?"

"They're all so busy with Kyle, his therapy, his crabbiness."

Eve grabbed her by the arm and started for the door. "We need to talk to Mom."

"She's gonna kill me."

"Right after she drags the name of the culprit out of you."

Angie shook off the memories. "My mom was awesome. She didn't kill me, and even when I wouldn't tell who the father was, she stood by me. They all did in the end. Well, Gage and Quinn grumbled some, but I think my dad probably rode them hard about letting me out of their sight in Vegas."

She took Matt's hand and pressed it against her

flat stomach. "I used to imagine you doing this, feeling our baby move. I kept hoping you'd contact me, and then I could tell you about him, and you could be there with me when he was born."

He pressed his lips to her forehead. "I wish there was something I could do to change things. To make up for not being there for you."

"Life happens." She tipped back to watch his face. "Once he was born, I was completely caught up in him, and absorbed with being a mom. I had a beautiful baby boy, and an amazing family supporting me, making sure I had breaks, got sleep, and then, once he was walking, my mom and Consuelo insisted I continue with my plans to become a pilot."

They'd fought over that. She didn't think she should be away from Dhillon, and they maintained that she'd be a better mother in the long run if she got the education she needed, and had the vocation she'd always dreamed of. It was pointed out that not many single moms were as lucky as she was, and she needed to take the opportunity offered to her.

Then her family did something incredible. They sponsored another single mom's education. A total stranger, a girl the same age as Angie, was also given everything she needed for her and her baby.

"Just as yours was, my life was busy and productive. I was happy, and being Dhillon's mom was, *is* the best thing that's ever happened to me. He's smart and funny and cheeky and thoughtful and a ton of fun to be around."

He never took his eyes off her, but lifted her hands, placed a kiss in each palm and her heart fluttered. "Although I wish I could have been a part of his life, he got something better, much better. An incredible mother, and an amazing extended family. For that, I will always be grateful."

Her eyes filled and spilled over.

"Oh, shit. I didn't mean to make you cry." He tried to draw her closer but she resisted, sniffed, and gave him a watery smile.

"They're happy tears, you idiot."

"Well. Okay then."

She blinked them back as best she could and dug a tissue from her pocket to mop up the rest. She wasn't a crier, but this man slayed her sometimes with the things he said. Stuff that seemed to come straight from his heart uncensored.

"The kid's had a charmed life for sure." The grin that had started faded just as quickly. "Until I nearly lost him."

He studied her face then. "You've never told me about that day."

"You already know the medical details."

His hands tightened on hers. "I want to see it through your eyes. How it unfolded, what you saw, how you felt."

She nodded. "You need to understand what you missed out on from a parent's point of view."

He shook his head. "It's more than that. It's like a piece of you I need to know. It changed your life. Your perspective. It's an integral part of who you are."

Entirely true. A woman didn't nearly lose a child without it affecting her profoundly. But she'd never put any thought into how it had changed her. She'd just gone on. Doggedly putting one foot in front of the other, feeling blessed that her son had lived.

"He'd gone to Quinn and Rachel's place to play

with her new dog, a greyhound rescue." She smiled. "A total failure on the track, because he wasn't the least bit interested in chasing anything, let alone a fake rabbit. Sighthound instincts had been left out when he was wired, and he was turning into a great pet."

Angie remembered joking with Rachel about moving Dhillon's stuff over there since he was spending so much time at her house with Chance.

"He spent every day for a week at their place, loving that dog. Anyway, *that* day he'd been there for a couple of hours when my phone rang, and it was Rachel. I'll never forget the words she screamed, 'Bring the Steed. Hurry!'" Angie shuddered.

"I was terrified. Had no idea what was going on. Rachel's voice had been barely recognizable—but the call came in from her line, so I knew it was her.

"Because the Steed was kept at the airfield back then, I had to drive over there to get it. And it was so fucking hard not to go to Rachel's instead. They were both only a few minutes away, but in opposite directions."

She ran a hand through her hair. "I tried to call her back while I drove, but the line was busy. I hit every speed dial on my phone and raised no one. Turned out the team was on an op, Consuelo and Mom were in town shopping, head of security was on one line with Rachel, while another talked to the closest hospital, and a third man was on directly with Eve, who was working at a different hospital." She grimaced.

"You know how they say time seems to stand still? I get that. Jumping out of the car and racing to the Steed felt like trying to run in waist-deep water." Matt nodded, but said nothing.

"But once my ass was in the seat, I chilled. I'd had the Steed out earlier in the day to set it up for rapid launch—that's a one button start-up—because it was the on-call craft for home emergencies. This had been procedure since Kyle's accident. Anyhow, I hit the button, brought her off the ground thirty seconds later, and barely skimmed the trees on the way to Quinn's house, set down in the driveway, and Rachel ran out the door with Dhillon cradled in her arms. He was limp. But instead of shock shutting me down, training took over."

Angie closed her eyes and saw it all again. "I auto-opened the back door, she jumped in, and within seconds I'd closed it, hit the control to switch the sound modifier off and got us airborne." Her heart pounded like she was back there again.

"Rachel filled me in quickly. Chance's frantic barking had taken her out back to check on them, and she found Dhillon on the ground. His heart had stopped, but she restarted it. She has healing powers in her hands. Anyway, she said his heart was beating, and he was breathing, but he hadn't woken up."

It was so close to the surface again. The horror of understanding that her child had actually died. The sheer terror of not knowing if she'd be able to get him to the hospital in time to keep him alive, if he'd ever wake up, if she'd ever see that cheeky grin, hear his smart-aleck remarks, feel the hug of skinny arms, or see her own attitude in one of his eye rolls. Would she be able to watch her son's hands cradle a duckling, or a kitten, or a minuscule tree frog again? Listen to his happy laughter, watch with pride while he studied his uncles' moves on the basketball court and tried to replicate them?

321

She took a long, deep breath and let it out slowly. Reconnected with where she was now.

"His life, or mine with him, played in my head like a movie in the background while I flew that helo at top speed and broke all kinds of aeronautical regulations, terrified I'd never see those big blue eyes again."

Her gaze met his. "That's when I thought of you. He has your eyes. How could he die without his father ever having known he existed? How could the universe be so fucking cruel? And then I was busy on the radio. Security had warned the hospital we were coming in, so they were ready for us, and we agreed that unloading hot was faster since every second counted.

"Once they were clear of the rotors, I shut down and raced after them, leaving Rachel with the bird." She suddenly felt shaky. Pushed off of Matt's lap and went to the fridge beside the desk for a soda. "You want something?"

He shook his head, and she popped the top, drank slowly.

"Are you okay?"

She nodded. Rested her butt on the edge of the desk. "It's been a long time since I thought about this."

"Can you finish it? Or do you want to stop?"

"I need to get the rest of it out." And then pack it away again, in the back corner of her mind.

"Because I couldn't tell them about Rachel's power, they assumed that since he was alive, and there'd been no CPR or defibrillator involved, his heart hadn't actually stopped. They tried to convince me he'd lost consciousness for an unknown reason.

They called in a neurologist, and I started to freak out that they would miss something." She took another long swallow, then set the can back in the fridge and went to sit beside Matt and stare down at her own hands.

"Luckily for me and for the people I was about to go off on, Eve arrived. Meyers Security had engaged a private medivac to bring her to us and then take Dhillon to her hospital. I followed in the Steed. And the next twenty-four hours blurred together. After a battery of tests, they identified Dhillon's heart abnormality and did the simple repair." She smiled at him. "The hardest thing I've ever done was let them wheel him away from me, into the operating room."

He tugged on her hands but she resisted. "While he was in hospital, I stayed in his room, only leaving when one of my family came to take my place. And when we got home, I hovered, never letting him out of my sight, until my mother dragged me into her office and had a long chat with me about smothering being the evil stepsister of good mothering."

Oh, how she'd fought that. Argued, and finally given in grudgingly. "They had a family meeting without me and discussed the merits of two options. One, kidnap me and keep me away from the ranch for a week, or let me do a slow self-weaning. I told her they'd have to knock me unconscious to get me off the ranch and away from him."

"We started slow. If I wasn't with him, someone else was, and once I got used to him being out of my sight for an hour, two hours and half days followed easily. In a month, I was able to get back in the Steed and leave the property." She smiled.

"And now that he's started talking about going

away to college?" She laughed. "I may never have a good night's sleep again."

"Come here," he said, tugging on her hand.

What was it about those two words that made her heart thump? Or was it the look in his eyes? Whatever it was had her leaning forward to meet his mouth with her own. It began softly, with a tenderness that made her eyes sting. His hand slid along her jaw to the back of her neck, tilted her head, and changed the angle of kiss. Went deeper as she opened to him, and her heart rose up the back of her throat.

More, she thought, while she gripped his shoulders, then slid her fingers into hair. Their tongues met, not dueling, but mating. Gently bending her back, he followed her down and she stretched out beneath him. Legs entwined, they explored. Celebrated who they were together.

CHAPTER 27

Stepping into the war room, Matt spotted the woman he assumed was Price and, studying her, was disappointed to feel no buzz of recognition.

After Angie told him about Price's uncle being connected to the Minnows and disappearing around the time of Matt's experience with them, he'd anticipated a sense of recognition, or some kind of visceral response. But his subconscious obviously picked up nothing familiar. He had no inkling of whether or not she was connected to the same dead man he was.

But then there'd been nothing when he met Kelton, either.

He crossed to the window. Stared out. But was brought right back to the present by Angie's hand on his back, rubbing in a soothing manner, as though fully aware of his disappointment. She got him. Understood the way his mind worked. Had somehow become an integral part of his life, and it was a helluva lot more than just sex. She stirred him on a myriad of levels. Made him more somehow, with her strength, support, acknowledgement, and the way she shared herself with him emotionally.

Was it only days ago that he'd considered freedom his goal?

Sure, he could explore the world, do what he liked once the Minnows were caught, but exploring would be much better, more fun, richer, because he'd have her and Dhillon to share the experience with him. He grinned. Even forty-eight hours ago that thought would have had him breaking out in hives. He hooked an arm across her shoulders, planted a kiss at her temple, and the startled look on her face made him laugh.

"Well, a PDA, what a lovely surprise," she said, then grabbed him by the collar and dragged him down for a steamy kiss.

Muttered suggestions that they get a room had him lifting his head.

"Ignore my brothers. They just need to get used to seeing us together. Besides, I've had to watch them constantly kissing and snuggling their wives, so payback's a bitch." And she laughed.

"That's different," said Gage.

"And," added Quinn, "we have company." He tipped his head toward Price and Broughton at the far end of the room talking to Logan, not paying any attention to what else was going on.

"What's the deal?" asked Angie.

"We're just waiting for Julia and Grace," said Quinn.

Matt whispered in her ear, "PDA?"

"Public Display of Affection."

"Ah. Of course." He hadn't had much public

exposure as an adult, and didn't have an opinion one way or the other. But if she kissed him like that again, his brain cells might not recover in time to pay attention to the meeting.

Luckily Julia and Grace entered moments later and everyone took their seats.

"Rollins has gone to ground, but his entire team was taken into custody late last night," said Julia. "At the same time, in a coordinated effort throughout this country and several others, one hundred and seventy-nine members of the Minnows were arrested, with solid charges laid against all of them."

Matt's jaw dropped and words came unbidden. "How the hell did they put that together so fast?" Could he really be free? To go where he wanted? Move around whenever and wherever he pleased?

Broughton's voice interrupted his thoughts. "This has been in the works for a very long time. Taking down an operation of such magnitude requires years of planning, investigating, and building cases that will put people in prison for a very long time. I was not only a plant inserted into the Rollins team, but when I retired, I became the silent coordinator of the only federally organized crime task force Rollins was unaware of."

Angie was nodding. "Torching your place in New Mexico when we picked you up makes much more sense in that light. But if you knew of Agent Price and her connection, why didn't you move on that sooner? Why wait for Meyers to be involved?"

"I interviewed Danica several times, but she refused to testify, because the only safety net the FBI was able to provide was witness protection through the US Marshals."

Angie addressed Price. "That wasn't good enough?"

"No, it wasn't," she replied. "Yes, they're damn good at what they do, but Rollins had been successful for too many years for me not to believe he had a marshal or two on his payroll. In contrast, I have no doubt that your family is not under his influence. Meyers Security has a stellar reputation, and I trusted you to give me a chance at a new life, and keep me safe from the Minnows. Period."

Grace was paying close attention to the agent in a way that had Matt's curiosity humming even before she spoke. "When you learned that Special Agent Broughton was to join us in a meeting, you said he was dirty. Explain that to me."

Price's shoulders went back. "He'd been after me to testify against Rollins for several years, and I turned him down every time, because he'd been on Rollins' team. How could I be sure whether he was fishing, or legitimately working toward taking Rollins down from the inside? There was no way for me to verify his position without giving myself away."

"Yet you spoke to him, shared your story."

Color rising, Price's hand went to her throat, and her eyes met Broughton's for an instant before going back to Julia's.

"I trusted my gut enough to take a chance with my own safety, but I would not endorse him to you and risk putting your family in jeopardy."

Grace nodded. Seemed satisfied with the answer.

"What about BDH?" Angie asked Broughton, and he held his hands out, palm up, obviously not recognizing the acronym.

"Agent Bellows," Julia explained. "James

imposed a code that is no longer necessary, Bellows Delta House."

"I see. A warrant has been issued. We're just working out the logistics for getting her to holding without encountering any of the men she has under her glossy fingertips. Luckily for the bureau—and mankind in general—she kept meticulous notes. Once we accessed them, we discovered enough documentation to add several powerful people to our warrant list. Two have yet to be picked up, but once they are, Bellows will be taken to headquarters for processing."

"Perfect, and that leaves Kelton," said Angie. "Where does he fit in this?"

Matt waited for the answer. Was his mentor to be trusted? Could Matt go back to his work at ETC if he wanted to? And why would he even consider giving up what he had here?

How *did* a research scientist look for a job in the real world?

Odd how no one seemed to want to answer the Kelton question. Finally Logan and Broughton both nodded toward Julia, but she shook her head, so Broughton responded. "He has been providing the FBI's Organized Crime Unit with valuable information about the Minnows for a very long time. He always appeared to be unaware of the Rollins connection, and we worked at making sure it stayed that way, because, knowing Kelton's reason for his quest, there was concern that he would try to get to the man himself, and ruin the entire operation."

"Where is Kelton now?"

"He's been relocated to Alpha," said Julia. "When he was finished his long walkabout yesterday, we decided that bringing him back into the house was unnecessary and possibly unwise."

Angie had explained the alphabets to Matt as self-contained and fully secured emergency bunkers in remote locations on the ranch. Alpha, Beta, and Charlie were set up inside as cottages, and Delta was equipped for detaining prisoners.

"Are you lifting lockdown?" asked Angie.

Julia shook her head. "Not yet. Your father still has some concerns, so we're keeping the house in safe mode."

That had Matt sitting back and his senses opening wide. There was something else going on in here. Current flowed between Logan, and Julia, telling Matt telepathy was back on the table. He opened channels in his mind, and waited, but picked up nothing. They'd layered on protection. But being a student of ETC for many years, he began working his way through.

Angie's tension level amped up because of the concern marring her mother's usually smooth features. Something was being left out. "Where is everyone else?"

"The children are with Rachel, Cass, and Consuelo in the security room."

Yes, something was definitely wrong, and it appeared her mother didn't plan to share, so she pushed. "Why?"

"Because, as you know, it's the safest place for them to be, and now we're done here, perhaps you would join them and give your sisters a break."

It might have sounded like a question or suggestion, but Angie recognized an order when she heard one. She gave Matt's hand a squeeze and headed out to join her sisters-in-law…or was it sister-in-laws? She could never get that one straight, so yeah, sisters worked. Julia hadn't mentioned Eve, but she was likely holed up in her lab programming some crazy machine to spit out answers about DNA markers and...

Pushing the pointless thoughts aside, Angie pressed her hand against the palm plate and waited, but the light didn't turn green, and the lock didn't click open. Icy fingers of fear crept up her spine while she waited for the biometric reader to reset. Counted off the requisite thirty seconds. Again put her palm against the reader for five seconds. Waited. The light stayed red. *Fuck.* Without taking her eyes off the door, she scurried backward toward the war room and was met halfway by Logan and Broughton.

"Security—"

"Copy. Stay here." They breezed past her.

"The door—" But she was only speaking to herself. Broughton already had the electronic panel open, rifling through wires. Logan had his hands pressed to the door. Right. He had extra powers. He'd likely picked up her fear, and now he was trying to access what was going on inside the room. Matt came up behind her.

"Julia wants you back in the war room."

No. She needed to stay here, to see what was happening. Dhillon. The others.

"You can't help out here, but Julia has an idea."

Angie marched in, stopped in front of her mother. "What the hell aren't you telling us?"

"Sit down, Angie."

"Dhillon—"

"Is fine."

"How do you *know* that?" She heard the shrillness in her own voice, swallowed. Fear wouldn't help. And panic was deadly. She needed to be calm. Focused and professional. She could do this. Took a deep-belly breath of air and flexed her fingers. Sat.

"Status update," said Julia in the tone of a leader, not a mother, not a grandmother. "We've gone code Zulu."

"What—"

She turned to Matt. "The security team may have been infiltrated. Only family members can be trusted." And that's when she noticed her brothers were missing.

"Where are Gage and Quinn?"

"Gone to the lab, Eve's not answering her comm." Oh, God.

Julia put a finger to her ear and Angie held her breath, waiting to find out what she was hearing.

"They've got her. She was bound, gagged, and locked in the cold room."

Logan came in with an update. "Broughton's working on a bypass. No security people in the room, only family, but there's something wrong with Eve."

"Eve?"

"I'm picking up her image, but her energy print is blurry because she's the farthest away, and the electronics must be interfering."

"Eve's been found in the lab, incapacitated."

"Bellows," said Angie. "Has to be." Her mother's fingers flew over the keyboard in front of her, brought up a video feed from Delta. Bellows was sitting on the sofa, flipping through a magazine.

"She's there," said Matt.

Angie shook her head and waited for the next

image. Julia scrolled, clicked, and up came the heat sensor data. Nothing. The room was empty.

"Fuck. Okay. We know who we're up against." Back on her feet, Angie paced the room while they brainstormed.

As soon as Logan, Gage, and Eve arrived, Matt said, "I've just made contact with Dhillon and everyone is fine."

"You've what?" Angie was stunned. Since when had they—

"Just now," Matt replied to her unasked question. "Startled him, but he's good now, and says everyone is sort of calm. Bellows kinda looks like Eve, has a knife, and is waiting for someone called Bill to phone her back. Consuelo is trying to talk Bellows into letting her go and get some food for everyone. The baby is sleeping, the twins are snuggled up with Puck and Stick, and he suspects that Cass and Rachel are hatching a plan, and he thinks Chance needs to pee, so he hopes we get them out of there soon."

That was her kid.

"Gage," Julia addressed her oldest son. "Any idea what direction Cassandra's thoughts will go?"

"First and foremost, protection of the children. She'll be pissed, but won't do anything rash that will jeopardize them. She'll think it through, and make sure everyone is out of the way in case we manage to break in."

"Quinn?"

"Rachel will be on the same page as Cass, and will probably let her lead."

"Are they aware of the other entrance?"

Both men shook their heads.

"Dhillon and Consuelo are," said Angie

Ten minutes later they were ready.

They'd hooked up to one of the cameras in the room and had a full view. Gage and Logan were in position. Julia connected with her two granddaughters, and prepared them for what would happen.

Quinn dialed the phone, engaging video in order to be visible on the computer screen directly in line with the escape route, and waited for Bellows to answer.

"About time."

"Hello, Agent Bellows." He was using his buttery-smooth therapist voice.

"Who the hell—" her words cut off when she saw him on the monitor beside her. She turned then, putting her back to the tall cupboard beside the coffee maker, and Angie prayed the hinges wouldn't squeak.

"You're not Bill."

"My name's Quinn Meyers. I'm sorry we haven't met in person yet."

While he continued to speak in quiet tones and keep her engaged, Dhillon signaled the dogs to stay, held his fingers to his lips, slid over and opened the cupboard door, pointed and the twins both went through to where waiting hands grabbed them. Quick-thinking Rachel jumped up, pushed the baby into Dhillon's arms then rushed toward Bellows, "Quinn! She won't let us out!"

Bellows jerked the knife toward her. "Get the fuck back and sit down."

Rachel edged away but continued to block the woman's peripheral view.

"Agent Bellows, what exactly is it you want from

us? Tell me now, so I can make arrangements. I'm sure you want transportation at the very least, and I expect you want safe passage as well. What is your destination? You do know, of course, that some aircraft have a longer range than others, so distance counts. Or would you prefer ground transpo? Money? Cash, of course. You name it, and I'll personally see it gets done. Of course a beautiful woman like you must be used to having your needs met. I'm sure you have men clamoring at your door." Quinn went on and on with a fast, slick torrent of words to keep her attention until Gage stepped up behind her.

"Game's over, Bellows."

When she spun with the knife aimed at his heart, Gage deflected with his forearm, stepped sideways to avoid the upward thrust of her knee, and drove his fist into her face. She dropped like a rock. "Nobody messes with what's mine."

***

It felt so right to have Matt's arms holding them both close while he muttered about how scared he'd been, and how proud he was of their son. She held on tight, wanting the moment to last forever.

"You're squishing Roger," said Dhillon, and stepped back to pull the kitten out from under his shirt. "I hid him the minute the crazy lady showed up waving a knife around." He stroked the dog leaning against him. "I couldn't hide Chance, but I told him to lie low. I nearly screwed up and left them all on stay when Rachel handed me Jamie. But as soon as Gage took him from me, I remembered the dogs. I peeked back out and they were staring at me, so I got them all with one signal."

"You did an awesome job in there today," said Matt. "Made *us* very proud."

Us, one little word, and it hit her right in the solar plexus. "And your dad was a great intermediary. Might be room for him in Meyers."

"Yeah," said Dhillon. "You could be part of the communications and intel team. That would be awesome."

"Be handy to have a job here," he said, watching Angie. "Course I'd have to find a place to live close by."

"Huh? You'd live with us. There's lots of room at our place, right, Mom?"

"Sure."

"I don't think your grandfather would be impressed. Not unless I married your mom."

Angie's heart pounded against her ribs.

"Well, then marry her. Heck, you guys have already got a kid. Get married, and then you can stay for always." He tugged on his mother's sleeve. "Mom, say yes."

Staring into Matt's serious blue eyes, she cleared her throat. "I haven't heard a question yet."

"Marry me."

"That's not a question."

"Mo-om," he stretched it out to two syllables, and she'd bet he rolled his eyes, too.

"Angie, will you marry me?"

"Yes," she held up her hand. "On one condition."

"And that would be?"

"No big wedding. A simple ceremony here. Outside. Casual. Just family."

"Deal."

"I've got a condition too," said Dhillon. "No getting all kissy-face in the living room or the kitchen."

"Deal." But, oh, behind the closed door of the bedroom there'd be lots of kissy-face going on.

"And one more thing."

"What's your one more thing, Dhillon?"

"Does this mean you'll be here with us for Christmas?"

Angie choked back the laugh when Matt pinned her with a look.

"Yeah. But I've gotta tell you, pal, I don't do Christmas."

Dhillon's arms shot up. "Yes! We can hang out at our place and not have to do all the sappy stuff up here. Well, after the presents anyway. And the food. And we'll have to hang out for dessert, and—"

"We'll work out a plan." Matt rumpled his son's hair. "Two choices for you now, kid. Stay here while I kiss your mother, or go find Consuelo and raid the cookie jar."

"Gone!" he shouted and ran down the hall laughing.

"Now. Angie Meyers, will you marry me?"

"I most definitely will. I love you, Matthias Alejandro Martinez."

His mouth came down to hers, and the kiss that began as sweet and tender, grew into passion as deep and endless as the love between them.

EPILOGUE

The noise of the group at the pool was starting to grow on Matt. He no longer winced when his nieces shrieked with the sheer joy of splashing water at their older cousin, and Dhillon was so patient with them that Matt was reminded of himself back when he looked after his sisters.

To have Cass back in his life, and to spend time with her and her daughters, was an opportunity he'd never dared to imagine.

And he couldn't imagine ever going back to his life at ETC. Angie, Dhillon, and the rest were his everything.

He watched Price swing Lola in the air, and was pleased that a glimpse of the mark on the agent's neck no longer made his breath catch in his throat or his heart pound with fear. The first time he'd seen it, he'd had an instant flash of memory, because it was identical to the tattoo on the man in the barn. The one the Minnows had murdered.

Turned out it was the man she'd known and called her uncle. The one who watched out for her as a child. Someone so special he'd had the shape of her birthmark tattooed on the back of his neck to prove to her it was something to be proud of, no matter what kids said at school.

And although confirmation of his death made her sad, she'd told Matt she was glad to know for sure.

You're looking awfully serious. Angie's internal voice made him smile. She'd become very adept at telepathy.

He took her hand. *All good thoughts, I promise.*

Julia heard from Dad. He's in Argentina.

Is that where Rollins is?

Not yet, but Kelton's certain he's headed there.

Does James have a plan?

Always. And, she grinned, *he promises to be home for Christmas.*

His glance moved from her laughing green eyes to the family spread out around pool. They were his now, and yeah. He'd be doing Christmas.

DEAR READER

I sincerely hope you enjoyed reading this story as much as I loved writing it!

I'm currently neck deep in the story of Julia and James. Did you know they met for the first time as children? Their path was a sometimes rocky one, and there are still a few more bumps in the road, but to get back to a life together will be so worth all the ups and downs.

Oh, and there's another romance budding in this book too, so now's probably a good time to pop over to my website and sign up for the newsletter. That way, you won't miss out on any of the great news about new characters, contests, prizes, and of course a sale or two!

Cheers!
Kathryn.

PS. If you have a minute and could leave a quick review for All She Wanted, you'd encourage happy dancing in my writing cave!

ACKNOWLEDGEMENTS

Writing a book might be a solitary endeavor, getting it polished and published takes teamwork, and I love my team!

Many thanks to: author L. j. Charles for your wonderful critiquing skills and advice; Demon For Details for fantastic editing; Judicious Revisions LLC and Barb for the sharp-eyed proof-reading; The Killion Group Inc. for the fabulous cover; Brenè Brown for Daring Greatly—an inspiration; Sandy James for encouraging me to rock the words; Al for keeping me, Bear, and Skye loved, fed, and cared for while I was immersed in this story; Bear for the constant purring company while I was holed up in the writing cave; Barb and Judy—how do I put it into words? You have loved and supported me my entire life. You are the constants in my journey. You've egged me on and believed in me, always. I love you both.

ABOUT THE AUTHOR

Award winning author Kathryn Jane writes about the kind of women she'd like to hang out with—smart, self-reliant, think on their feet ladies just as happy eating a loaded hot dog at a ballgame as they are sipping champagne in the back of a limo. Women who laugh as hard as they cry, appreciate good sweaty sex, and know how to keep a secret.

Kathryn lives on the west coast of Canada with her very own charming prince. Among her favorite things are the smell of the ocean, crisp sunny days, the warm breath of a horse, cats with a sense of humor, dogs, music, sunflowers, orange gerbera daisies, beach glass and rocks, and kind people. She loves to walk on the beach with her sisters.

For more information about Kathryn and her other books, check out her website and sign up for her newsletter. http://kathrynjane.com/.

OTHER BOOKS BY KATHRYN JANE

Do Not Tell Me No
Touch Me
Daring To Love
Voices
Lies
All She Wanted
Secrets (Fall 2016)